APPROACHING OUR DESTINATION

Peter Campbell lives in the chilly north of Scotland with his partner and three demanding cats.

Also by Peter Campbell

Strange Attractor
This Time We Go Down to the Green Together

APPROACHING OUR DESTINATION

PETER CAMPBELL

Dojoba Press
2016

Published by Dojoba Press 2016

First published by Lulu Press 2008
Blowing Hot and Cold first published by
Lulu Press 2008
This revised, combined, edition
published 2016

ISBN 978-0-9930314-1-0

For Douglas

Approaching Our Destination

On the day of his fifteenth birthday, Gordon ran away from home. Home was that part of Scotland which would never be forgotten because it had never been remembered in the first place. All those misty, soft-focus pictures in travel brochures, they looked so romantic, but the truth was a sheep wandered out onto a road while a car bore down with headlights gleaming. Ah, the smell of cow shit in the morning.

London had none of that. Oh, God, the glamour of those glass-fronted streets then the back alleys with their stench of cider. Needles in the metal bowls of toilets and Eros pissing in full view of a bank of tourists, Gordon knew it all: he'd seen it on TV.

So to the train which clicked and clacked along its never-ending length of track, first through the green and then into the grey that lit up at night, just as he knew it would, into a gorgeous electric display that was better than Christmas. Sitting with his elbows propped on the failed oblong table, he sipped coffee from a plastic cup and watched the window pull the long, light-cut street inwards. There were red-bricked walls and tunnels that pressed hard into the ears. There were cars and then the sea, then plushed yellow fields. There were houses he could look into and see people undressed. Sometimes another train would pass in the other direction with its impacting noise and then he was travelling twice as fast, he was faster than light on the defining edge of the universe, weightless with everything spread out before him.

All the station names in London were known to him: King's Cross, Waterloo, Victoria. The map of their

3

routes was drawn in brown and black and red and green in the rear of a cheap plastic diary that arched in his back trouser pocket. Each time he passed a station he knew, he traced a path with a finger, its nail bitten so short it revealed its soft undershell of pink. When finally the train stopped, stepping onto the platform in Euston was like entering a new mythology. The high, constant rush of hot and cold air brought its announcements and apologies, and there were so many people, all moving at once along the bewildering accumulation of platforms, driven by the timetable overhead lit up and chattering. Gordon loved the way the letters spun, like a clever card trick. Oh yes, this was to be his new home.

As though this was a holiday, he travelled light, his belongings slung into a loose green holdall that hung from his shoulder. That, and five twenty pound notes, was all he had taken with him to offer to the city. Breakfast - a greasy mound inside a polystyrene tray - both multiplied and reduced his money. It was served by a girl in a red check overall whose pasted smile was curling from her face. When he winked at her it fell away and revealed something new beneath.

This was the truth: he had the looks of an Adonis and aware of this, he let his reflection spill out and reproduce in polished surfaces and mirrors. That lank hair thrown foppishly over his eyes, that slight, knowing smile. While others hung around ticket machines begging for fifty pence pieces and pound coins, cultivating their forceful, hesitant manner, he leaned against the glass doors of the information office, catching the eyes of the men who entered. Again, that smile. There, in that city that was completely alien, he knew exactly what he was doing.

In the cubicle of a toilet with a faulty door, he jerked off a desperate businessman who came so hard that he ejaculated an enthusiastic spit all over his briefcase. For this five minute act, Gordon was given a twenty pound note and a shy kiss on the cheek, as though that transaction had been motivated by affection, not desire.

A black, antiquated taxi took him into the city. It moved with the stuttering exactness of a film advancing frame by frame. All along the route tourists pointed their cameras towards him, they pointed and waved, and he wondered why: but then he looked behind and saw another car with smoked glass screens and neverending, the revelation of a face seen daily in the papers. Somehow he trapped fame like a butterfly, he held it tenderly in the cave of his fingers. So many photographs and his face would be on every one.

Then a room for the night, a bed. Oh, the softness. Flat on his belly with the covers cowled over him, the motion of the train seemed to propel him forward still. Someone coughing in the bed alongside him and music rising from the street. Yes, the dreamy rocking and then he was escaping again, away from the farm, it was this terrible muddy darkness and he was racing flatfoot ever quicker into the light and the cough cough coughing in the same room.

Morning was a collision. It was cutlery and newspaper vendors and the tube going screeclatterclatterclatter. Electricity was blue and liquid over the dirty brick patterns of the tunnels, cutting through Gordon's reflection as he was crushed against the window. Well this was a galleon, this was a spaceship. Water or stars for me boy, oh!

Euston again, now it was a homecoming. Some dirty old cunt with the filth shiny on his clothes filched his last pound coin but that was alright because his hand had done faithful service the day before and would do again. Just look at that smile, keep it pinned there.

It was still the vestiges of rush hour, all those tireless suits, it was exhausting to watch them. The clatter of their shoes as they ran up the rising escalators would cause an earthquake in Japan. There was a strange sort of glamour in the spreading pattern of their expensive cloth and the flotsam of their luggage, the way it forced tourists into the nearest WH Smith, blank behind newspapers.

Nearby, bent over a rucksack, unshaven, squeezed into a shiny blue kagoul that was not too small but rather he was too large, a willing punter if there ever was. Yes, yes, punter, now the new words were swelling in his brain. He sashayed over, with the click of camera shutter eyes.

Minutes later they were in the toilet with the smell of disinfectant all around them, the man's balls swollen with eagerness in his hand.

"Yes, yes," the man whispered in his ear, "oh yesss."

Unconcerned, bored even, Gordon watched the shiver of their reflections on the wet floor. His coat lay by his feet where he had let it fall. In an adjoining cubicle there was the sound of someone's piss striking the pan.

"Almost coming," whispered the man, "nearly there."

There was a knock, sharp and insistent on the toilet door. There was a voice, determinedly official.

"Sorry to bother you," said the voice, "but we've received notification to evacuate the area."

The man groaned, and ejaculated all over the back of Gordon's coat.

"Be right there," said Gordon, "be right with you." And waited until the footsteps had moved on, the message repeated.

They fled out into the hurried, disordered crowds then, the overweight tourist wheezing, dragging the bulk of his rucksack along the ground, while Gordon, conscious that he had not been paid, followed just behind. The evacuation message, continually relayed across the loudspeaker, distorted into feedback. Ahead there were glass doorways pulled open, there was light, there was a street that turned people into water. Petrol fumes had the fragrance of flowers. Words were treacherous candy: he heard the word BOMB at every moment, somewhere, fissioned through the crowd.

In those moments, at some junction where commuters emerged into a wider road, police gesturing, hurry, hurry, no telling when there would be the screaming cut of glass, yes in those moments Gordon lost the tourist who left behind not money but the melting jewels of come.

Later, he stood in the street with his spit and paper hanky, trying to wipe away the stains. The crowds split past him on both sides. There were bumps and knocks, annoyed exclamations. A girl in a black leather jacket and dyed orange hair almost knocked him over. Sheepishly, he looked around, and gestured to the mark on his jacket.

"Seagull," he said.

"Must have been a fuck of an excited then," she replied.

That was the start of it. Her name was Diana and she was Irish and she came over from Dublin on a ferry with the sea blowing an oily slick into her face. Oh, a brave Oirish lass. They had this in common, the need to run away to something, anything, as long as it was not what they had left behind.

He had thought that London was all television, but she knew it better than that. With her, he came to see that even filth was a varnish that had to be scraped away. Hanging around the ticket machines in railway stations and it was, "Fifty pee, mister, got fifty pee?" Catch their eye and give them an aggressive stare, that was the way. Evading the other groups, ruthlessly organised, doing the same thing: to avoid being described by a Stanley knife. Diana showed him how.

"Got fifty pee, mister? My name's Diana, just like the fuckin' princess. Got fifty pee?"

The world became an anticipation of commuters.

The first night they met, she took him to a nightclub. Under a night turned violent by the effects of speed, they fed on sweat. Were faces really so white, so hard, so defined? The music was so loud it animated their bodies. They kissed for the occasion, and then in the toilet Gordon gave a blow-job to a braided punk, just because he felt like it. The speed made his ears buzz and he had a nose bleed: it was the odour of disinfectant, it was so strong.

Diana waited by an open door, smoking a cigarette and being cooled by the night air. Her jeans had a melting patch of wet where someone, perhaps herself, had spilled a drink over it.

"Come on out now," she said, "we'll go to the station."

There was another drug then, it was sticky and tasted of treacle. The world was razored by a pillow. Lights burned with an inner heat, taxis flowed black and luminous along the roads. There were bodies boxed or dossing in doorways. One of them called out.

"Fifty pee? You got fifty pee?"

"Oh bugger your fifty pee, you dirty cunt," said Diana. She really was, Gordon thought, as foul-mouthed as fuck.

Then the tube station was before them. A metal grille had been slid over its entrance, but Diana only had to wave at the attendant who stood nearby for it to be opened.

"Fancies me madly," she said. "One day I'll drop my knickers and give him a thrill."

The tube station was not deserted as Gordon had imagined it would be. Instead there was an entire workforce here, labourers, cleaners, electricians, and there was battering and clanging and the brusque hiss of brooms among along the concrete floors. Some of the workers greeted Diana by name. They had bodies of soft chocolate and marzipan and when Gordon saw this, he let out a laugh that spilled out the alphabet, so loud, and he was embarrassed; but then he saw that no-one had noticed, and the realisation came that he had not laughed at all.

The tracks were not electrified; he remembered being surprised at this, and that even down from the platform into the tunnels, noise and work continued, the repairs, the collection of refuse, the men so primitive with their shovels and axes, stripped to the waist and stinking with sweat. He passed them by. Diana passed them by.

"Go on," she said, "they won't stop us."

There was no sound then, and no light. They had gone further than the trains, with their velocity of metal, had ever been. Even the air was old here, it was the gasping of penny farthings and Hansom cabs. A rusting of colour lay over the walls and on the uneven stones underfoot, revealed by an illumination that seemed to have its source at the very edges of darkness.

"Up there, look," she said, "you see?"

Up in the curve of the roof, stuck to the frayed edge of dirty brick, a face looked down at him. The face was smeared with black and stubbled, and there was a distinct smell of alcohol. Its skin glowed like an insect's. Behind the face was a body, but the body was shapeless, it was like jelly slopped into a sack. Its mouth moved, it formed shapes, but no sound came out. Gordon was held in its sight, unable to move.

"And down there, by your feet," Diana said, whispering now, and when he looked there was a tumble of something on its hands and knees, grey-haired, hands in fingerless gloves, and this something dragged itself around his legs and mewled like a cat.

Gordon crouched to see, and the entire world was plastic, it was liquid rushing down along with him. The creature rolled away before he could touch it, it left the scent of mildewed cloth. Diana's hand was on his shoulder then, and he looked up, and at that moment the face above chose to speak.

"Gordon," it said, "Gordon, have you got fifty pee?" And then it burst into tears, and all of its features withered like an old flower.

In the following days, the city turned to dust, or that was how it seemed. The sun became a blurred whiteness in a hard, blue sky, and the buildings, the bridges, all of the city's glittering, gaudy architectures became as flat as card. They were props to punch through. On the radio that Diana carried, a voice said, "...as hot as Nairobi," and if the city had turned to a dusty, tropical jungle, then the commuters, wilting, frustrated, were its weltering vegetation.

To Gordon, to Diana, who together had become savages, nature children of this unrelenting landscape, it was oppressive. Not even the parks with their rows of tall, burdened trees could shield them. They wanted to leap into fountains: fizzy drinks were not the answer. Doorways became arbours, shops were places to seek out icy gusts of air conditioning. Tube stations became anxious, frantic places, and money dried up in the impatience. Their clothes and bodies began to smell, their hair so stiff from the dirt of the traffic that when they ran their fingers through it, it stood straight on end.

What happened, days became strips of cardboard folded in boredom into concertina shapes that were then left free to expand like a crazy snake, jack-in-the-box, an accordion played with one hand. Avoiding the dead oasis of the city's heart, together they explored an underworld of back alleys and dead-end streets that had not yet discovered pin-stripes and mirrored glass. Here, time was counted out in dead bottles, close your eyes and this could be Bowery Row, the reek of clothes grown heavy with sweat and bodies that had bloated as though overfed. Able to skirt them by, Gordon conjured a curious romanticism, he stole a smile from a woman with grey hair and rotted teeth.

Diana had a map of London, metal and acid inside her head. Street signs were unnecessary; faces and names were landmarks they travelled by. When the heat warped the air like sheet plastic, they retreated to these places, the spots where Arthur or was it Benjamin or was it Peter, Gordon always forgot, lived. They lived in cardboard boxes or under newspaper sheets spread in a canopy; and these walls and roofs had grown brittle with the heat, so that when they got drunk or took pills that stretched or deepened the frail plains of reality, they would crash through habitations like dogs bounding through paper hoops.

These were moments so real that Gordon expected people to burst into song. The score was already written on their lips, waiting to fall like a rope ladder. If they themselves did not realise it, it was only because they had never imagined themselves being in the last reel, or had seen themselves in the self-reflecting glory of a mirror. But then there were no mirrors here, in this city-within-a-city, because the beauty of its inhabitants was such that it would shame the glass and send it cracking into pieces.

One of Diana's friends had hair tied up in a knot, with a screwdriver plunged through it. He lived in a packing case with a sheet of plastic sacking drifted on top, and somehow they would crawl in there, the three of them, to abandon themselves to whatever treacherous narcotic route they could administer.

There were times when they had no food, but always there were drugs. Unremarked, all the days merged together, they lost their boundaries so that day slid into night like melted chocolate into water, and the hours they passed through grew convoluted as the recesses of leafy plants are convoluted, or the body's sexual organs. Perhaps the heatwave only lasted days but it seemed to last forever.

They crossed the city in the rain. It was growing dark, and the city had turned a uniform grey. Diana had a limp, there was a cut, long and crusted, along the sole of her foot, but neither of them could remember what had happened to put it there. Cars turned on their headlights to pierce the wet, falling gauze, and they were moths spinning blinded into their glare. Gordon thought about sheep then, but this was different, he had a cinematographer gliding overhead to give their situation glamour.

Yes: running to the big screen, in cinemascope. The rain jetting upwards on the hard road, running in brown, twisted streams, their feet splashing through puddles. In close focus, the wet glistened on their skin.

"Where are we going?" asked Diana, but the truth was, he didn't know. There was something tidal in the city, a roar that was not only traffic, pressing against the matte backdrop of bridges, buildings, picture-postcard landmarks. If this new life was paint on card, then the flooding would burst through and drive them both away.

They came to a railway station, it was King's Cross, and this station was so bright it was like heaven. There, they sat and dried out in the heat. Gordon ate an abandoned hamburger someone had left in the waiting room, but Diana refused when he offered half of it to her. He wondered if she had ever gone hungry before; or rather, if she had ever been able to notice it. There were pools of shadow around them, cast down by the overhead lights, and slowly these pools filled with water. An old woman wheeled a trolley filled with rotting vegetables and sat down beside them. Her hands trembled and she talked constantly to herself, the syllables she let slip running into each other and suddenly combining in a bark. Spit flew from her lips with the words. She was suddenly sick onto the floor. The sick was acid and had the smell of old green things. When a guard led her away, her body broke out in a series of ticks, she screamed, "I had *orange* for you!" and shook and cried at the same time.

Gordon was filled with desire to be just like her. Diana had folded over his arm like paper, but this woman with her sweat-stiffened clothes carried herself like a demented warrior, she charged with her chariot of wasted carrots and yellowed cabbage before her. Beside him she had left an oily, burnished mark on the plastic of the bench, and he lifted this with his finger and rubbed it on the centre of his forehead, like a mark of desire.

When he looked at Diana again, he saw her lips were turning blue. It was the cold: it seemed to press out of her flesh in the way that it would normally radiate heat. Her bird's nest of hair was matted, it was a colony of secret things. The way her coat lay over her body was like a brightly-coloured shroud, yes, that was the way it was all going. To slip this way into the land of the unliving: that was a great honour.

Later, he carried her out of the station like a kite, along with the handbag belonging to a woman who still sat, unaware of its disappearance, at a snack bar where she famished herself with cups of coffee. The woman had hair whorled up like a snail's shell and wore too much lipstick and she drank her drinks staring at herself in the ornamented glass of a mirror that hung over the back of the bar.

Under an iron bridge that leaked a rusty, brown rain, they emptied the contents of the bag which was an unravelling of tack, memories, essential trivia. This photograph - was it the woman herself? Pigtails and checked shirt, a background that may have been foreign. Eastern Europe, perhaps. An address book with too few names. Buttons that had severed from clothing, with tails of coloured thread still attached. A ring grown tarnished. Gordon examined these things and felt a

15

sadness, but when he discovered the purse with its rustling notes like peacock feathers, there was only elation, and he let the other objects fall to the ground where they were drowned in the pools of water. Diana ground them under her feet which had turned blue, like the rest of her body.

Night brought its sirens and they slept in a doorway with a single blanket to cover the two of them. The purse with its money lay in the hollow between their bodies, barely touched, as fragile as chaff waiting for the first wind.

"Tomorrow," Diana had said, "that's when we'll buy the whole fucking city and make it dance." He went to sleep with his head on her shoulder. Her breath smelt of an exotic spice.

In the morning she was gone, and the money had gone with her. The blanket slumped where she had been, still containing the warmth of her body. The treaded print of her shoes was scuffed on the wet concrete of the doorway, gradually being eaten by the acid of the wet.

Where had she run to? That was what had bound the two of them, the desire for movement, the need to run away. The air, which was thundery and dense, and the rain which scattered down with the swish of sophisticated curtains had covered the sound of her departure. The advancing of clock hands did not bring her return, even though he stretched each second to its fullest, to give her time. When he acknowledged finally what she had done, he looked up, up into the camera eye, and gave his most sincere smile of pleasure.

If he had a photograph of Diana he would have prayed to it nightly. Her face should have been in stained glass on the windows of Harrods and Fortnum and Mason. It was such a sweet betrayal. Had he thought, there would have been nights when he masturbated himself to sleep over this very action. Instead, there was only a footprint, a few loose tangled hairs that clung to his jacket, to remind him she had gone.

A policeman moved him on. The policeman wore gloves in this hottest of weather, it was something reptilian brushing against his skin. If this was a jungle, if the rain that fell was a monsoon, then there were jungle creatures everywhere with verdant plumage to lure and distract him. Still he knew: he had the starring role.

Someone had spilled an ice-cream into the gutter. How absurd: to eat ice cream in the rain. Kneeling, he scooped it up into his hands and pressed it into his mouth. The ice cream was studded with diamonds of grit. Diana would have said, "It's like a fucking chocolate chip, but tasty," and then they would have taken some more drugs and the world would have burned white from the inside. Already he had grown nostalgic for that sensation.

Perhaps if he retraced his footsteps he would rediscover the past. The streets, which had been embroidered with light, had let the stitching unravel. Still, if he followed the white of the pavement kerb and kept his head bent low, it would lead to somewhere.

There was a parade. It slipped past in the rain, with its mocking reflections in the wet, and its untimely squeal of music. Traffic had become paper and glue to let it past. A woman dressed in a costume monstrous and furry approached, shaking a tin, but when she saw his face, the way he was clothed, she passed him by. Someone spat at his feet in tribute. It was better than golden coins.

He went to the station then. This was where it had all begun, wasn't it? At the station. Before that there had only been the farm, and that was the scattering of dust as the coffin was lowered. In the morning he would rise and part the curtains to see the breaded landscape before him, and it reminded him of chicken shit, the mealy lumps he would have to clean out of the hen house each day.

There were crowds and the crowds were soft like butter. People were banana skins, apple cores, the pith of grapes, they had nectarine odours. That was what the woman had collected in her basket, there in the waiting room. No wonder insects clustered around bodies.

"Got fifty pee?"

He was in a tunnel. The tunnel was dark, with no light at the end. Tracks beneath his feet absorbed brilliance into their metal. They were old tracks with flawed wood broken into untidy chunks. There was a skeleton of an animal, it may have been a cat, lying there on the oily stones. He trod alongside it and it fell into pieces.

The area was growing familiar now, its route traced out by memory. Recollections bloomed like flowers. If he crushed their petals, he could make an exotic perfume to dab about his skin. Their breathy pollen would leave yellow daubs on his fingers.

Then seeds spilt open and there were the green threads of shoots growing. Filaments, which were like his fingers, traced over the high archway of the tunnel, breathing in the dead, sooty air. Near: yes, it was near. His footsteps fell so quickly now, it was almost running. On his back he carried Diana's ghost, and her instructions whispered into his ear, like a bad monkey. There was a familiar tightness in the region of his thighs, and he thought he would shit himself, but he came instead, buckling at the knees and bowing on the hard stone.

There was luminescence then. Noises - the dry scraping of cloth, whisperings, high, childish tittering - approached out of the dark. Shapes, almost human, came into view. He had seen the faces before, with Diana, but their presence was more intimate now. They carried their scents like wasps. Faces pressed against his own, stubbled hard, wattled as an elephant's skin, wet with saliva. Hands or almost hands pressed to his chest, his legs, his arms, his cock. He let himself be raised, carried away on the backs of these creatures who paraded him like a golden god. The noise they made increased; perhaps they were singing. He felt himself joining in. His voice made baroque, unfamiliar sounds. The tunnel walls passed so quickly by that it was like being on a train again, only this was not an arrival but a departure; up and up into the tunnel's blackened thread where he was lifted and where he hung and clung to the deepest recesses, fingers dug into the Victorian brick, looking down into the smiling darkness which stretched on and on, neverending.

House, Family Moorland

The rain approached from the west. It fell in graphite slants, ragged where it touched the land, that flatness with its dwarf, crooked-back trees and grass combed to one side that seemed to reflect the light. Donald watched it from the unlatched window, which brought the scent of living and dead things off the moors. The window was of the type that swings open in two halves, and when the rain, wind-fed, reached the house, it snapped inwards with a cracking of hinges. A concave dampness sprayed over the floorboards and pictures clipped from magazines fluttered on the walls. This was Donald's bedroom.

He sat on his bed until the shower passed, propped against its rising iron back, his body finding a groove against the striped, suffocated mattress that long ago had given up the illusion of support. In his lap he rested an ashtray with its cemetery of crushed, hand-rolled cigarettes, to which another three were added during the rain's advance. A lash of wet sometimes blew in his face, and when he wiped it away he could smell his fingers with their edging of nicotine. At some point he may have slept, but he could not be sure.

Sun strobed through speeding cloud by the time the car arrived. It drove up the mud track to the house, in competition with untidy land which deviated into puddles, and sometimes it stalled and threw surges of dirt over its red, newly-polished exterior. Around the house ran a lopped stone dike with a sinking iron gate held in place with twine, which the driver had to get out of the car to open and let the vehicle through. A woman emerged. Even if Donald had not known who she was, he could have told she was a social worker. She looked like social workers are supposed to: greying hair pulled back from her forehead in a cusp, round face protected by large, owl glasses, chunk-knitted sweater with a neckline obeying the law of gravity, black stretch slacks that made her all bottom. Her foreign, dangerous name was Claudia and her speech was full of heavy stresses that fell in the wrong places. When she knocked on the door one two three times, he did not move but only lay on the bed listening, hearing the knocks matched by his heart's amplified beat. Silence, then the same three sharp interruptions. He moved back to the window, crouching beneath it and trying to see the woman, what she was doing, if she was preparing to leave yet. The floor cracked in a much-too-evident way beneath his feet.

"Mr Minter?"

She was calling to him. She was standing back from the house and looking up at the window, hands on hips, calling to him.

"Mr Minter, it's Claudia. You remember me, don't you? I'd like us to have a little chat if we could."

He pressed his eye to the gap between window and windowframe, watching. Somehow this reduced her to a badly-defined smudge of colour. She was speaking again.

"Mr Minter? I know you're there, Mr Minter. It's Claudia. I don't think it's very nice of you to let me come all this way and then not speak to me."

Even his breathing must be controlled. It was tight in his chest.

24

"Mr Minter?"

Moments later he heard the snap of the letter box. The woman was walking back to her car, avoiding the ground's muddied overflow. He could move again.

He went down the stairs. These, like his bedroom, were uncarpeted and the heels of his shoes made a sharp, impacting noise, but that was alright because now there was no-one to hear. A postcard was caught in the letterbox flap, hanging from one corner like a lazy tongue. On it, written in blue, looped writing was the message *I came to see you but you weren't in. I'll call again soon. Claudia, Social Services.* A dirty thumbprint covered the words 'Social Services'. Message in hand, Donald ran back up the stairs to his bedroom. There he tacked the postcard to the wall, alongside all the other letters, pictures, foodwrappers and envelopes that he had pinned there over the years.

Among the pictures fastened to the bedroom wall was a photograph of Donald's mother. It was an old photograph, in black and white, and age made the corners cusp inwards until they threatened to touch. In it, a woman in her early thirties laughed towards the camera, caught with her mouth yawning open. Some sort of special occasion: she wore a modest, polka-dotted dress and her hair was brushed thickly down over the shoulders. She sat on a blanket spread over grass, her legs tucked beneath her and an unlooped ribbon in her lap. Behind her, the bonnet of a car could be seen with someone, it may have been her husband, emerging from the driver's seat. Donald was represented by one child's foot intruding at the photograph's edge. Probably his sister had held the camera.

How long ago was that? To Donald it was barely years, not decades. When he remembered those times they came to him in primary colours and he would recall and mouth old conversations, as though they were still taking place. Empty and fading, the rooms of the house he lived in were nonetheless, for him, full of memories.

There were six rooms in all, in a building once handsome, finding its way out of the moorlands by means of a solitary, rutted path that was gradually losing its distinction. It led onto an exposed, single track road along which a bus travelled twice a day, inevitably empty apart from one or two passengers whose faces he may or may not once have known. Sometimes he travelled on the bus himself, choosing a seat near to the back where he could sit and ignore any other people travelling with him. The moorlands revealed their unvarying heart then, the planed land on which nothing could grow tall, brown knotted except where there was water, and then the ground cratered away and reeds emerged, as did thin, whipping grasses.

It was always a shock when the town came into sight, strutted and grey, as though it had no right to intrude so far into this wilderness. Here he always used the same store and bought the same things, food in cans mostly, shreds of meat that came out garbled with vegetables, and there was invariably a landscape of fat at the bottom, waiting to fall out after the rest.

Often he ate this food cold. He would sit in the kitchen and empty the food in a pan and then he would eat without heating it up, using a spoon that clacked on the pan's bottom and left scores in the metal. He did this sitting on the floor, on linoleum bubbled and discoloured, even though a table stood alongside him, drop-leafed, red-formica'd at one time.

This room reminded him of his mother. It was what a farmer's wife did, work in the kitchen or out in the yard at the back, feeding chickens. She cooked over a large, metal Raeburn set in one corner, its top painted black and giving off the smell of hot brick and metal. Pans sat, burbling, their lids clumping up and down, and gusts of steam rose to the ceiling. Then, as now, he sat on the floor, in a corner, watching the staunch passage of his mother's legs which were skirted and bare, her feet fitted with blue, acrylic slippers given the false glamour of nylon fur. The heat had mottled the skin of his mother's thighs and the pattern disappeared into the wary darkness of her skirt. She had blue eyes, his mother, and dark, curly hair, and her fat arms would lift him up and press his face into her chest. "You're coddling that boy," his father would say, his voice suggesting this was not quite right. Donald would feel ashamed of this weakness but would not move, intoxicated by a feeling of protection. Sometimes he caught the scent of his mother's perfume through her clothes, and it could only be called cheap. There was a fissure of lines around her neck.

She was the first of them to go, although he was too young to remember all the details. He was the only one to see her leave though, catching her as she walked out onto the moor in her best coat and shoes. Her hair had been made perfect and he wondered where she was heading. It was night then, and misty and cold. Even the farm's outlying buildings had begun to disappear, gone soft at the edges, their light gauzy. In Donald's bedroom, condensation had formed onto the window, and he pressed his palm against the glass then removed it, and when he had done this his mother was there, stepping into its runneled imprint, a handbag clasped into both hands, as though it were precious.

She was never seen again.

Later, he was asked: did he hear the sound of any cars, had anyone come to meet her, but he could only tell them about the single image, the fingerclick moment he had slowed down until it was grainy. Sometimes he imagined he had tapped on the windowpane and she had looked up, smiling and giving a brief wave, but it was only imagination, he knew that. At night he lay in bed and told himself she was still out there somewhere on the moors, in some corner where the mist never cleared, still walking, just as he had last seen her.

Life became harder after that. His sister found herself prematurely confined to the kitchen, and he had to go out to help his father, rising when it was only just turning light and the birds started to call; and then in the evening he worked in the stifling darkness of the barn, where animals moved in thick clots and the air stunk with grassy, regurgitated gases. The cattle were the worst, stirring about in their own shit and giving out their angry, mournful calls. This only stopped when he started to fall asleep in class at school, and there had been notes and inspectors, and things began to improve a little.

People said his father was a hard man. That was the phrase they always used. He had a clumsy body and a blunt face that held a nose that had been broken twice and eyes that were pitted. His hair was razored close and he wore a cloth bonnet pulled down over his head, causing or hiding his baldness. His cold, callused fingers were described by nicotine. He never laughed, not anymore: only his wife had been able to make him do that. When he and Donald went out into the fields together, they sometimes did not speak all day, except out of necessity. Still, these were the moments Donald remembered best of the times he spent with his father: that he had been there when the lambs had come, emerging hot and wet and bloodied; or how they navigated the marshlands with nested birds exploding furious and screaming from beneath their feet; or the day they were caught in a clearing when a shower of hail had driven in suddenly, huge stinging stones the size of his father's thumbnails. They hunkered on the ground with his father's coat tented over them, and then sat listening to the sharp cracks impacting from the material, while a cold damp rose from the ground to wet their trousers.

He visited these same places now, when he left the house. The detail of the land was known to him, streams having gouged their same muddy course, crossed by two-plank bridges, ever since he was a child. Nothing had changed, not really; this was not a place people came to, but rather it was a place they left behind. Sometimes he rose in the early morning with the sun still pallid and the ground retaining its frosty crust, and he would go out into the land spanning the back of the house, walking far enough for the building to become a dim scoring on the horizon, and he stood there, becoming as much of the landscape as the slant-rooted trees or the cupped, battered flowers that only dared grow so far. Sheep shifted their mudded bodies from where they sheltered and started to graze. Once they had been his family's, but now they wandered wild, their saturated wool torn loose and unravelling, caught on the ground's close stones and heather. Most were lame and sometimes they could not get up after they had fallen, their leathered carcasses sinking slowly into the soil. If anyone else was around at that time of the morning, it was always khaki-coated men who carried rifles. Often they waved to him, but he never waved back.

One day his father shot himself in the stomach. People were so insistent it was an accident that Donald knew it was not, and that the man he visited in hospital, bandaged and silent with the colour gone from his cheeks, had turned a rifle against himself and fired. Donald's sister Margaret looked after him then, she was old enough, and when their father came home she had to look after him too. He had to be spoon-fed soup like a child, he was useless, and even though people came and money came it was not enough, and the farm was sold in pieces, just as it had been built up, diminishing and decaying in slow gradations.

His father could no longer work. He grew breathless with exertion and sometimes folded over with pain. If he was fed too swiftly he would vomit. Twice a day he had to have three sets of pills, bright-coloured things that came in capsules. On a good day he would go out into the yard and do what his wife had once done, feed the chickens, but most of the time he sat on a chair, in a room cloudy with the smoke of his cigarettes, to stare at a newspaper, pretending to read. In part it was the medicine's fault: it made him feeble.

At first Margaret looked after her father well. She was a plain girl, lank and awkward and pigtailed, but at school she was clever and the other pupils liked her. Leaving was difficult because she valued the school's protection. In its place, all she had was Donald, and her father who sometimes pissed in his pants and threw up his food. When the cattle were sold, they bought a colour television, and in the evening she watched the programmes in which every girl seemed to wear mini skirts or trouser suits, spending their lives in restaurants or nightclubs, and when she saw this she felt like something sharp toothed and clawed, scrabbling around frenziedly in a cage of her own making.

Donald was the first to see the change. His sister wore make-up sometimes, in the kitchen, clumsily applied so her lips were overbright, and the powder she dusted on her face only made her seem gaunt. Steam beaded on it like dew, and then it streaked down her cheeks as though she was crying. If the radio was playing, she danced to pop songs emerging brash and tinny, but only when she imagined no-one was looking. Donald spied on her when he was out in the back yard, seeing the way her body swivelled, and he listened to the music too, but out in the open, with the moors equidistant, it sounded isolated and lonely, unnaturally cheerful, like a pasted-on smile.

Winter came, its winds attacking and carrying snows, locking the three of them in together, so Donald could not escape outdoors, nor Margaret to do the shopping in the town. Their father spent all day watching television, but he did so vacantly, the same way that he ate food. If someone spoke to him, there was a three-second delay before replying, like a message bounced off the other side of the world. He grew fat, and the springs gave way in his armchair so he sat lop-sided, an idiot king, but he did not even seem to notice. The arms of the chair were cratered from the falling ash of his cigarettes. Sometimes he cried, for no apparent reason. Rain started to leak in from the roof, smacking irrhythmically on the floor. They sat there and listened to it, the three of them.

When summer arrived, Margaret was the one to escape. Wearing her one good dress - bright, floral, the fashion of a decade gone - she caught the last bus into town. Then, in the morning, when it was still dark, Donald would be woken by the sound of an arriving car, its door slam and risen voices, and after that she would climb uncertainly up the stairs, her shoes held in one hand but her body giving her away all the same, clumping against walls, as her legs discovered they were not too definite about where they were going. She still rose early, at the usual time, before her father or brother stirred, but her face, white and puffy and shadowed, proved traitorous. Cooking breakfast with a grimace, a slaver of sausage and eggs stirred about in grease, she had at times to hurl to the toilet, leaving Donald to look after the skillet which cracked and exploded, sending sprays of hot, smoking fat into the air.

Only at these moments did her father tried to regain his former authority. "You're going out too much," he said, and he slurred his words as a drunk does. "That's how a girl gets a reputation". Margaret paid him no attention. It was impossible to take him seriously, this shambling, corpulent creature with a fool's abandoned expression, who now only saw daylight through a window or framed by a doorway. Pity, exasperation, resentment, the need to protect him; these were the emotions accorded to their father, not respect.

He went missing one Sunday evening. Margaret was away and Donald asleep. A mist drifted in over the moor, as it had on the day their mother disappeared, and perhaps this was the enticement or torment that took him outdoors. His absence was not noticed until the following morning, when a coldness marked the house and the back door was found standing open. All the chickens had been let free during the night and had come in to roost on the chairs, in the dresser, on the table, marking their new nests with feathers and ammonia droppings, leaving these deposits behind when they leapt off and cackled as Margaret shooed them outside again. Of their father though, there was no sign. It was said he could not have gone far, not in his plodding, dreamy state, but who knows what those drugs did, where they could have taken him. Perhaps it was deliberate, and that was why they never found the body, not any of the men who covered the moor's concealing wastes. There were marshes, after all, and vicious streams and fissured passages in stone leading downwards into a stale blackness. People said it was a wonder they never found him, but Donald never thought that. He had been the one, after all, to see his mother's parallel disappearance, how quickly it happened, becoming lost in the mist's drifting edge.

Margaret changed after that. Strung out on guilt, she carried out the household chores with a repetitive, obsessive ferocity, as though attending to these things could make her father return. Despite this, the house continued to decline. It was the framework for the condition it would find itself in when Donald lived there alone. What was salvageable was sold: all the equipment, most of the livestock and the land. They only kept a few chickens and sheep for themselves, and even the sheep went astray, in time. It hardly seemed worth the bother. The cheques from the social security covered them otherwise, counting out the days, week to week. Donald left school knowing only that expectation.

In later years, even that expectation had gone. He slobbed about the house in stretched-long cardigans and polyester trousers, prematurely old, avoiding the people who came to the door - strangers most of them, looking for directions. They carried binoculars and hiking sticks, and they all had glasses and beards and wore the same blue, expensive jackets. Sometimes they tried the door, imagining no-one lived there any longer, and he would yell at them then, GET AWAY, GET AWAY, in a voice grown husky with disuse, and they would start and sometimes even run on hearing evidence of life emerging from the dilapidation.

Even in daylight the moor was not safe, carrying old echoes, and perhaps the house had come to embody that, standing at the end of a mud track with its paint-peeled door and card-patched windows. Apart from a paraffin heater with which he fumigated the rooms on the coldest nights, the house was never heated, and patches of damp bloomed on the walls. Rain made the carpets sodden, and insects colonised the rotten backing that once had been foam, so he threw them all out one day, into the yard at the back, in a mound that petrified in the sun. Around the roof, the guttering had become a garden, grass-mounded, a place where birds nested, sending down spats of lime to break against the windowsills. The chicken coop still stood, in a lop-sided fashion, but there were no chickens any more, and the wood crashed dryly inwards if too much pressure was placed upon it. Something rusting that had once been a piece of machinery lay like an altarpiece, near to the back door, leaking a brown frost when it rained.

Had it been like that when Margaret had been there? The two of them had grown dotty in the house together, their movements synchronised in the days' long indifference, becoming like an old, married couple in the toleration and encouragement of each other's eccentricities. Margaret seldom went out any longer, never socially, and her face gained the pulled-taut expression of a woman who has been a waitress all her life. In the mornings she turned on the radio, to a station that was bland, singing along to songs popular a generation before, while she polished and swept the rooms into a tidy magnificence; even as the building itself grew dilapidated around her. Donald did nothing: he went out and came in, and he stared at the red-cusped fireplace or at the moor's long unravel. Margaret had to encourage him to wash, because otherwise he let himself grow grimy and ripe, and his clothes built up a sediment of dirt. Sometimes he refused and then she would have to say to him, "You're getting just like our dad," which always worked, always: it was like an incantation. Of course the truth was that he *was* becoming like their father, as he had been in his last, gloomy years, and perhaps she in turn was stepping into her mother's trapped, limited role, the one she ultimately ran away from.

Donald did not say, but sometimes he still looked for them, his mother and father, out on the moors. He tramped over the lagged land, alert to its variations, the disturbed ground that had not been cut the day before, or the stream that ran less freely than it should, its edges collapsed-in and its bottom dense and silted. Something would streak the rabbits, watchlight tails flickering, and he would look but it would only be a scrying hawk or a deer that disturbed them. Normally sounds were limited by the wind's bevelled hiss or the calls of birds rising from the ground, detonated by the approach of his feet, but sometimes gunshots came, distant, their blast snapped and unreeling, often only an echo of an echo. Once, he found a handbag, driven in the mud, but when he opened it and emptied it, all that came out was a reluctant sludge.

No matter how far he went, the house could still be seen. From a distance its defects were not obvious and it sent up a spiral of smoke as perfect as that in a child's drawing. When he returned, his sister would still be in the kitchen, finding things to be done. A slam of heat and cooking scents assaulted him when he entered, and usually she would not even look up from what she was doing. Who else could it be, after all?

It was years they stayed together like that, repetitive, decrepit years that merged incompletely, with only the season's passage to define one month's movement to the next. On some days Margaret stood before the mirror (cracking, as all mirrors must), and imagined herself prematurely lined, but then she would see her brother and found he too carried the same defining marks. They had become tangled, the two of them, like ravelled pieces of string. Those were the same days she noticed how the house itself was failing, how the wallpaper had blemished and the windows no longer properly fastened, and how the tiled roof had become a chessboard and the back yard a mortuary. The television, once new, lashed now with white bands of static. The radio died, and they did not bother replacing it. On her trips for supplies, the town became an alien thing. She did not discuss these matters with Donald, but he knew all the same.

It was not surprising somehow, that the day came when Margaret walked up the track towards the bus and did not return. Her brother watched her leave, shopping basket bumping against her leg, but he did not watch for long and so never discovered whether she reached the bus or detoured along the way, distracted or fleeing. Naturally, the day was misty. Nothing was ever found. Donald kept all her belongings, even when her face had become hard to define. His world, although assaulted by outside authorities, from the moment of his sister's disappearance, closed in further. Now he lived his existence in monotone, a listless life in which he was impelled only occasionally to go out on the moors. Sometimes he would find a room and hide there all day.

He was still in the bedroom, but now it was dark. The pictures he had been examining merged to become part of the larger, uneven surface of the bedroom wall. Insects explored the ceiling's corners with their clattering needle sounds. There was warmth in the air but a coldness too, and when he looked out the window, the moors had a cataract depth, the result of a spreading mist obscuring his vision. Once, there had been an outdoors light he would turn on to thin the impenetrability, but he had let it fail, like everything else in the house had failed. Instead, he had to endure the mist's density, with the birds and animals calling out of its interior like flaws.

There was light downstairs, but it seemed overbright. In the kitchen he drank three cupfuls of water he had run until it was painfully cold. The water came out of the taps threaded brown, as if it was still dirty. Whenever he tried to lift out one of the impurities, it dissolved over his finger, as if denying its own existence. This never seemed right, somehow: it was too much like the water that ran through the striated land. Putting the cup down, he moved to the window. The cup stood alongside seven empty cans displaying their sharp tongues and an unopened carton of milk grown bloated. At the window, he inclined his head, looking out into the back yard, as if acknowledging a conversation.

Someone was calling out of the mist. It may have been one person or it may have been many. *Don-ald*, the voice or voices went, sharper in their focus when he was not listening directly. The mist did upsetting things to sounds, it made them list and waver, as if they could lose their way too, like people. This was when the moor was at its most foreign, all the strangeness seeping out when it was safe to, careful to retain its distance and yet almost in reach.

He did not mean to go outdoors, but this is where he found himself, wearing no coat and attacking the ground with blown-out slippers. Apart from the focus of his body, nothing could be seen, and in the yard he fell over the wasted machinery, making his knees and the palms of his hands bloody as they impacted against the ground's sharp grit. Disturbed, the old coop sank in on itself and made sleepy, dying noises. With his hands, he anticipated the wall's cold assault and then he was out on the moor, blinded, humble before the unexpected bobs of rock and the yielding earth that sucked up to his ankles. Streams warned of their presence but the sound diffused and hid everywhere at once. He had not gone far when he could not even see the house, its shape consumed, like everything else.

When the voices came, it was only briefly, as if they remained deliberately elusive, and sometimes it was his father's voice he heard, or it was his mother's or his sister's. He heard and recognised them, even though he no longer remembered what their voices sounded like. Their cries had a slim vigour and they were elusive, even in their urgency. They came from before and behind and they led him to balance at the edge of a fissured pool, no telling how deep. He stood there, cold-skewered, and acknowledged his numbness.

This was an area where the ground grew more pliant. Reeds bundled and a collusion of iris leaves grew together in tattered oblongs. The mist had cleared enough to see that, and it revealed other danger signs too: the sucking grey of the mud and the shallow rim of water giving off its phosphorescent wisps. It was here that the cries came from, close now, not voices but cries, sharply fearful. He could not imagine how he thought they had been saying his name.

Unexpectedly, they fell quiet, and all that could be heard then was the loneliness of smaller creatures around him, a wheeping of birds and the rarity of calling frogs, their cross-reference of signals. Then it started again, all the cries at once, terrified. When he moved now, it was a passage through memory: his mother, dressed up and hurrying for an unknown assignation; his drugged, feeble father sitting by the television, protected by a circle of fallen ash; his sister with her guilty bloom, watchful of the clock, waiting for her moments of freedom.

The marshland revealed itself to him, in glimpses. Mist peeled back and returned, renewed each time, and then he was in the midst of it, uncomprehending. Here the voices seemed close enough to touch, but their origin remained hidden. He would choose a direction and then realise it was the wrong one, and his feet would sink in the unresisting, grabbing stodge. A bird flew close enough for him to feel the waft of its wings on his face. The sound was ahead now, he was certain, and he moved forward, determined, listening. They were not human cries, no, he realised that, but animal sounds, quick and frightened. What else could have they been, out here on the moor? This was their source, at last before him, pooled by the mist, their outlines visible and their hard utterances definite. When he reached out, they nudged wet and shuddering to the touch of his hands, because now he was amongst them: a flock of sheep caught drowned to their necks, pushing up with their desperate breath and fixing him with their terrified eyes.

Fabled

"Love me tender, Elvis dear," remarked Little Miss Piggy. Her eyes, which were red, spat like coals being nudged when she said this. Elvis, who lay opposite her like a great, uncooked hamburger, belched up vanilla-flavoured gases in reply.

"Now is that any way to talk to your beloved, your adored one, your one-and-only." Miss Piggy, who was wearing a kimono that barely covered the pinkness of her rump, crawled on her hands and knees to Elvis' berth and kissed him on the chin. As he had forgotten to shave for the last week, the kiss, although delicate, was turned into something brutal. When she attempted to kiss him again, this time on the forehead, he shifted away by means of his fabulously blubbery, prehensile buttocks, and stared up at the blushed, rhinestone-studded ceiling. Elvis yawned then belched and the room wafted strawberry-vanilla.

This is what he had to eat that day: six hot dogs spooned with relish and slimy with onions; half a chicken, crisp with fat; three strawberry milk shakes; a self-immolating chocolate gateaux and a plate of flapjacks in maple syrup. But best of all, his favourite, he had consumed two whole family-sized cartons of ice cream. And it was only morning! No wonder he was fat.

What about Miss Piggy, though? Well, despite her considerable girth, and those thighs that slapped like newly-tenderised meat, she barely ate at all. Not enough for a sparrow or a titmouse, or a reedy bulwark frog: something to do with the glands, you see. A few years back and the finger down the throat was not unknown to her.

That was before she met Elvis. Elvis, dizzy, and letting those stoned stardust phrases giddy their way from the stage while she grasped them like the confetti that they were, piecemeal, afraid that they would dissolve in the sweat of her hands.

What made him notice her? Was it an acknowledgement that, out there in the crowd, in those faces he could barely see, much less differentiate, there was a piece of his own, cracked mirror? Ah, Elvis, you should never have let them cut your hair. First came the hair, but then it'd be the teeth so indulgently dissolved in sugary feasts, and finally they'd be using your bones to fill the cavities of walls. Wasn't that a familiar pattern? Was it ever allowed that black should become white or vice-versa? Ask Miss Piggy, she'll tell you. Somewhere inside her was a person as thin as a thread caught from a nylon stocking.

Think on this: when falling stars fission in the night sky and then crash through the roof of a house belonging to some old codger who makes it to page five of the national newspapers next morning, Elvis is in there too, clinging to its tail. Poor Miss Piggy would never even make it that far, she's still somewhere in the centre of the earth, waiting to be spat out in a blob of molten ore.

Look at her, risen like some badly-made cake. Those feet were never made for walking, they were baby feet, with rounded baby toes. The pink varnish that she spent so long applying yesterday had begun to peel and chip already. And she was never going to dance! But yes, there she was, each step dragged through cement, singing 'Love Me Tender', more passably than her companion ever could these days.

Elvis wanted another milk shake, he wanted another tub of full-fat, udder-creamy vanilla ice cream. To express this desire, he thumped loudly on the floor twice with his barrelled, sequinned arm and grunted the way that cavemen do in cheap fifties movies. Somehow deciphering this code, Miss Piggy ceased her dance mid-step and fell like a pressed flower through a strung and beaded side door. Shortly, she returned with the required food, and spoon-fed Elvis as you would a baby. Out of indulgence, and because she was feeling expansive, she allowed herself a sip of milk. Just a sip, mind, just enough for the foam to melt along her lips. When he finished, Elvis sighed and gave what may have been a smile. Miss Piggy would have spooned a whole frothy ocean for that.

She watched him as he rolled back his eyes, seeing himself ride with Jimmy Dean on some ghostly Cadillac, faster now, faster than he would ever move again, the great lumbering sloth. Roads described Bluegrass Mountains here, and the clouds surrounding those distant, shivered peaks were the torn tissue from the latest, loving, expensive gift he'd received, inscribed with hearts, the writing on the card in simple loops and the i's dotted with circles. *To Elvis With*, well, that was so predictable, why even read the rest? The lawn at Gracelands fed on the fallen petals of discarded bouquets, it had the green lushness of death. Look! There was a thief come in the moonlight to scoop up a few of the faded flowers, his tulle bridal dress drifting upwards as he dropped. Could it be salt or could it be sugar that made the heads bloom so suddenly alive and fill the air with the unmistakable scent of attar? But too late to wonder - he'd escaped with his pocketful of evanescent fame. Had Elvis known, he could have introduced him to Colonel Parker.

Oh, but that was right, the good Colonel had gone, hadn't he? And Elvis surely would follow. Look at the polarity of his chest which took such an effort to rise and fall, and the way his mouth hung open and bubbled wetly. Miss Piggy noticed but daren't say. Unimaginable. I mean, the very possibility...

Still, something haunted Gracelands that night. Every movie Elvis ever made was shining celluloid bright somewhere in the world, but here the dust was growing greedy, the discs that described the walls were becoming tarnished, the vinyl stacked in racks had been played too often. Look how the speed had been getting slower: 78, 45, 33. Isn't that inevitable, you say, and of course it is, but don't let Miss Piggy hear.

Yes, Miss Piggy, sat there with starry eyes a-jangle, knees crooked and compact with the fold of her arms. She thought about, well, one day, a mingling, a meshing of genes. Something that was not a polarity but a grid of their desires, venturing out into the world.

Here is a secret: Elvis was a mask. What lay behind the mask? The child would know, that lightless thing with Elvis spittle and Elvis lips and Miss Piggy eyes and Miss Piggy nose. Crawl and hump and slither, blackened creature. If it found a voice (would it inherit those essential cords?) it would modulate between southern growl and obese squeal, vacillating like a radio signal, the type that every day, every moment, let drift one of Elvis' songs to the cupped ear of the world. It was a rhetorical process of course, and Gracelands carried a New York of antennae on its back. We all know how the legend ends: pills and diapers and the muted attention of a TV screen. What would have become of Miss Piggy by then? Better not to ask. Maybe she never existed at all, maybe Elvis' mind only pulled her from the adoration of a crowd and brought her here, a ghost to fill Gracelands' empty, populated rooms.

Best not tell Miss Piggy that. It's all her self-confidence would need, to learn she was the product of some dreaming god's mind. An incident from her childhood rose here like heat: "PUSH and PULL Katie," (because, yes, that was Miss Piggy's real name), "or you'll have thighs like a walrus' fins forever." Where else did she learn those dance steps but at ballet class? And did you ever see such a lumpen, heavy creature forced into a pair of leotards? Her teacher, whose name was, oh well I forget, but who was clouds and sheet lightning, drove the rhythm into her pupil's body, but every step, every perfected bend, arc or curve was mettled with an insult. Bestial names: elephant, hippopotamus, rhino, ape, and here was the one, "*What a little Miss Piggy you are. I swear, what a child.*" Well, that was yeast to her dreams.

There, she was arching her toes because the memory returned again. Barefoot, but with a ghost of pink satin. If she could make that leap, it would take her to outer

49

space. No chance for Elvis though, lying there anchor-heavy, waiting for the pennies on his eyes.

"Treat me like a fool, treat me mean and cruel". That's another song, isn't it? Elvis sang it many times, drama-laden, but he never meant it. It was only the love he wanted, swept-up affection like flower petals left on stage when the curtain had fallen and the lights had risen, too bright. While the audience filed out for coolness and the torn membrane of a dream, he sat backstage drinking fizzy drinks and - it was to become a habit - a pill to wash down the memories.

It is a natural process to rise and fall. See how, poised, Miss Piggy toppled towards Elvis. Her head rested on his chest, her fingers sought his hair. Elvis, too sated perhaps, did not resist. In moments like these, with their quiet loneliness, they were not separate but fused somehow, like colliding atoms, or slices of bread and butter pudding stacked the wrong way.

"But love me." Miss Piggy said the words aloud, with just enough force for her to hear, while the rest of the room filled with the rough breath of Elvis' dreams.

Sleepwalkers

What disturbed her that night? She still didn't know, even though everything else had become clear on that trail of memory she'd travelled so many times. The clue must have lain in the blood roar of fear accompanying her as she woke in the middle of the room, far from the bed from which she'd risen, as it must in the covers thrown back as if in panic. Yet there was nothing, no trace of dream or nightmare to have driven her to stand in her nightdress in the room's dark centre, night bird call and insect burr crusading the unlatched windows her only accompaniment. Perhaps there was nothing. Perhaps the process of waking was enough for terror. She was only seven.

Standing there, she became aware of the sound. Faint, a tremor in the house's far recesses, but present all the same. It came from downstairs, a footstep or an object disturbed in the passing. She imagined it would be her parents. They'd taken to staying up late, sitting at the kitchen table, caught in an earnest reminisce that chose its path between grief and nostalgia.

This ritual had begun when her grandmother died. She had been found at the bottom of the stairs from which she had not fallen or attempted to ascend but simply chosen as a place to die. It was her heart. Everyone expected it; they'd wondered how the previous attacks hadn't finished her off. "She was a resilient old bird," they said, sigh and admiration in one, before adding, "You'll miss your grandmother, won't you Catherine?" And she did, it was true, but only in the way you miss a piece of furniture that suddenly isn't there, or a favourite television programme not on at the appointed time. It was natural, that was what she understood, people die. Still, she would not tread on the step on which her grandmother had been found, nor would she go near the room in which she had lain, waiting for burial. Choosing to brave these areas at night was an indication of how deep her disturbance lay. She wanted comfort. She wanted her mother or father to take her in their arms and say, "What are you doing up at this time of night? Are you thinking about your Granny, is that it?" And then they'd sit in the blued haze of the kitchen, the scatter of conversation broken around her, words she'd ignore but gain comfort from, their untidy rhythm, and then she'd fall asleep, waking in her bed to morning, sun or rain on the window to accompany her.

This is what drove her down the stairs. They were darkened, the last step skipped past, but then where she expected brightness there was only further darkness, and somewhere amongst it the merest of sounds, half a dimension away from where she stepped, between waking and sleep. The possibility of danger didn't occur to her: she was at an age in which fear took on less mundane, less specific forms. The house, her parents, these were solid, unmovable things which did not allow the possibility of uncertainty or crisis.

This same certainty led her into the kitchen, from which the noises emerged. It too was dark, her eyes taking time to adjust and register the figure standing there. It was her grandfather. He was in his pyjamas, jacket undone to reveal the frailty of his chest, and she couldn't see what he was doing exactly, but it seemed to be some sort of circling dance, a ritual compulsion sending him first this way and then turning him back again, tracing with circumspection the linoleum, the pattern which may have been pavement cracks or stone-earthed abyss. His face, turned to her, was nothing human but instead resembled a mask, set in the expression of despair. He made a low keening noise and his body rocked from side to side in time to this sound.

"Grandad?" she said, "What's wrong?" As she spoke, he circled away from her and began to beat at his body with his fists. "Grandad, what are you doing? Stop it. Please."

She ran to him, and tried to halt his movements by holding onto his arms, but he was a strong man and pulled away from her. There was a force in him greater than muscle or compulsion. Greater, certainly, than Catherine who was slippers and ribbons and acrylic toys. When she looked up at his face, she saw he didn't recognise her at all, didn't even see her, and he was instead looking at something distant, something she couldn't see, something existing only in the recesses of his mind.

That was the first time Catherine saw anyone sleepwalk, at least as far as she could remember. She thought about it often, one of those childhood incidents recurring with ferocity in idle or distracted moments. Did this influence her choice of career? It was difficult to say, but it must have, if not consciously then at some other level, forming a guiding principle leading her first from this place then to that, from medicine to physics to biology to neurology. Maybe it would have happened anyway. Who could say? Time's ravel was too complex to unfold the moments of what might have been from the implacable, the events over which she exercised no control. Only the destination was certain, the position she now held, working as a research assistant in an institute for sleep disorders, her first and only job. It was like an object that's been hidden around a corner, unseen, but present all the time.

In the process she'd moved to the city. If her childhood was tied inextricably with the country, then adulthood was the collusion of concrete and steel, the nerve endings of speed and light she'd only encountered askance, years before, on school outings and trips to shopping arcades bleeding from the city centres. Then, experienced in hours or days, it seemed both enthralling and intimidating. Only when she lived there did she discover how mundane much of it could be. She rented a flat weathering the city's undesirable areas, close enough to feel the thrill of danger, but aloof enough to offer protection: locks on the doors and windows and a spy hole to look through when someone came calling. Each morning she'd travel to work by tube or bus and then the day would expand into a world of diagrams and questions and long hours of observation fed into reports. A depth to the job she hadn't expected pulled her in so deeply that after work and travel little else remained. The friends she made in the city were work colleagues, there was that intimacy and coldness, but that was the way she wanted it. Her career came first. The rest could come later.

Jaime was first admitted to the clinic two months ago. Unusually, while his sleep patterns show signs of disturbance manifesting themselves in episodes of somnambulism, no instances of trauma seem to exist that could be held responsible for these incidents.

He is five years old. His parents are both wealthy immigrants who have lived in this country for three years now. Jaime has little recollection of his life before this time and has settled in to his new surroundings with no real difficulties. The sleepwalking episodes began two years ago for no apparent reason. He is not known to have experienced any prior occurrences.

Each incident follows a similar pattern. On a nightly basis he rises and travels as far as he is able from his place of sleep. Sometimes this takes him out the house and into the garden. There he proceeds to play what appears to be a complex game with invisible companions. The game involves catching and chasing but is performed in a very elaborate manner. Neither his parents nor staff observing him have seen any precedent or variation of this game. It seems to follow very definite rules, and once the game has ended, he will either fall asleep at the same spot or find his way back to bed.

Although this is a nightly occurrence, there are no discernible causes or signs of stress. Its only effect is to cause the child to complain of tiredness and cause long periods of lethargy. Medical checks have found nothing untoward. Furthermore...

Jaime was throwing an object of some sort. Invisible, undefined. You rather imagined the object might be a ball, but it was difficult to tell. Maybe it was war games, and weapons, the things boys really like, a programming unravelled from the genes. His laughter, seemingly so innocent as he ducked and hid, may have been malicious, or a cover for distress washing in from his dreams.

Catherine watched him through a two-way mirror, of the sort she'd once thought only existed in police programmes and spy films. The room it looked into was sparsely functional: a bed, a table, a token picture on the wall, the mirror through which she made her observations. It wasn't the sort of place she'd have been inclined to sleep in, although in actuality her bedroom at home had something of its studied practicality. This was an area with no free exits, no intrusion allowed beyond her own, and the cameras, the confessional hooked down from opposite ends of the ceiling to catch their subject in anglepoise.

Even in sleep, the child had an aura of invulnerability. She'd noticed that when she'd first met him, and it took some time for her to work out the cause, which was wealth. It provided a level of protection she could only imagine from her own middle-class perspective. Nothing intruded there, and if the child claimed no worries or traumas, then probably he had none. The world she wanted him to inhabit was one of crayon and crushed chalk, pastel colours, a paintbox thinness. She wouldn't allow the possibility of muddier tones seeping in.

Giggling, he danced around in a circle. Wherever he found himself, he wasn't alone. Did he see other children? Was this a phantomed game of chase or tig? In the darkened room he moved in and out of shadow, towards and away from the observation screen. There was never any suggestion he'd collide with the objects around him, even with his eyes closed. He danced through a new geometry, something fractal, dimensions not quite expanding to another level. Left on the outside, watching, trying to comprehend, Catherine took notes that didn't quite cohere. At one point she'd even considered the possibility that he wasn't even asleep, but this was an act too elaborate and regular. She doubted a child of his age would have the stamina to continue with such deception for a long period of time. Looking at him, she felt she was entering the realms of demons and angels; there was a sort of primacy to the occasion. An atavistic fear, here, in the painted walls and neon lit rooms that would allow nothing else but the purest scientific calibration.

That night she finished late and Roy offered to drive her home. It was out of his way but he said he didn't mind. It was the first time she spoken to him really, he'd only been with the department for a fortnight, and their relationship was one of nods and muttered hellos in passing. To look at, you'd have thought he'd been derived from some sort of archetype, stocky, bearded, clumsy hands with stub fingers, glasses that could only be described as practical. He had an appetite for gaudy things, the credit rush giving him protection by designer brand, the payment on abeyance. His car was new enough to smell of leather and plastic.

"You're not really getting the opportunity to see how it moves," he said, "not stuck in the traffic like this. We should be out in the country, you'd see the speed it travels at then."

He talked incessantly, from the moment they left work together, subjects appearing in freefall, a morass of words substituting for conversation. Catherine was astute enough to hear nervousness in his voice signifying attraction, or at least the desire to impress. This didn't stop her mind wandering, and every so often she'd interrupt his monologue at what she hoped were appropriate moments with murmurs of approval or understanding.

They were travelling through the outskirts of the city. This was where buildings had been demolished by a bomb blast a year before, and at the time every newspaper had carried the same photographs of concrete slabs clinging to steel girders, of shards of glass fallen in such quantities it gathered in drifts, like some bizarre meteorological phenomenon. Now it was being rebuilt and new synapses of cables and plinths formed their surroundings. Catherine didn't usually take this route and she found herself staring at the construction with the intensity of a tourist.

Roy said, "When they build them high like that, it's an invitation to knock them down. You never hear of terrorists attacking hovels. My brother works there, you know. He was the one that got the phone call, warning about the blast."

"What does he do?"

"Something in finance, I don't know exactly. You know the sort of thing, sums and suits. I don't speak to him much, he just tries to make me feel inadequate."

"Brothers do that. It's a man thing"

"You know -"

"I'm sorry?" She hadn't been listening.

"I've got two tickets for Macbeth, tomorrow night at the National. Do you want to go? It's had good reviews."

"What, Shakespeare? I'm not sure it's my sort of thing. Besides, I'll be working late again."

"Go on, a night off won't kill you. I'm ambitious too, but you've got to have some sort of life outside of work. Think of it as research, if you have to. The most famous depiction of sleepwalking in literature. 'Out, damn spot; out, I say.'"

"Oh, I know the one. That's the wife, isn't it, washing her hands. I remember it from my school days, vaguely. It might be interesting."

"You'll come, then?"

"If you'll pick me up."

"Sleepwalking and ambition. You'll enjoy it."

Catherine wasn't sure where he'd got the notion she was ambitious. It might look that way, she supposed, to an outsider, but her work was really a pit she fell into and couldn't find her way back out of again.

He dropped her off at her flat. Dark now, the streets near to where she lived began to fill with the disenchanted, the hopeless, the desperate. Drunk, stoned, aimless. It was her life's polar opposite. Roy dropped her off outside the main entrance.

"You won't forget about tomorrow night? Six-thirty, I'll pick you up then."

"I'll see you at work anyway, remind me just in case."

As he drove away, there was the sound of gunfire, or it may only have been a car backfiring. Living in the city, she tended to assume the worst.

She climbed to her flat up stairs smelling of cat piss. This was the middle class barrier, this expensive tawdriness. What was it like in the places she distantly saw but didn't dare visit? The ones with chicken wire on the windows and graffiti and the groups of youths standing around on the pavement, the ones she crossed the opposite side of the street to avoid? At times she'd be lying in bed, not yet asleep, and noises would rise off the street, remote and alien. She knew where the noises came from, but she couldn't imagine what caused them, these sharp, dangerous sounds that were frightening and attractive at the same time. Out there in the city somewhere, in that stretch of patterned light and dark.

It was later than she'd imagined. She'd eat then sleep and then it would be morning again. A lengthening cycle to the working day made the hours disappear without even an awareness they were passing. Supper came in foil and plastic, cooked beneath the bright-lit eye of the microwave. Ready-made meals for one. Standing in the kitchen she looked out over the city. It was a mirror constellation, giving birth to sounds of traffic, car horns and sirens, shouts seeming to have no purpose beyond their own expression. Behind her, the radio played. Reports of the threat of war in the Middle East; a disaster - earthquake, famine, flood? - in somewhere yet more obscure, a country whose name was a congress of syllables on the tongue; the death of a television star whose life had proven as flimsy as celluloid. The usual. The babble of uncertainty. How the days were measured out, in moments of catastrophe and glamour.

She lifted the cover from the meal she'd prepared and spooned it out onto a dish, burning her fingers on the film lid. A compounded smell rose from the food, the product of a culture in which everything had become amalgamated, indecisive. The necessity for speed, the blurring at the edges of familiar things, this is what the meal represented. All the time that her body performed its automatic movements, she thought about Jaime. Jaime, and then Roy, who intruded unexpectedly into her thoughts.

The meal grew cold quickly and tasted of plastic. She was used to it. Her life was like that.

With his face close to the glass, Catherine could see the forehead riven by the scar. A deep cut had formed a tightly puckered wound, a geological formation he attempted but failed to disguise by combing down his hair. It was the most visible evidence of damage, but there was more: a broken wrist, bruises, scoured flesh, a limp, black eye, bashed ear, the bloody swab of his nose. Seemingly no part of his body had not at some point suffered impact, piercing, general trauma. Many of the injuries were negligible, but all had been inflicted in his sleep.

"One morning I'll wake up in my bed," he had said, "and find part of me's missing." He said this jokingly, but since she'd had him under observation, Catherine understood how inattentive to his own safety he could be.

What he was doing now, for example? Down on his hands and knees, trying to crawl beneath the bed, bashing his head in the process, then scraping his back on the metal bedsprings. There must have been pain, but he didn't even wake up. Perhaps he'd been conferred some sort of invulnerability in his dreams. It was hard not to believe the injuries weren't deliberate, at least on some level: even asleep, people tended to retain at least a tangential awareness of their surroundings.

The subject: male, thirty seven years old. Divorced, two children, job on a fixed term contract coming to a close. Who wouldn't be insecure in a situation like that? Coming up to middle age, you're supposed to be looking for stability, settling down to the cosy inevitability of rut. Catherine thought this threat must carry over into his sleep, taking physical form: that was her theory.

Roy poked his head around the door to remind her he'd be picking her up at half-past-six. Was that ok? She nodded, distracted, before realising what he was saying. She'd been more interested in the events taking place in the observation room, and had genuinely forgotten.

"Do you think I wouldn't remember?" she lied.

The man was feeling along the walls now, as if searching for weaknesses or cracks. The yellowed light gave the scene the cast of lurid drama. When Catherine had spoken to him before, when he was awake, lucid, she'd discovered he had a love of action adventure films, fantastic drama, he followed the progress of UFO groups on the Internet. Asleep, was this the world he inhabited? More malleable than his own, limitations stretched by desire, mundanities replaced by the fantastic. If it was, he gave no indication, and claimed no recollection when awake. There was a link here with the child, yes, it was speculative and tangential, but she was sure she had found one. She made a note of this in her book.

The man stubbed his toe.

Roy said, "I didn't think it would hurt, before you got too wrapped up in things," but she only nodded again, not hearing him at all now, drawn into the events before her, the dream's fever allowing no possibility of escape.

The phone rang when she was half-undressed, tights flapping around one leg, blouse unbuttoned and caped around her shoulders. It was her mother, she could tell even before she lifted up the receiver: the telephone's tone shrieked more insistently somehow when she was on the other end.

"I thought I'd just give you a ring to see how you were," her mother said. "We hear so seldom from you these days."

"It's work, you know that, it's always busy."

"Too much work isn't good for you. You need some time to relax. Go out and enjoy yourself with friends. And," she added, on the offensive, "it would be nice if you could spend a little time for your parents now and then. When are you coming to visit us?"

"It'll be soon, I promise. I've some leave coming up." Then, as a means of distraction, "Besides, I am going out, tonight, in fact. I've a friend coming round to pick me up soon."

"Mm. A male friend?"

"Oh, mother, I can't say anything without you sniffing out the possibility of marriage and children somewhere down the line." Then, switching the topic again, an old hand at the practice, "Is dad there? Put him on, then."

She talked to her father, the husk of his voice down the other end of the line. Words were hard to pull out of him; he was the opposite of her mother. He wasn't keeping well, she could tell, there was an ache of disease in his voice when he spoke, but she couldn't get him to admit this. When her mother came back on the phone, Catherine promised faithfully that, yes, she would visit soon and, yes, she was keeping well. Yes, it was safe where she lived, her mother shouldn't pay any attention to the news stories: they were all exaggeration. It was a litany of reassurance, a mantra to defend against the corroding rain and random attacks fissioning the city. Each time her mother called, she had to repeat it, as if the words themselves were protection. This ritual was expected, on both sides. To end the conversation she lied and said her lift had arrived, she could hear the car horn beeping, and yes really she must go. That left her mother spitting out words, at the line's far end, trying to form a bridge of syllables across the electronic continent to where her daughter lived.

She'd thought a play would be like a film with bad acting. There had been a vision in her head of actors on the stage in stilted poses, reciting dialogue the texture of concrete. Costumes made out of curtain material and prompts whispered from the wings. That was what it had been like in her school days. What she hadn't expected was the tension, the taut snare of emotion that held and released the audience. Yes, it was artificial, but it was an artificiality that drew her entirely in. Nor had it occurred to her before, how many parallels her working day had with the theatre. The same props, the lit stage, the detachment between observer and observed. And then there was Lady Macbeth, somnambulant, giving the recital that even Catherine knew, the play's moral centre expressed in one still moment where repressed emotions seep out in the form of compulsion.

"It's everything you need to know about psychology," Roy said, "in a single scene." He was leaning over, whispering in her ear. He smelt of soap and mint, there was a scented chemical something that came from his hair.

She smiled and squeezed the tips of his fingers, aware of the act of intimacy she'd performed. On the stage, the set had changed to one involving intrigue, plots, hints of the future. What a strange place for romance, surrounded by hundreds, in the theatre's blued light, watching a play about murderous ambition, guilt and retribution.

Later, they stood in the bar, speaking in the warm alcohol-fuelled fuzz of sociability. She felt giggly and affectionate, the way she'd felt when she'd had schoolgirl crushes on popstars and teachers. She'd trouble enunciating her words.

"My brain's like sherbet. It's all fizzy and popping in different directions. I really didn't expect to enjoy this evening so much. Thank you for invot-inva-inviting me." Then, after a moment's consideration, "It's the wine, it's going to my head."

"It's only three glasses."

"I don't usually drink. You're a corrupting influence."

Afterwards, they drove home through a city made of light, all danger sealed out by speed and glass. She leaned her head on Roy's shoulder, experimentally. An unreality to the scene made her give way to softer emotions. What she'd constructed was a world drawn from celluloid, romantic fiction, womens' magazines she never read but whose ideas she was aware of anyway. It was infant gratification.

Outside of her flat, she waited for the opportunity to invite him in, but he only smiled and said goodnight, and didn't even give her a goodbye kiss. Yes, it was disappointing, no matter how much she tried to pretend otherwise. Her job to was see below the surface, to read the props and signs, but that evening she'd misplaced the ability, it had been distorted by an unexpected, rising ache, and all the signs she'd seen, she'd misread them, she hadn't understood them at all.

The woman was always crying. She'd stand then grasp her hands to her chest, and the tears proved limitless. There didn't seem to be any obstruction, no barrier of retained emotion. To look at her you would have thought there would have been. Early fifties, make up, immaculate hair. Well off: evidently life had treated her kindly. Age hadn't really hit her, face a bit jowelly, perhaps. Yet there she'd be, shivering with grief, saying, "Oh please, please, you mustn't," until suddenly she'd wake, and the moment of terror would carry over from one state to the next, without her knowing why, leaving her bewildered.

Here was a coincidence: she'd been to see Macbeth on the same night as Catherine. It wasn't a topic Catherine encouraged, because it brought up associations she didn't want to follow. Yes, an excellent performance But we'll assume your sleepwalking doesn't spring from quite the same cause as Lady Macbeth's. Polite laughter. The woman was that sort of person.

Asleep, she was different. Her grief was oracular, the look on her face distant. She'd perch on the bed's edge in her recalcitrant pose, displaying a strangely impersonal suffering, one not directed at anyone or anything in particular. It was sorrow for sorrow's sake, it was a glimpse into the future and the fact of her own death, it was a longing martyrdom for the world she found herself in. It was any or none of these things: Catherine couldn't tell, it was something she couldn't penetrate. What her life had become was embodied there, acid around the edges. It was a blankness, it was white noise, it was the disquiet that had grown, without reason, until it formed her life's hollow centre.

The news was full of the conflict in the middle east. People spoke seriously about prophecy and the end of the world, as if a war in one part of the globe was more significant than any other. A group of people had committed suicide in one of the wealthy areas of the city. Twenty of them, in the same building, lying in a circle with their arms crossed over their chests like Egyptian mummies. They called it a doomsday cult. The new century's particular manifestation of hysteria.

In the clinic, the doctors discussed share prices rising and falling. Would this one be a good investment now, or later? Roy had started to hang around with the more senior members, laughing at their unfunny jokes, trying to impress with his fawning. He'd hardly spoken to Catherine since their night out together. She didn't know what she'd done to offend him, or even if she had. It was difficult to broach the subject, especially at work. More than ever, nothing existed beyond work. More patients arrived daily, the centre could hardly cope. Catherine worked all the hours they asked and it was tiring, all she ever saw now was the world of sleep. She was starting to look forward to the leave she'd booked, even if it did mean honouring her promise to see her father and mother. The city was such an alien place, with no room for comfort. Leaving the clinic each night was like travelling into the set of a science fiction movie.

It was the middle of summer but it had started to snow. Freak weather patterns, the effect of tides and winds across the other end of the world. In the city it was only a rim on the buildings and a wetness underfoot, but in the country drifts reached to the tops of the hedgerows.

When she woke up in the middle of the night, having walked to the front door of her flat without knowing how she'd got there, she knew it was time to go home.

There was an interrogating moon. Had that woken her? Her mother and father were still asleep. When she rose it was to walk not through space but time, back to the limits of her childhood, as if she hadn't left this place at all, wooded, gabled, with odours in the rooms sweet and floral and overbearing. She looked out the window.

Her bedroom overlooked the neighbour's garden. There, lit by the moonlight in a way that recalled the stage, were three girls. They were sisters, she knew, late to early teens, wandering about the garden in their night-dresses. The girls were barefoot and somnolent. One reached up to the branches of a weeping willow. Another knelt, staring into the surface of the ornamental pond. The third capered along the stone set path, her hands raised in a wild jig, her clothing rising to reveal her nakedness beneath. At first Catherine thought she'd tumbled upon some sisterly midnight rite, an arcane companion to midnight feasts and pillow fights, but the girls were a little too old for that, and, besides, the gravity of their movements gave them away. They were sleepwalking, the three of them, all at once. Was

71

that what had drawn her here? The years she'd spent studying, taking notes, guessing intentions and motivations, had they attuned her to the very fact of a sleepwalker's presence? She opened the window and looked out, the night air still warm, laced with the trace of burnt wood and insect wings. She didn't know why it was necessary to do that, she wasn't going to call or speak, but it was as if the window formed a barrier between her and them. The window was stiff and paint-dried, and the sisters must have heard the noise of it opening, the crack and groan registering in the strata of their sleep-controlled minds. They looked up, the three of them. Their eyes were wide open, and it was a pleasure and a terror, their collective stare, with its numbness of expression, its lack of decision or judgement. The three of them, looking up, in the garden, in their night-dresses, barefoot, longhaired. To Catherine they looked like vestal virgins.

The Progeny of Jean Genet

It was a difficult birth. She lay alone in a bare, cold room, lying on a paint-stained sheet, naked from the waist down. Belly raised and knees levered up, her breath hissed out between cries. There was a monstrous pushing outwards, a ripping of flesh, the hot sting of blood. This heat sustained the morning.

She laboured in a derelict house close to the metro, its windows rattling when the train passed. Heedful, her child emerged with the precise arrival of the 11:30, headfirst, while her shriek mixed in with the train's, the clutching of brakes forcing out sparks. Then the sigh as the engines settled, mingled with her sigh: with the relief of having that enormousness thrust out of her.

After resting for a moment or two, she managed to lift her body forwards to see the child she had given birth to. Alarmingly, it had not seen fit to cry, although she could feel it move between her thighs. Pummelling legs revealed its sex: a boy, blue-veined, wrinkled and covered with bloody slime. He was large too, much larger than other newly-born babies she had seen. No wonder it had hurt so, emerging. The child had a snub nose and creased-shut eyes, and his ears were glued to the side of his head. Out of affection, she touched his face. Disturbed, his eyes opened. He had the clearest blue eyes, focusing in on her. Was that a look of distress? Surely not.

The child spoke. "Chipie," he said, and spat in her face. This done, he crawled away from her. The unexpected assault left his mother too startled to move, and she watched his progress instead, hindered as it was by an uneven clump of afterbirth dragging behind him.

His hands and knees left bloody imprints on the floorboards. On reaching the doorway, he turned to face her. His soft claw fingers lifted the string of afterbirth attached to his middle and, plucking the cord over the head of a nail hammered unevenly into the floorboards, he severed it from his body. Then, looking at his mother, he repeated the phrase *Chipie* before rising to his feet and padding out the doorway. Still too bewildered to follow, all she could do was listen to his clumsy descent on the stairs.

This was the last she ever saw of him. Where did he go after that? Down back alleys, under grates, into the glittering mica of the sewers. His diet consisted of shiningly carapaced insects, eggshells raided from unlidded bins, cold, congealed takeaways left by drunken, would-be philanderers on their way home at night. His gaudy mismatch of clothes was pilfered from unwary toddlers whose mothers had left them unattended for minutes, seconds: time enough. In pink dungarees and blue woollen cardigans he drifted around shops during the unwelcoming spring days, grateful for their ventilated warmth. Then, when it was summer, he made a more permanent home among the flower beds in parks where he lay on a matting of petals, falling asleep breathing in the scent of roses.

During this time he grew quickly, because he must. At three months he resembled a child of seven. At six months he could have been mistaken for a thirteen year old, even though he had not yet seen a single winter come and go. To commemorate this half-year coming of age, he chose a name for himself, an act of self-determination that would typify his life. The name he chose was Jacky. Oddly this was also the name his mother had chosen for him while he still lay in her womb. Jackie if it was a girl, Jacky if it was a boy.

Emboldened by this self-christening, his tactics for survival became more elaborate. In the autumn, on cold nights, he would allow himself to be taken back to unappealing hotels by randy sailors whose passion on shore leave extended no further than relentlessly screwing bored prostitutes in brothels. The hotels were usually dirty and unheated, but at least the bodies he pressed against offered warmth, his skin smooth against their hirsute chests. Some of them expressed love, which was sometimes reciprocated, but he always left before they did, and he always took their wallets with him.

Even when he had money he stole. It was a compulsion. Department stores with their clumsy electronic eyes proved no match for the deft manner in which he slipped clothing beneath his coat. Windows left open, even three or four stories up, were simply an invitation to intrude into their heated, scented interiors. The belongings he stole were stored in a disused railway shack to which he must have been drawn by an atavistic memory of the moment of his birth. Outside, it was broken wood and flapping tarpaper. Inside, it was a monument to gaudiness, he had a jackdaw's eye. Here were electrical appliances in all their shiny redundance; designer clothes, too large or small, or for the wrong sex; costume jewellery to rifle around in and let slip through his fingers; an enormity of toys in requiem for the childhood he would never have; and books, dustjacketed, so many that it was impossible he would ever read them all.

Books? Yes, because Jacky was a reader. The words, catching his eye, had their own riverflow torrent. There was never any question of his having to learn, because from the first he knew. Deciphering street signs and shop hoardings advanced to newspaper headlines. When he pilfered and read his first books, the world transformed, its brilliance described by the sharp intervention of words. He imagined creating his own language which would redefine the world for others, much as these books had done for him, but it was a solipsistic dialogue because the words seldom ventured further than the thoughts in his head. Sometimes he would begin a conversation with the sailors who nightly fucked him, but he was met with incomprehension. Most of these men were of the type where you could count the syllables in a sentence and be sure to come up with a number less than ten.

Here then was the contradiction: although he had no commitments he had also no freedom, because freedom is freedom of expression, and he had no-one to express himself to. When he dreamt, it was always that his body was hollow and porcelain and it was breaking open, like cracking laminate, to reveal a fairy tale briar of thorns underneath.

The day this changed was the day he met Java.

It began ordinarily enough, dawn still bleeding as he made his way to the park and the bed of flowers he had made his home. Here, his routine was to sit, watching the city waken, hearing the traffic sounds thicken while he counted out money usurped from a sailor who still slept alongside his body's warm indentation. On this particular morning it was darker than usual. Autumn had come and threatened to push prematurely into winter. Making his way over the chained, spiked gates that obscured even the isolated patches of the streetlights, he arrived at a circular bed of roses, withered now, leaving only a compressed thicket of thorns he had to manoeuvre, skilful enough with practice to avoid obtaining the red, inflamed scratches that still left their scars on his skin. Nevertheless, it took some concentration. Perhaps that was why he did not see another person had arrived before him, lying in the spot he usually occupied himself, a black knot of flesh gathered like a cat with its tail curled around itself. Only when he trod on an unseen limb, causing its owner to cry out with exaggerated pain, did it become evident anyone was there.

"Who's that?" Jacky called, suspended in the act of stepping forward. Before him, the darkness unfolded into a form, stood up to reveal a figure, male, around his own height. The figure spoke.

"I'd fallen asleep thinking you were never coming. I told the others, he won't be back until the morning. Would they listen? Oh, no. 'It's too important,' they said, 'what if you miss him and he moves on? We all move on, it's our nature'. Yet here you are, same as the morning before, and the morning before that. Well, it's too late now. Give me your hand."

Jackie remained frozen, hesitant.

"Give me your hand," repeated the figure, with such force that Jacky found himself automatically responding, his palm offered.

"That's better."

Saying this, the boy unfolded, he unpeeled like the delicate petals of the oneday flower he must be, the grasping stamen embracing Jacky who was too firmly held now to break free, and in the narcoticised grip of which he swooned, like an actress in a Victorian melodrama. Then they were gone, the two of them, with only a scarring of earth to show they had ever been there.

Jacky awoke in the midst of a marvellous jungle. Silver clagged pipes ran the length of the roof, spitting steam. A boiler with a flame-coloured spy panel made sporadic and terrifying outbursts of noise, turning the walls a pumpkin orange. It was as humid as the onset of a tropical storm. Lying on a sprawl of folded, yellowed newspapers, it seemed to him at first that he was alone, but the sound of a foot scraping on concrete made him turn. A shaven-headed youth looked down at him. He had a downward scar across both lips that made them pucker into four and a homemade tattoo scored into one cheek spelled out the word DIVINE. He was young, yes, but already he had the face of a middle-aged tough. This made his choice of clothing all the more startling, his thickset body awkward beneath a purple sheath dress. A fur boa purled around his shoulder.

"Look," he said, "he's awake." Saying this, the tough gave a speeded-up cartoon giggle.

With this announcement, others moved out of the darkness or from behind the obstacles the pipes created. There were six in all, amongst them the one who had brought Jacky here. None had the willed outlandishness of the thug in the dress, but seeing them together made definite what they had in common. It was their looks. Their features, while not identical, had a genetic similarity, like inbred cousins. They had broad noses and round faces, and their bodies were squat and stocky. All were boys. All were of the same age, or at least as far as could be gathered. One of them, dressed in the most sober of suits, and with a fedora tilted back from his head, hunkered down level with him.

"We were waiting for you to find us," he said, "but eventually we had to find you. Look," he continued, "you're bleeding."

On Jacky's chest, bright abstracts of blood began to appear. It was his nose. He pressed his hand against it to stop the flow.

"The heat -" he began, but Divine interrupted, saying, "It's the curse of the invert, the bleeding nose."

As though this were a further signal, all six moved closer, bending down to prod at his body, smearing fingers into the rush of blood beneath his nose, tasting it, marking their faces with it like a rite of passage.

Jacky demanded, quite loudly, that they stop. This quietened them for a few moments, but then they began again.

"Quite feisty, isn't he?"

"Certainly one of us."

"See his eyes flash."

"*Quel courage.*"

He faced them with silence, which seemed to work, because they grew silent too. The youth in the dress sat down beside him.

"Don't be alarmed. One always imagines a precedent is being set, but what you are feeling is known to us because we've been in the same situation. The fact is, we're your family."

"My family? You mean we share the same -" he spat "- mother?"

"Not quite, although it could be wished that the answer was as simple as that."

The youth's name, as it turned out, was not Divine at all but Maurice. "The tattoo's a commentary, not an appellation," he said, pushing his hand over his razored hair. All the others had equally forgettable names: Java, William, Mustapha, Dennis, Joe. Their names pushed against the remarkable quality of their lives.

"At first our meetings were only chance. Imagine the moment when Java and I met, how struck we must have been by the likeness of our features. Even in a city of this size, how unusual to find another made from same template. Questions revealed other similarities. Our remarkable birth, for one."

Yes, it was true, they all shared the same birthday, and if they could not narrow their emergence to minutes and seconds, it could at least be said they were born at roughly the same time. Their families, unrelated as far as could be told, were abandoned, before they abandoned them. All were precocious, their growth accelerated. How did they live? By theft and prostitution, at least until they discovered each other. The existence of others seemed certain when a third was found. Two? Coincidence. Three? More than chance. Something deeper drew them together, a taut line regulating their lives even while they worked in the pretence of freedom.

"Naturally you will ask yourself what it means, to be born in this way. We have all asked that question, if only to give our lives the deception of purpose."

"And the answer?"

"That we've still to discover. In the meantime, we have discovered a number of amusing diversions."

Yes, what mattered was the thrill of depleting shops, and the not unpleasant task of sucking men off in doorways and hotel rooms. They all knew the elaborate glamour of night, the neon city emerging with the sun's descent, the lurid texture of skin under sodium light. During the day they would return, dormouse-drowsy, to this place they had made their home.

"Which is your home now too."

This was a statement, not a question or an invitation, and it was one Jacky did not contradict.

He joined them to live in the basement of a nobleman's house, one commandeered during the war to become a governmental outpost. It had never been given back. Now it was used for storing papers. At night they stole upstairs and wandered between long rows of archived boxes, their labels age-yellowed and with an encrustation of dust along the top. It was a thrill to break the silence of that place with their footsteps, or to pry among the papers marked '*In Strictest Confidence*', even though their formulated language was a bore. It was not revelation that excited them so but desecration. If it had not been for the fact that they lived there, they would have dropped a match, just for the thrill of seeing it burn. Instead, they shuffled the documents and threw them quite at random back into the boxes they had been taken from. On some of the pages they scored out all the adjectives, on others the nouns. Several of the papers became nothing more than lists of conjunctives. When Jacky joined them, they adopted his suggestion of finding stories hidden among the texts, whole sentences scored out bar a word or two, pages curling shining and black apart from a few boxed words illuminated in white. Read one after the other, these papers created disjointed aphorisms lacking a moral. It was a process simultaneously both destructive and creative.

How long does it take to subvert fifty years of endless documentation? A long time: more time than they had. Besides, apart from the thin wattage of officials spending their day filing these objects away, carefully catalogued, no-one ever came here, and certainly no-one ever looked at the documents. This realisation caused their ambition to find another form.

One evening they were lying in the basement, sprawled like languid cats amidst the leaking, steamy pipes, with the heating cracking on and off to preserve the temperature just so, when the idea came to them. It came as Maurice was recounting the day's exploits.

"A Chinese sailor," he said. "Lugubrious 'til I met him. His prick was the size of a pencil stub. We played innocent lovers, holding hands in the cinema he took me to, but afterwards we fucked at the back exit while the music we heard played formed a soundtrack to our own activities. I came during an arpeggio, the moment in the film, I believe, when they failed to defuse a bomb. My little Chinaman, I'm afraid, hadn't lasted past the opening credits. Still, he was supremely grateful. Less so, one would imagine, when he discovered I had taken his wallet."

"That's what we need. A bomb." William, lying on his back, smoking, blew out disjointed smoke rings. "Something to enliven the city. Turn it inside out. Cause riots in dancehalls. Mothers will be afraid to let their children out in case their minds are corrupted. Fathers will roam the boulevards with primed shotguns threatening the lives of those who have defaced civility."

"And what shall we do to earn such notoriety?"

"We shall break into the offices of La Figaro."

Two weeks later, when the early editions of la Figaro appeared on the streets, the blandly inoffensive headline gave no indication of what lay inside. There, staunchly conservative columnists used their space to praise the accidental release from prison of a mass murderer who subsequently raped two toddlers while on the run. The centre pages were devoted to a full colour spread on Algerian militants who had been making random bomb attacks throughout the city, including a favourable appraisal of their demands. In the arts section three whole pages detailed the techniques of pederasty. The political cartoon depicted Jean-Marie le Pen metamorphosed into a pig, enthusiastically buggering a Jew.

These ersatz copies, smuggled into the paper's distribution centre and sold nationally, became the subject of a great scandal. Questions were asked in the highest offices. A special task force was assigned to tracking down the culprits. Copies quickly became collector's items, creating a market for counterfeit editions. Counterfeits of counterfeits, if you will.

The attention given such a prank was worldwide, and quite naturally the group were delighted with the success of their first attempt at media terrorism. The problem now was how to follow what they had just achieved. In the winter afternoons, when it became too cold to go outdoors, they sat in the humid, belching basement, making plans.

"Cover the billboards with absurdist slogans," suggested Joe.

"Daub the Eiffel Tower with graffiti of a libidinous nature," countered Maurice.

"Corrupt the databases of the world's publishers, so they only print out random phrases." That was Bill.

"Spike the coffee of the city's actors. You'd see them on talk shows or on stage reciting these perverse hallucinatory visions. That'd be so cool." Dennis speaking.

These ideas were debated, but nothing was ever settled. Instead they merged, quite without conscious decision, into a single plan, the sole purpose of which was to disrupt the workings of the city. Who else could have been responsible for defacing the signs and hoardings of the department stores they had previously stolen from with so little effort? Advertisements were adjusted to find or illuminate lewd connotations in their aspirational slogans. Place names and store signs, slyly adjusted, linked together to form situationist expressions, provoking debate in intellectual journals and prime-time TV as to their meaning. Following the routes of these slogans became a new, briefly-fashionable pastime. Chic teenagers on scooters conjoined with earnestly pondering Marxist deconstructionists who created learned and quite unoriginal papers on the meaning of these brief, emblematic phrases. For the children, there was the satisfaction of knowing they had moved from paper to glass and wood and paint, decoding the city's motorcades and boulevards.

Still, it was not enough. These activities had their limitations, no matter how skilfully carried out. The impulse they all felt had become defined and greedy, providing a need to continually better what had been done in the past. Their written acts of subversion occupied nearly all their evenings now, so they had to make daytime excursions to perform those acts of love and theft previously executed in the twilight. What time remained was spent on the debate of how their work should progress, a question endlessly argued over, never realised.

It was a debate to which Jacky hardly contributed. Instead he lay listening, drowsy, searching for a vision that would be grander, more outré, more true than the others.

One evening he had a dream. He dreamt the city turned to paper, and he and his brothers filled in every space on that paper with their finest handwriting. The whole city then was nothing but letters, words, phrases of his own devising. He awoke, excited at what he had seen, ready to tell the others of this grandiloquent vision, but when he lifted his head it was to find a rifle pointed at his head. A policeman, buffeted in riot gear, directed it towards him. Jacky tried to see the face, but the policeman's mask was polarised, and only his own features reflected back at him.

"Put your hands out," instructed the policemen. "There, where I can see them. Don't move."

Although he did as he was told, the butt of the rifle still swung into Jacky's side, and he folded over, breathless, almost crying, while his wrists were handcuffed behind his back. Then, when he looked up again, the boiler gave its sharp ignition of light, so the scene was caught like the impact of a camera flashlight, the seven of them bound and twisting, leathered policemen with their guns and truncheons astride them.

It emerged they had been careless. Faces had been caught on surveillance cameras. Sailors threatened with discharge from the navy supplied details of where the group had been, what they looked like, where they were likely to be found. Thin lipped Mafia bosses, alarmed at the children's sudden and efficient crime wave, squeezed out information and, once this had been obtained, had the children trailed. They too had an interest in preserving the current order.

The trial that followed was reported in lurid detail by the press, who all loved a villain but even more loved his downfall. The children sat in the dock, the seven of them, listening to police reports, psychiatric reports, traumatised witnesses for the prosecution, a team of semiotics experts assembled for the defence. When it came to their turn in the witness stand, they said nothing, standing muted by their unfamiliar suits, pinned by the eyes in the press gallery, European, American, Asian, looking at them. It was so silent in those moments that the combined scraping of pens on reporter's pads could be heard.

Certain facts emerged. The prosecuted were only over a little over two years old. Judge: "Is this verifiable?" Witness for the defence: "Milord, it is medically proven." This produced ethical quandaries. Was an infant morally responsible for a crime it had committed? "Milord, consider the psychological damage it must have caused ones so young to have found themselves trapped in the body of an adult. All are self-confessed homosexuals. To discover oneself so alone and vulnerable in an uncaring world. Imagine!"

Rather disappointingly for those assembled, the case ended in indecision. Of course they would have to be sent for incarceration, but the seven were to find themselves in a reformatory rather than prison. They were to undergo further psychiatric evaluation, while the press returned to their offices to file their sensationalist story without an ending.

"Even the legal system can't contain us," remarked Java, somewhat gleefully.

"One imagines it can," replied Maurice, "at least until we're seventeen."

So their sentence was almost equivalent to life. Seventeen years, without appeal, and who knew whether their own bodies would respect time or whether they would continue accelerating, into infirmity, decrepitude, death, the mouldering of ashes. They thought they had won, but they had not won at all. Still, if this was defeat, it must have its pleasures. In a reformatory there would be a degree of freedom, and undoubtedly there would be certain other boys around, the kind that attracted them, crop-haired and with self-inflicted tattoos on the backs of their hands.

Quite how mistaken this assumption was became clear when the reformatory first came into view, revealed when the van taking them there turned a bend in the road. It was an old building with high walls, slate roof, tall, barred windows set against a grey sky turning black. At one time it had been a ward of the insane. Its block stone walls were so thick they exceeded the length of a man's body. The courtyard was concrete, the walls barbed, the high metal gates topped with impaling spikes. On their arrival, each was given a uniform to wear, dun and harsh-clothed, and they would only have needed to rub ash on their bodies to complete the effect. Their heads were shaven, so it became even more difficult to tell them apart. A wing was provided for them alone, long disused, and here they all slept in the same room in which seven metalframed beds were lined, their corners tight-tucked, beneath high ceilings hung with saucer lampshades dangling from an extraordinary length of wire. In this place the enfeebled had been sent to die, and the children would wake in the night to cries they alone heard, glossalalia slipped through from another time when the insanity of the patients had found itself matched and bettered by the supposed cures of their wardens.

The children were treated quite differently from other inmates, with whom they were never allowed to socialise. They would see them sometimes, in the windows opposite, or down in the courtyard, playing volleyball. These inmates wore the same sort of clothing they would have worn in the street, and they seemed to move with a freedom confined only by the walls that enclosed the reformatory.

"Frankly," confined Maurice to Jacky one night, "I don't know whether I ought to feel jealous or superior."

Did the authorities fear for the safety of the seven? Perhaps. Or perhaps it was the safety of the other inmates they worried about, afraid the virus of ideas would spread, causing the others to become more than addicts, thieves, thugs. Perhaps this too explained the circling guards, watching warily while the seven ate their homogenised dinners, or while they sewed brown hemp mailbags, pricking their fingers as well as the material with sharp needles. This was how their days were spent. Every so often a doctor would come, or a psychologist. Examinations were made, ("Hmm," went the doctor), questions were asked ("Aah," said the psychologist), but any conclusions reached were never made known to them. At noon each day they were allowed to exercise, treading in a circle around the grey concrete courtyard.

At first they were unhappy about this situation, but as the period of confinement increased, their complaints became muted. Even routine has its comforts, and the longer they followed that routine, the more indistinct became the memory of those first anarchic years of freedom. Sometimes not even their separate identities were clear to them any longer, it seemed as though they had converged, so that Jacky would be called William, or William would be called Joe. Even if recognition was made of the mistake, it hardly seemed to matter, because their personalities had become as similar as their faces.

Perhaps this is the way it would have stayed, the seven of them unrecognised apart from the occasional coda of a newspaper article, but one night while they slept, an angel came. He was the strangest angel, dressed in the white of a bridal dress, his shiny pate struck with moonlight. A long, ledged window ran the length of the room beneath which the heads of the beds ran parallel, and he perched on this, barefoot, bridal veil obscuring his face, the train of his dress brushing down over their heads. He watched them while they slept. Curiously, the angel's face resembled theirs, only his features were older, more worn.

"Boys," he whispered.

The seven twisted in their sleep, made muttering sounds, answering conversation in their dreams.

"Boys fly free," he continued, and the bars fell away from the windows. They fell in serrated lengths, as though they had been cut through with a hacksaw.

"No locks, no doors."

The great iron door of the dormitory clicked open, swung wide. At night, a metal grille was placed at the end of the corridor, and on this the padlocks snapped open, fell to the ground.

"No-one will stop you."

Alerted by the noise, the guards turned, panicked, twisted on their feet, then collapsed face down in an opium fervour.

"The whole city awaits you."

The power in the building went out, alarms disabled. Although it had been a calm night, the wind blew fierce and burst open the walled gate, the front door. The glass in the window cracked, scimitar fragments leant inwards. Caught in a shared, ecstatic dream the children slept through it all.

Leaping down from the windowsill, the angel walked the length of the room, looking at each sleeping body in turn. The moonlight that cut in through the window seemed to follow his path, the enveloping bridal dress, the long train that trailed over splintered wood, glass and metal. He walked barefoot and when the glass cut his feet he bled, leaving dark, pressed stains along the floor. Perhaps he was not an angel at all.

Then he was gone, as inexplicably as he had come. When he had left, the children awoke. They were not surprised to find the destruction around about because it had been signalled to them in their dreams.

Everyone else in the building must have been asleep for they stepped away from that place with nothing to accompany them, apart from the sound of their footsteps grinding in the debris, and their breathing grown loud in their ears, excited by the memory of freedom. In the courtyard, the dogs that usually patrolled at night were found curled against each other, trawled into unconsciousness, legs entangled, teeth bared as they had been when they first sensed danger.

The wind had grown calm again. Walking out of the front gates, they found themselves on the outskirts of the city which was spread, scored with light, before them. It came to them on the air too, in the blunt scent of smoke and petrol. A car passed, and the driver offered them a lift. Even they thought it strange that he did not remark on their harsh dress, nor the fact that they should be out so late at night. The driver said nothing for the length of the journey, but when he let them out in the city centre, Jacky noticed a lacy flap of tulle peeking out from his shirt cuffs.

As they moved through the city, the moon was so bright it was almost a cold, submerged daylight. They strode abreast through side streets that were barely enough to contain their width, the gaps between the arrondissements of commerce where the walls grew mildewed, a gathering of back entrances, no-one else foolish enough to linger there at that time of night, because these were the spaces where the uncivilised collected, taut beneath untested fire escapes, junk hungry, attached and repulsed by the security of wealth.

With their passage, the city changed. The libraries were the first to go. Animated by the language they contained, books leapt from shelves, their dust jackets bent back and the pages purling, a susurration of paper that blew a dusty fervour through the corridors, doors slapping, banging, the edges of carpets lifting, snapping. Then, unwatched, from beneath the book's pages there flew an assault of flowers, their petals only, reddened, lilac, pollen yellow. They rose circling in the breeze then gathered in lurid piles against walls, against doors.

In the streets, similar events were occurring. From the painted letters of shop signs briars grew, a long twisting of thorns ravelled down to the pavement, pure blood-red roses bursting and opening their petalled maws, roiling around lampposts, parked cars, prising open doors which filled the air with their electronic shrieks until these defences were defeated by the clogging of spores. Newspaper stands, tarpaulined, waiting for the morning to come, vomited out a sudden carpet of microheaded blooms. In supermarkets, the carefully stacked products grew a mossy covering where the instructions had been, and these in turn produced thin, pin blossoms that overgrew the metal shelving, subsided the floor, crashed through the windows where the day's special offers had been posted. In apartments, love letters stored in the back of drawers tumbled out and became bouquets. On the back of electrical appliances, the polyglot of languages took on a common vegetative form. Advertising hoardings became vast, ornamental displays, producing horizontal gardens of flowers that spelt out ESSO and PEPSI before they were totally overwhelmed. Wherever they passed, it happened; nothing survived this process. The city, twisting language inside out, was cracking, transforming, becoming a hallucinatory jungle through which the seven wandered while others screamed either from delight or fear. When the streetlights blew out one by one, it became a darkened place, growing sultry in the density of vegetation, hotter than it had been in the months of summer. So many places for the plants to grow, in the printed cavity of the written word.

The seven walked to other parts of the city, and the air was filled with the scent of roses.

Why Men Carry Bullets in Their Guns

There are some places less precious than dust. A main street, a saloon, some bare, narrow rooms, that's all they have. The buildings are made out of wood, which is better than straw, but it lacks the permanence of brick. It's how it is in the Wild West.

Men come here in search of their fortunes, dragging their families like animals on a leash. The prairies are so vast that some of them are never seen again. In the tall, illuminated cornfields children hide, growing as hard and pious as savages. Their chattering exists only to fill the silence.

Even the town is better than that. There's the bottle there, and love, and the gun. Sometimes all of them fall together in a lopsided pattern. It as common, in fact, as three pennies falling heads in a row.

On the street of the town there is a man called McGrath and a man called Tangiers and they are fighting. They fight under a full noon sun with incomplete bodies that are lopsided and balanced on precarious wooden carts. Hand meets hand, chests crush against the other. Tangiers has his teeth bitten deep into McGrath's nose. The carts supporting them tremble with a seismic vigour. If it was a measure of the passion being generated here, then the earth would split and then draw them into its dark, sulphurous gullet.

Directly alongside the two men is a saloon. Above the saloon, a series of rooms. Each of the rooms has a balcony, uneven and plainly cut. On one of these, Rosa sits. She is prominent in a dress of rough pink and white striped calico from which peacock feathers elaborately sprout. Her feet are bare, the tangle of her hair falls about her neck like a sad disease. She is drinking absinthe. Even from where she sits the sounds the men make can be heard: grunts mostly, but sometimes short, brutal words too. "Cocksucker," they say. "Cunt." "Bastard." "Fucker." "Shit." Their carts butt together so that they threaten to become overturned crabs, stranded with a scrabbling of amputated limbs.

It is very hot. Rosa does not know how they have the energy to fight in this heat. Directly above, the sun is burnished to a hard gloss. The dust in the air is a pepper itch. She can see the glare of their loved and polished boots. One wears spurs that clink like counterfeit gold. The other wears a belt of bullets that he has been known to rub excitedly over his crotch at night. Both are familiar with the fever of powder burns and the prickle of sweat on flesh.

As they grapple, a gun falls from a holster and a horse on the opposite side of the street collapses in a bloody froth. Something happens to the two men then and they fall into each other's bodies that are both liquid and hard at once. Rosa looks on, and it is like a premonition of a movie screen spread before her.

McGrath first met Rosa when he had a corpse in one hand and a gun in the other. He stood in a street with the dust gusting hard and a spray of blood blown in his face. His teeth showed up much too white. Rosa hid her eyes as she passed, but he bowed for her anyway and then fired his gun up into the air so birds gathered split apart like spores or ink on wax.

That same evening he turned up at the saloon where she worked. The backward clatter of doors announced his arrival, deliberate in his best, pressed dark suit, as though he were attending a funeral. His thinning hair had been lashed to one side by means of an unfamiliar comb. Flowers clasped in his hand had been pruned by the wind.

"For you," he said, and pushed them towards her.

"Two dollars," she said, "and you can have me flat on my back."

So in this way the basis of their relationship was established from the first: no-one could claim any ambiguity in that respect. Still, for McGrath it was not enough. Emerging from the hot cave of her bed with the scent of her body still on his skin, he was aware that this scent was the only thing of hers he now possessed and that it too would fade, too quickly.

At that time he and Tangiers were friends, not enemies, and the frustration McGrath felt led him to express a number of confidences.

"Fuck her stupid every night, I would," he said, "if'n she'd give me a chance."

These words did not express exactly what he felt, indeed they bore little resemblance, but within the confines of his limited vocabulary they articulated considerable tenderness. The confessions slopped out in droplets. Out on the prairie the two of them would sit below the ascending sun and watch the colour being burnt from the land. Lizards, birds and strange, skittling rodents ended up bloody and unravelled on the ground because their guns were as faithful as dogs. Each time he pulled the trigger, McGrath thought of Rosa and her brilliant cotton bloomers crumpled around her legs.

Rosa lived in a plainly-furnished room above the saloon, and the nature of her profession was such that the door was always shut. Like the rest of the building, it was impregnated by the odour of whisky which rose from the bar below and penetrated into the fabric of her most supple and intimate clothing, so that to bury your head in it and then inhale was like breathing in fermented rye and barley.

There was another woman, Antionette, who shared the room with Rosa. A claim of sisterhood was made, but her olive-coloured skin and an accent that clattered like the clash of steel pins suggested otherwise. The rumour was that the affections the two displayed for each other was more than sisterly, but these coded words never reached the ears of McGrath. Had they done so, perhaps he would have understood better the way Antionette assaulted him with oaths of remarkable inventiveness when Rosa received his requests for sexual favours. Even down below, in the saloon, her voice could be heard. The men raised their bottles and cheered when this happened, turning it into a ritual.

It was for this reason that he persuaded Tangiers to accompany him on his visits, his purpose not only that of companion but also as distraction. In that room with its incendiary temperature, McGrath and Tangiers folded and grunted in separate corners, trying and failing to prove they had equal durability. Drying bedding was strung from one side of the room to the other and warm drops of water fell and impacted on their naked bodies. In the gaps between the stiff and swaying sheets, they could see the pinkness of each other's flesh. Their groans foreshadowed the telephone.

Someone is playing a piano. Rosa is on the balcony and the men are fighting on the street and someone is playing a piano. The music rises up in pockets, it is as though the wind has bound the melody together, and it animates the scene, gives it definable purpose. Antionette joins Rosa and they hold hands. It is like the end of the world. Together they drink absinthe from glasses that pout in the same way the opening buds of flowers pout. The notes of the music are like coloured panes that can be pushed from the windows of churches. Once, when she was a child, Rosa cut her feet on shards that had risen like grass between the rocks of the desert. The scar still remains, tight and knotted around her heel.

Her name was not Rosa then, it was something plain, as plain as porridge. There were pigtails in her hair and her clothes were unelaborate and she had calluses on her hands, risen from having to help her daddy each day clear the land. The new name did away with all that. It was the exoticism of the *a* at the end that did it, she could have come from the continent, like Antionette, drifted into town on a scent of stock or wisteria.

"Down there," that was Antionette now. "Do you see what they're up to?" Rosa bent closer, leaned over the balcony to look.

Tangiers fell in love with Rosa too. Daily he would arrive with flowers and poems and the hard, gutted hides of rabbits. These things were precious to him, and he imagined they would be precious to her as well, but they only lay unattended outside the door of her room, growing ripe in the day's heat. The letters were picked open by curious passers-by.

Among their number was McGrath, who regarded this discovery as the most despicable sort of treachery. The hand in which he held the paper with its blunt, crooked letters shook with a delighted fervour. When, from behind Rosa's door came a groan which may have been pleasure or distress or fear, the tremor travelled from his hand and filled his whole body.

That same night, he waited outside the saloon until Tangiers walked out with a step that prefigured the first landings on the moon. Then, with a sharp, heavy stone he battered at his friend's head until others managed to pull him away. Tangiers, bloodied, lying face down on the hard, dirt ground, washed so far down towards death it was like touching a membrane. His heart gave several unimagined jumps, and his limbs fluttered. This was the condition in which he lay for many weeks, his wounds healing slowly as he lay on his back in a flat, iron bed so worn the springs pushed through the mattress and into his spine. Sometimes, Rosa came to visit him.

To McGrath, it was as though a great barrier had fallen, but in actuality nothing had changed. Without the money that brought him those moments with Rosa each day, he would have had nothing beyond the vision of her face in the far corner of the bar, her voice stripped like paper into transparency, curled up at the edges. She wore a hat as elaborate as a galleon, its feathers curved and dyed, that sailed over the heads of men. When McGrath paid for her sex, he would let coins fall into its upturned felt interior.

The desire for revenge pulled Tangiers upwards. Weakness had no defence against that persistent, deliberate force. When he was able to walk, he left town. Then, his face still disfigured by the redness of scar tissue, his skull wrapped in bandages that turned him into a figure out of the orient, he rode back one hot August morning, propelled by the weight of the sun. In his hand was a rifle that pivoted alarmingly, and his horse had a bubbling white froth that set its teeth in a grin. Perhaps there were even sparks of flame leaping from the impact of its hooves.

McGrath was asleep in the shade of a porch, and his dreams were those of a snake that has swallowed its tail. All of them involved the close wetness of flesh. Sitting there with his legs stretched out and his hands cupped protectively over his crotch, he smiled to himself, secretly, which is the only betrayal dreams can have. Tangiers came then. He came and went and McGrath woke to a screaming redness in which he discovered he had been shot in both feet and fire had been set to the ruins of flesh.

I tell you, months were swallowed by that. Rosa got older, more beautiful, more indifferent. McGrath lost one foot and dragged the other like pitch bundled on the end of a stick. Each day it had to be bathed or else it gained the shiny tautness of overcooked pork. Antionette would sometimes do that, while he lay crushed in Rosa's arms.

If there was affection it was in those moments, but there was no declaration of love now, not when it took him minutes to limp from one end of the saloon to the other: and besides, Tangiers still came some nights, a hat pulled down over his eyes to help disguise his face which had the crazy glamour of patchwork. Rosa never pretended otherwise.

Evening brought the scent of blooms in from the desert. Cactus flowers had become partially-turned cups which spilled a sullen perfume that McGrath gathered in his arms like a disinterested woman. He had taken to sitting out in this way, on the serrated rocks that began at the town's edge and fed into a darkness turned as cold and penetrating as his own fear. In the darkness there were different creatures to shoot. Each carried a mask of Tangier's face over its own.

Money was becoming a memory but still he had enough to buy himself a horse. Up there, perched on its chestnut back, the crippling of his body became less important. He could even ignore the pain when he dug in the blackened stump of his foot.

And then too he brought a rope and its fibres were as harsh as a martyr's vest. Each day when he was done handling its coils, weals would rise on the palms of his hands. They became as familiar, in time, as the vortices that made a map on his skin.

No surprise then that the day came when Tangiers was found bound and lying in the centre of the town.

One arm had been lopped off and he was missing both ears. His knees were bleeding and broken. Such was the pitch and intensity of his screams that they brought answering cries from the coyotes on the prairie. A full moon that had taken the place of the sun turned his body the colour of bone. Onlookers gathered around in a circle and asked questions like "Is he still alive?" above the sound of his screams.

Surgery in those days was a brutal process, as cruel in some ways as the injury that had first made it necessary; and the assault of burnt flesh and alcohol that met Rosa when she arrived at the doctor's to take Tangiers home was intense as the horrifying vapours that had risen when she had first seen a cow being slaughtered.

Why did she do these things? Out of a sense of guilt perhaps, as the one who had begun this long, ricocheting motion of destruction with her brief, fervid smiles and the scent of her body which had the perfumed cleanliness of soap. Certainly, something kept her awake at night and sent her into long, introspective silences when she would stare, aimlessly transfixed, out of her window.

Antionette: "Is it your fault that they do these things, hm? Answer me that."

Rosa: "But I take their money."

Antionette: "Darling, you eat like a pauper then worry about men whose bellies droop over their belts."

Rosa: "But still..."

Tangiers moved into a room alongside Rosa's own. The walls were bare, the floors were bare and the chairs hard and wooden. Through the thin panels of board that separated this room from the next he could hear the excited squeals of men and the feigned sighs of women. Sometimes, McGrath's unsteady limp could be heard passing the doorway, but until Tangier's legs healed he was fixed in one place and could not rise to confront his attacker. Except when the women were with him, the days were endless. There were times he could catch the odours of other mens' bodies on their fingers.

Antionette had a cart built to carry him in. It was as flat and practical as a tray, with two iron bound wheels on either side propelled by a single lever mechanism that he turned with his one good hand. As it advanced, it flip-flopped in a random and determined way and sometimes it flung him entirely back so his poor, crippled legs were thrown straight up in the air. Children would gather to collect coins that fell from his pockets. Life was mercenary in the Wild West.

On day a small boy wheeled him into the desert. The boy had blue hair and blue eyes, just like a painting Tangiers had once seen of an angel from the Bible. Clouds should have been there to support his feet, but if there were any, they were only composed of dust.

Rattlesnakes hid beneath rocks. They had the lovely allure of poisoned jewellery. Without fear, the boy seized one at the base of the head and placed it in a bag. He passed it to Tangiers. Inside its prison, the snake thrashed briefly and then was still. The journey back to town was made in silence.

McGrath's habit, when drunk, was to sit at the door of the saloon and kick off his boots. Even with the alcohol to disguise the pain, it was as if the fire was still there, corroding its way through the reset skin. Sometimes it seemed to lift him into a kind of delirium, and he would say to each stranger that passed, "Tangiers, is that you? Is that you? What you doing, Tangiers you cunt. What you doing?" And then often he would scream and lurch and vomit and fall still.

On the night about to be described, events were no different. He lay in a puddle of his own bile. A man who appeared to him as Tangiers lifted him upright. When he had passed, another man who looked like Tangiers helped him on with his boots. Inside one of the boots was a rattlesnake. In its fury it bit McGrath several times. The hide that had built around the stump of his foot provided some protection but still, the moments before he folded in on himself were very few. His skin darkened to an alarming colour, it gained the purple lustre of berries, and his eyes flipped back in their sockets until only the whites were showing. To those who watched, it seemed this time death was certain.

Still, he did not die, and if he did not die it was not because of love but because of hate. When Rosa pushed open the door of her room and wheeled him out into daylight for the first time in months, he had the white, boneless appearance of a creature that lives in the soil. Lips pulled back to display gums shrunken away from teeth, while his eyes had the fixed intensity of a man who has faced death, and still carries it with him. If they were struck together, his limbs would clatter like sticks.

"Rosa," he said, "I hate him more than the poison in my gut."

When she bent over to hear the whisper of his voice, he could catch the cheap, pretty scent of her perfume. The first time she helped him to his feet, he collapsed in the blanket of his clothes and lay on the ground, looking up at her with a combination of self-pity and awe. She had petticoats the colour of buttermilk.

McGrath now lived in a room alongside Rosa, directly opposite the one occupied by Tangiers. In this way he gravitated towards the one he loved. Unable to carry himself further than the door, he would press his ears to the harsh grain of the wood and listen to the sound of Tangier's cart clumsily propelled along the floor. When it was quiet, it was worse, because then he imagined Rosa and Tangiers together, in a grotesque, lopsided embrace. Down in his dreams they merged into one double-faced being that spat and smiled as it bit into his flesh.

In his bed he carried a gun. The gun was shiny and oiled and had never been fired. When he slept, it pressed against his thighs with its heavy, cold metal. On the back of the chair by the bed hung a bandolier of bullets, Mexican style. It was his intention that each one of these bullets should find its way, someday, somehow, into Tangier's body. To this end, he had a cart built himself, identical to the one his enemy owned.

And what of Tangiers himself? What did he dream of, now his revenge had been completed, his body rendered untouchable? He dreamed of escape, to the cities that lay to the east, where the crowds were large enough to lose him and the wind sifting into his room was not as hot as the breath from a feverish man's mouth. If he did not go, it was not for want of money, no, nor of familial ties; but rather he recognised the shape of the triangle formed here, in the noisy, constant air above a small-town saloon, and its shape pinned him, it held him, until the time that one of its pieces was permanently removed.

So this is how we move to the day of the final execution. A few, gruff words exchanged on the stairwell were the means, rather than the slap of some fop's silk gloves. McGrath and Tangiers moved through town on their carts, mirrored even when apart, and burnished their guns in private, polishing the long shafts. Both had been known the shoot the eye from a penny hurled randomly through the air. A date was set, and the time? Well, that could only be High Noon, the sun above heavy and constant, avoiding eye contact, like someone with a guilty secret. During the crush and press of other mens' bodies, Rosa learned of it all and stood there on the balcony the day the carts lined up either end of the street. She sipped absinthe and leaned over the rails.

And it is the rails she leans over now. The two men have clambered from their carts to fall into the dust and the movements their bodies make has changed from aggression to violent seduction. Yes! Clothes come free with the taut ripping later associated with Velcro; arms intertwine, legs too, tongues seek out the body's secret hollows, things like that. Then even as Rosa watches, they explore the true nature of each others' desire, and spits and squeals and small gasping noises come rising up to where she stands. The smile on her face is not entirely free from condescension: after all, she has known these same forbidden impulses longer than they, her mouth has shared with Antionette's a secret cachet of saliva and longing.

McGrath rocks on his back like a cradle, his damaged feet unable to find stability in the hard, defeating road. Tangiers has his one good arm wrapped around McGrath's neck; their penises chafe, there is a tongue wet on Tangier's shoulder, the sharp indentation of teeth. Tangiers whispers something briefly, urgently, he repeats it. On the ground by McGrath's hand is the fallen revolver. He lifts it and brutally, without consideration, slides its shaft into Tangier's anus; it has been oiled recently, and slides in smoothly, without effort. "Oh yes yes YES!" exclaims Tangiers, bouncing up and down, pistoning the cool metal in and out while McGrath holds onto the barrel. The excitement is definitely growing here, something spontaneous is going to happen soon, McGrath can feel the swelling in his balls. The voice is in his ear, it's saying, " Yes yes yes YES yes YES!" and his own body is buckling, look out now, he's going to come...

He screams, his torso flexes. Tangiers rolls off with the unexpected jolting, and onto the ground, the pistol still drooping from his sphincter. Its handle strikes the ground and well, it is one of those unlucky things, but it's primed for use, isn't it? Yes, the handle strikes the rock, the gun detonates, and bloody pieces of Tangier's gut and brain joins McGrath's come as it goes jolting into the sky.

I will tell this last part quickly. After a period of guilty seclusion, Rosa once more became the town's primary, attraction. In this she was assisted of course by Antionette. Both lived to a considerable old age due to the daily exertions of their profession, and then there was the carefully banked hoard of coins to see them through the inactive, golden years. Often they were to be seen together, on the balcony, while the town grew into something miraculous around them.

Unfortunately, the same happy ending did not exist for McGrath. Overcome by remorse, he hurled himself into the path of a speeding train, one of those heavy, endless, steaming vehicles they had back then. Still, the vultures had their share, so it was not a life entirely wasted.

Tangier's remains were buried in an unmarked grave, out on the prairie somewhere. He would have liked that. Coyotes came to snuffle around the spot in the moonlight.

As for the gun? Well, there's no point in wasting a good gun, is there? It was sold by the sheriff to a trader, who sold it to a gunslinger in town, who lived somewhat longer than its original owner, long enough to raise a family, and for the gun to be passed down, generation to generation, blasting away at bottles, birds and even the odd human being. Today it sits behind glass in a museum in Wisconsin, but the plaque identifying it has faded, and nobody looks at it anyway. It's only a gun after all, and that's an object you can see everywhere, all about you, every day.

Narcolepsy

A blue angel. Not the automatic evocation – Dietrich grainily imagined, leaning back, stockinged legs tantalisingly crossed, her voice reduced by the soundtrack to a modular imbalance. No, not that but instead a real angel in a film tinted blue, the matrix of his skin visible up close, body honed to a homoerotic musculature, hair tight Michelangelo curls, unseen features flipped down over the crotch of some geek he's blowing. "Uuh," says the geek when he comes, and he sits up to show this businessman's face, black heavy-rimmed glasses over vaguely Jewish looks. His cock, when it rolls back, is shown to be circumcised, lolling blue on a blue sac of balls. He says something to the angel and then the angel turns too, his head twisted up towards the camera so his dimpled bottom and features fill the screen at the same time. I think: *I know that face.*

When I push the button on the remote control, the image stutters then holds, a thick band of white jumping through it. A couple on the bed beside me who have been making it protest in unison, and then one of them says "Come off it mate," but it's a perfunctory objection and when I don't reply they return to their grunting and kissing again.

The face stares up through the screen. I can see the lick of his partly opened Renaissance lips, the smudge of cheekbones, the twist of hair that's looped wet over one eye. He has blue eyes, blue skin, blue hair. From the swoop of his back which is all muscle and spine, the wings grow miraculously, a dendril pushed through the skin to emerge scooped and feathered, not card and paste and turkey pluckings but a half-raised plumage, caught temporarily in the image's enforced stammer. I ask the couple, "Do you know this guy, who he is?" and one of them looks up sweat-layered and flushing and he says, "Him? He's through in the party there, with all the others." *That's* why I know the face.

Through the bedroom door the party beats something speeded up and metal, a sequence of chopped notes and phrases. When I open it there's smoke and voices and a sharp chemical odour. Behind me the video lapses into movement, the angel forced across the screen again. I close the door.

A girl comes to me. She looks familiar but I can't place her name. A running water silver slips across her eyes and her pupils are loose, like a furry toy's. Drugs of some sort: their scent rises up sour through her sweat which has eclipsed her ruined, expensive clothing. "David," she says, "do you remember me?" I'm not David though. I don't even know who she's referring to. Without waiting for a reply, she pulls back the hair from her forehead to display a fashionably trepanned hole, puckered around the edges to a taut, mortified purple. "I had it done three weeks ago, you can't imagine what it's like, it's so..so..." She clicks her fingers twice, trying to conjure up the missing word. Behind her, bodies are in collision, pooling in the coloured light, in sync or out of sync with the music which is renegade, which can be felt underfoot or in the surface of the glass I'm holding and can't remember picking up. There, half-hidden, disappearing, reappearing, is a crown of tight curls which may belong to the angel. He never turns my way though, so I can't be certain.

The girl has her head pressed to my shoulder now, dribbling a damp patch on my arm. "..always liked you, you know that," she's saying, turning up to me with those three primed eyes of hers, and I can see that the hole in her forehead is infected, spilling out a clear, viscous fluid when she moves. She presses her hand to my face and it's entirely without warmth, it's a mortuary cold stealing the sensation from my fingertips, and I'm staring past her, trying to see the man with the cherub hair, and she keeps on pawing at my hand to retain my attention, and I'm reflexively slapping her away and –

I had to walk the last two hundred meters to my apartment tonight. The taxi driver abandoned me at the street's end, looned, his talk of guns and plague and kidnapping for illegal experiments. He shone his headlights down the pavements and pointed at the polyps of makeshift dwellings, tottered wood and plastic constructs grouped together in shadow, curled black clots of figures revealed behind plastic walls and doorways. There was, he assured me, no way he was going down there. Had I heard the story about the girl who..? I had, but he was confusing this area with another part of town. Still, he refused to take me any further. Fear made his face, which was rolled with fat, look gaunt.

Outside, it was raining. Flecked, oily blooms burst on the pavement. I was cowled and the lower part of my face blanked and protected by a filtration mask, but still

I worried about my eyes. Behind me, the taxi pulled away, despite the driver having made assurances he would watch me until I had arrived safely. With his retreat the street became sullen, lit only by a few globular baubles of street lamps whose power had been tapped into, leaving them with a dull orange splutter. For safety I remained on the road, out of range of the people who occupied the pavements. I had been told they could pick out strangers by the perfume they wore, or by the cloying smell of soap that came from their bodies. They could recognise footsteps too, the sharp-heeled clatter of wealth. Thinking of this I hurried on, trying not to move too fast or too slow.

It appeared most of the people here were asleep in any case. There was one street fire, built under a sagging corrugated metal canopy, a stubborn foul-smoking thing that glowered white at its centre and frazzled whatever tatter of food had been pushed into it. I could taste the fluorocarbons even through the protection of my mask. Behind the fire, made amorphous by layers of clothing, something humped and shadowed crouched and feasted. I wondered what was being eaten. Some of these people hunted with panthers. They caught them on the moors and brought them here where they trained them to hunt down other animals and sometimes humans. For protection I always carry a knife, the kind that snaps open and glitters, but it would not be much defence against a panther.

Ahead was the building I was looking for. It was a screened multiplex of light punched up in an oblong from which nothing fell, no sound or thrown invitation, no sight of faces curious at windows. At its base, sliding glass doors opened onto a volley of bored armed guards, one of whom would escort visitors up to their destination. I had been there before, in the daytime, and had thought the security lax, but now it felt welcoming, a safe haven.

"Hey, mister."

At some point when I had been looking at the building, one of the people had come off the pavement and now stood before me, half-hidden, dipped in and out of shadow. It was a man, blundering beneath a too-large coat, and it was impossible to tell whether he was young or old, but I could see he had only one eye, the dead one turned towards me like a collapsed star. Presumably he had sold it for money. He had a terrible cabbage reek.

"Hey mister, want to feel me dong?" I stuttered away from him at this, and grasped the knife in my pocket.

"Go away," I said. "I am not at all interested in your sordid transactions." My voice, I am pleased to report, was resolutely firm, and I outstretched one hand towards him so that he would keep his distance.

"Come on," he insisted, "ten for a feel of me dong," and he grabbed my hand and pushed it in the vicinity of his crotch. Something smooth and sticky slid into my palm. When I backed away, it remained there. I held it up to the almost-light. It was a stick, whittled smooth and smeared with...

"Dog shit, mister. That's all you are. Fucking dog shit." He was laughing as he said this, something horrid in that laugh, and I was shaking my hand, disgusted, fearful of the plague, imagining all the germs already blooming about my skin. When I ran, I did not worry about the way my feet smacked with such obvious wealth on the pavement, nor that I veered much too close to the shanty dwellings with their reluctant walls and doors. No, I only wanted the building I was heading for, and the light, and the doors that slid open so perfectly at my approach.

"Are you all right, man?"

Someone is looking down at me, goat-bearded, eyes intent out of a pudgy face. At first I think it's the devil, but that notion's soon drowned in the rush of music. He holds out his hand and helps raise me up to sit on the settee cantilevered by his bulk. When I look to where I've been lying on the floor, tacked to a sticky mess of spilt drink and ash, I see a border of smudged footprints marking out where I had lain, indented crescents of heel and toe.

"You been smoking too much, then?" The man hands me a glass of water and simultaneously pulls on a pipe that's being passed around. There's a rush, a grey, exhaled smoke with its bitter scent, and he gags momentarily, spitting out black crumbs of shrivelled vegetation.

"No, it's a medical condition I have. Narcolepsy – sleeping sickness? Essentially it means I fall asleep without warning. It unnerves some people."

"Uh-huh."

"The doctors aren't sure what causes it, but they think perhaps there's a failure of the mechanism in the brain that stops the dreaming state from overtaking the waking state."

"Riiight."

Looking at him, I realise I'm talking to myself. There's a defaulted look to his face, his mouth ovalled open, still wisping out smoke, and when it closes again, it closes in slow motion.

"You want some of this? It's real intense."

He holds out the pipe to me, but I shake my head, having long ago discovered that all it makes me do is vomit violently. The pipe is made out of an upturned skull, foiled over, with a metal tube protruding out of its base.

"Skull of William Burroughs. Gives it a real hit."

I can't help smiling at this. So many of these pipes claim to be made from Burrough's skull, all of them fake, and some evidently plastic so the smoke comes out laced with additional toxins.

"Who-oo-oo." He's melting into the cushions now, neurons unravelled in the spin of his features, his hands making the fluttering movements of crippled birds. The skull lolls in his lap. It falls as I rise, sleep still dulling my body. I've remembered the blue struck features of the angel. "See you later, maybe," I say to my companion, but there's no reply, his body still spasmed with the drug's acceleration. When I leave him he's making the wet, tonguing noises that predicate sickness. Perhaps I'll return hours later and find him in the same position, having vomited in his lap.

In the density of the crowd I'm looking for a golden-topped head, but the coloured light here makes everything something it is not, and there is no blue light to enable recognition. I think of him turning towards me, looking out of the screen, and of the wings risen out of bone, half-aloft, as if preparing for flight. There is no resemblance in the faces I pass, pierced, dyed, tattooed. One man has a skewer between his cheeks and a smear of something red down his forehead. He smiles and says "Hello," and the impediment in his mouth makes his tongue lazy. Worried he'll bore me with his religion, I don't reply, but instead wonder in an abstract sort of way if he removes the skewer before kissing anybody. Perhaps he just doesn't kiss.

By now everybody seems to be either dancing or talking. The dances have become capricious, the talk simultaneously shrill and gravitas. Smoke greys the air, making it impossible not to get a secondary buzz, misjudging where bodies stand and feet fall, and eyes gain that look that says they've been rolled over with glass. A woman in retrogressive scarlet slaps against me and pierces my foot with her high, gaudy stiletto. "Why don't you look where you're going?" she snaps, and I stupidly apologise before limping away.

Someone is mentioning angels. It has come from that crowd there, bundled fascistically, their conversation a shared incestuousness. Their backs form a carapace, but recognising some of the people, I push my way in. There are nods and skimped greetings, but these are moments of attention stolen from the depth-charged words of the man who is speaking. His voice is a barbered monotone, all sibilants and vowels, issuing from a face so nondescript as to be lacking identity, only his clothes betraying his wealth and the flick of his eyes his power. Disappointingly he is not talking about angels at all, but UFO abductions. Perhaps it was a comparison.

"Twenty five percent of all people registered now claim to have experiences," he is saying in that manufactured non-voice, and in the people around about there are intimations of assent, little orgasmic cries of recognition. The woman next to me has stitched her scarf through the tines of her fingers. Her hair is pulled back in such a way that I can see the pink thread scars of cosmetic surgery behind her ears.

"...twice a week I go to the contactee group run by doctor David. He's been though it himself, you understand, so he doesn't belittle our trauma – the fear of aliens with the darkened eyes..."

"...the sensation of floating," the woman is saying, and the scarf has become a knot now. I've seen this all before, and may even have had my own experience, a memory of a dark figure emaciated beside my bed, but my therapist tells me this was probably ritual abuse. The possibility of angels is much more intriguing, sculpted and blue, turning towards me...

"...a silver ball pushed into one's nose..."

There is a tension growing in the group, nearly tangible, a capillary whiteness that almost suggests something is going to spontaneously manifest.

"...lying on the operating table while they obtain sperm or ovum..."

"But what do they *mean*," the woman beside me suddenly insists, and something is broken by that display of emphasis, the unwebbed heads of the gathering spin, and other voices join in. I take the opportunity to sidle out, crushing layers of expense that give off their perfumes like broken flowers. As I do so, someone familiar moves out of the rivet of dancers, not the angel but the Jewish businessman who so enthusiastically received his affections. He's holding someone's hand, but I can't see who. The crowd won't part to let me pass.

"Hey," I say, pushing people out of the way. "Hey -"

When I wake, the Jewish businessman is sitting beside me. He has a kinder face than appeared on the video, crumpling up when he smiles like seized polythene. Beside him is the angel. He looks odd, pale, and his hair has grown so that it ringlets down the length of his neck. I can't decide if this makes him look more or less biblical. When he speaks it is a disaster of half-learned elocution lessons and an east London accent.

"One simply cannot have him attending functions and sitting there not saying anything, so this is something of a compromise," the businessman explains, "though it is admittedly an unsuccessful one."

The angel smiles at this, and shows his teeth which are perfectly white but somewhat crooked. They ought to be blue, like his eyes are blue, even without a colour filter on the camera lens. His name is Paul. The businessman's name is Winston, except he is not a businessman as I imagined but a senior civil servant of some sort. Something to do with public relations. I may have seen him on TV at one time, I decide. Quite by chance they were the ones to pull me out of the crowd when I fell, lifting me here to the place I had been taken before, talking to the man smoking out of a skull. He sits here now, at the settee's end, comatose. He has vomited in his lap. The skull has rolled extinguished on the floor beside him. Winston looks and says, "It is just so unfortunate about the side-effects one experiences sometimes," while Paul retrieves the skull from where it has fallen and examines it for damage.

On the dancefloor a fight has broken out, an uncoupled spiral, the music too loud to overhear its cause, but by the end a woman is half-lying on the floor, her nose bleeding, a man beside her holding a cusped broken glass. Everyone else has pulled away, a retreat from the blood that goes drip drip drip from her nose onto the suffering carpet. The back of her hand is smeared ferrous, and her torn dress has been turned a new pattern.

"Life is so much simpler when a monetary transaction is involved," Winston observes, and kisses Paul on the cheek. Paul smiles back, dumb and beautiful. I watch him, trying to see the shift of wings beneath his jacket. Seeing me look, there is a shutter of recognition in his eyes.

"It will not surprise you to learn that we met in London," Winston says. "I had some tiresome diplomatic affair to attend to with regard to those children that went missing. There were all sorts of rumours, you know, about what had happened to them – that they'd been found half-eaten or with their organs removed, that sort of thing. Of course, it wouldn't have surprised me if they had been kidnapped for use in some sordid little slave trade, but naturally one mustn't publicly admit to anything like that. Besides, there was no evidence. Anyhow, I had this tiresome speech to make, and you can imagine quite how squalid it is down there. They cleared the streets for the cameras, really one couldn't even walk on the pavements for the shanties that had been built, but when I came to speak, my God if the people they had all thrown out didn't come back and stand amongst the crowd! It was very unpleasant, I must tell you, especially when some of them tried to come up to me afterwards. Of course, the security teams managed to keep them away. It appears they imagined I could cure them of disease if they touched my body. It was an effort to avoid them, I must say. This was how, probably," – he turns to Paul – "he managed to slip through and publicly proposition me. It was terribly romantic, though quite how he knew I found him attractive, I cannot imagine."

"I could see the way your cock stood in your trousers," Paul reveals. He is heating the base of the pipe where the bone has been thinned, and inside there is a tarry bubbling and a tempered liquorice scent escapes. When he puts it to his mouth and expertly inhales, the foil snaps taut over the sockets of the nose and eyes.

A squad of cleaners in bodysuits and facemasks have arrived to clean up the spill of blood. They spray and vacuum the dotted mess, the machine's mantra another layer in the music which is still playing, and a hard, artificial scent mixes in with all the other odours in the air. It is done quickly, efficiently, and they are gone even before the spray of cleaning droplets settles through the crossed beams of the ceiling lights. When the dancing resumes, there is a superstitious avoidance of the disinfected spot. The woman with the trepanned forehead is passing in front of me. She is missing one shoe.

Beside me, Winston is patting my arm and pushing the pipe into my hands. There is an afterimage of smoke on his breath and I discover he's sucked the life from the pipe which spills a black ash from its stem, still warm. "I'm sorry my boy, you'll need to...." And there's a waver in his voice and body that tells me his mind's retreating, folding out from itself in a detailed, repetitive expansiveness. That's why the drug's called *Fractal*. When he lets his head roll onto my shoulder, I can catch the musty scent of his scalp and an acid base of shampoo. He's combed his hair sideways to cover a bald patch on top. Across the slump of his body, I look at Paul who retains the fixity of my gaze, making it a covenant. When I reach over and touch his neck, slipping a few considered fingers down to the bare of his shoulder, he doesn't stop me. We rise together and Winston slides down to occupy two seats, his mouth pumiced open on the fabric of the cushion. His shirt has pulled above the band of his trousers to reveal a roll of fading-tan flesh.

Paul looks at me. "You'll have to pay, of course," he says.

In the bedroom the video is no longer playing and the television screen is muted to noiseless static. Less real somehow, its creation has emerged to stand before me in a plain, tailored suit, greedy, amorous, certain of his own beauty. On the way here I had whispered to him, "You're an angel," and he had smiled and said "Yes," in a self-congratulatory way. The smile remains on his face now, but it has become unfocussed.

Apart from the two of us, there is no-one else in the room. Crushed-open capsules have been trodden into the carpet, while the bed bears the marks of several earlier couplings. Paul sits down on its edge and his face has a gradually-diminishing expression, as if the personality is leaking out. It's the drugs that are doing it. In his cheek there's a nervous twitch that has synchronised itself with the beat of music through the door.

"Is Paul your real name?" I ask as he lies back swooning, perfectly-realised onto the bed.

"Paul-Michael-Andrew...my parents are Catholic...."

I'm pulling off his clothes with an undignified hurry but he's still attempting and failing to undo the catch of his trousers. Assisting him, it appears that he is only just capable of lifting and bending his legs.

"There was a video I saw in here tonight – you and Winston –"

"His joke...wanting to shock. We did it because he thought I looked like..like..."

Now his trousers are rucked around one foot. His pants snap briskly down around his ankles. I have to lift him to remove his jacket. His torso feels more normal than it should.

"Your wings?"

"From a theatre…he bought them…taped to my shoulders…"

Not real wings then, not real. His unbuttoned shirt slipping free confirms this, revealing a smooth, undeformed back. In my mind I can see the wings lifting, ready to beat. I can see the way they rise out of his skin, and how they respond to the shift of the muscles in his body. There was no tape; the wings were not theatrical cast-offs. Pushing Paul onto his stomach I sit astride him and examine his back with my fingers, as if the evidence might be hidden under the skin. There is nothing though, only bone and the flared ridges of anticipatory muscle. For some reason I think of the man who pushed a shit-smeared stick into my hand, and of the terrible fear caused by his presence. Paul sighs, responding to my touch, drifting off into some narcotic half-world. His eyes are closed and trembling, and I remember their blue promise, looking up at me from the screen. By the time that I fuck him brutally, angrily, he's desensitised into feeling nothing at all. The bed's headboard beats against the wall in response to my emotion and I come into something as useless as tissue.

In revenge I take the knife from my pocket and carve red, seeping wings onto his back.

Blowing Hot and Cold

ONE

It was midsummer when we found the body. Martin was twelve, I was nine, and the man we discovered could have been no older than the combined total of our years. He wore a green uniform and there was a thin scar down one side of his face. He reminded me of my brother.

The weather was hotter in those days, so the tar on the roads would blister and stick to the soles of our feet. Flowering bushes grew wild in untended gardens and filled the air with the scent of honeysuckle. Sometimes we would steal in among them and pretend we were soldiers. The game always ended with Martin shooting me down with a burst of gunfire. When I was resurrected we would return home and say our prayers.

Martin was my brother and I adored him. He was all the things that at my age seemed to be the most desirable: he was older and taller, slimmer, was able to run faster and could recite the names of countries I had never heard of. By contrast, I could barely name the places around the city we lived in, their names exotic and distant. Whenever people talked about him, he was always *good looking* and a *real charmer*, words never applied to me. Of course, they only saw what he wanted them to see, hardly ever the angry, rebellious side of his personality that emerged when we were alone. But that was the aspect of his character that appealed to me most of all.

We lived in a house in the prosperous part of the city. It was a gloomy, gothic building left over from the last part of the previous century and it had remained largely unaltered since that time. All of its rooms were filled with antique furniture, the scent of accumulated polish, and sounds carried unforgivingly through its long passageways. Unused, some of the rooms remained locked, accumulating dust. Except when they had to, my parents never left this place. It was their way, I think, of hiding from the war.

To see them, they seemed an unlikely couple. My father was a great, portly figure with a beard that almost entirely obscured his face. Once he had been a preacher. My mother was a drab nothing who had come from nothing and would go to nothing, yet it was her I loved and my father I feared, and when I dreamed, I dreamed he had somehow vanished, leaving the three of us alone. Martin, I knew, felt no differently. To escape from him, we would lose ourselves in the house's many rooms or, if that was not possible, play outdoors in the streets. Children of the war, our distrust was not nearly as great as that of our parents. Invariably we were warned not to go further than the end of the road, but usually we did anyway. There were no other children around our way, most of the houses standing empty, their families moved out long before to the relative safety of the countryside. White-sheeted furniture could be glimpsed through the windows, utilised in one case by a group of squatters who had taken possession in the owner's absence. ("Don't you ever go near them," we had been told). Boredom took us further afield.

Martin would lead the way. He seemed to know every road and street that ever was. One route took us past filaments of glass and concrete, buildings between which sparse traffic passed anxiously. The opposite direction led to dockyards and slums and whole areas levelled by the bombing. This was where we went most often. Here the buildings were derelict and greedy for territory. People seemed to spill out onto the streets during the day, and then at night some of them remained there. Rumpled bedding could be seen heaped in the doorway of a deserted warehouse, or makeshift shanties of cardboard and plastic erected down unwelcoming alleyways. The people who lived in them were never around. Maybe they were the same ones who stood around street corners smelling foul and begging money from passers-by. We avoided them.

Other people in the street turned to stare at us as we passed. Our good fortune was always evident enough to make us conspicuous. Usually the attention was just curiosity, but sometimes it was hostile as well. Children kicking a ball frustratedly around pavements would stop to call names, while adults halted mid-conversation to pointedly glare and make snide comments. After a safe distance had passed, we would turn and call the vilest names we could imagine, then run off laughing.

From open windows came the smell of mildew. Washing was slung out to dry, hanging from window frames. Sometimes there stood the friable shells of buildings recently bombed, but often not even that, only a desolation of rubble from which carbonated wood and torn metal emerged. Picking amongst the stones, we looked for remnants of other peoples' lives. What we found was unremarkable – coins melted to a dirty slag, jars miraculously preserved with their contents intact – but to us they seemed like treasures. On returning home we hid these in the bottom of a neighbour's garden. We did not dare say where we had been.

At night our mother would read me chapters from a children's Bible. It was a large book, full of colour pictures that seemed much more interesting than the stories themselves, and I could tell from my mother's tone that she also found its contents dreary. Martin had a Bible of his own, bound in black leather. He never read it, but instead manhandled a few pages a day to make it seem as though he was slowly progressing through its contents. If he read at all, it was lurid horror novels secretly devoured beneath the bedclothes by the light of a torch.

The Bible studies were my mother's initiative. My father did not seem to care much one way of the other, although sometimes we would see him looking from behind the pages of his newspaper to see how things were progressing. The newspapers he bought were the trashy, sensationalistic sort, certainly not what would have been expected of a man who had once been a preacher. We never saw him open a Bible, nor did he go to church, although at the dinner table he would sometimes say grace. Perhaps my mother only did as she did out of a misplaced sense of duty because, looking back, she did not seem to have much of a grasp of what was going on around her at all.

On nights when the war was at its most evident – sirens cutting and planes ominous overhead – we watched the city burn. Orange flames tore at the horizon, casting up heavy clouds of smoke spreading the length of the sky. Voices travelled on the wind, mixed in with the fire's roar. Excited, our own voices rose an octave, our laughter came too easily, and this excitability was mistaken for fear. Protesting, we would be led down to the cellar where we wrapped ourselves in blankets and slept beneath the light of a naked bulb. The sounds of destruction could still be heard, muted, but it was more thrilling to spread our hands on the floor, feeling tremors transmitted through the earth. When an especially violent vibration was detected, we would giggle simultaneously. "What are you two laughing at?" we would be told. "Go back to sleep." Naturally this was the last thing we intended to do, and our elation lifted us into the early hours of the morning until, finally, we would drop exhausted into our dreams.

The following day the air still carried the scent of smoke and, if it rained, the ground was flecked with blackly impacted soot. For the remainder of the week we would not be allowed to leave the confines of the garden or, if there was school, then we would be led by the hand to and from the school gates. Faced with the embarrassing prospect of facing other children whilst still in the company of our parents, we would break free at the last moment, running as quickly as possible through the entranceway. At night we dawdled long enough to be among the last to leave, ensuring in this way that our journey home remained unobserved.

Still, school was an escape of sorts. Both my brother and I were considered clever, although this was not reflected in our work. Martin in particular was thought a disruptive influence. He sat at the back of the class, cracking lewd jokes and generally ignoring any attempts to interest him in schoolwork. "You're a bright lad," he was told, "so why don't you give yourself a chance?" He would smile then and nod, feigning humility, but when we met in the school grounds, he cursed the teachers with amazingly inventive oaths. It was a side our parents seldom saw. Because I admired him, his rebelliousness also spread to me.

The angriest I ever saw my father was the result of this rebelliousness. It began with a class trip to a local exhibition of ethnic art. Our teacher, who accompanied us, was a flamboyant, foppish figure who dressed in hideous tie-and-die T-shirts and went barefoot in sandals. He smelled of linseed oil and cardamom. Looking back, thinking about him, I add a little black beret on his head, so he resembles more than ever a cartoon depiction of a painter. Conversation for him was a long, enthusiastic monologue we could barely follow, and this was especially true when he spoke of his great (and, you thought sadly, perhaps only) passion, art. Wandering around the items on display, he espoused the value of the masks and paintings hanging from the walls while we giggled behind his back and mocked his mannerisms. Besides, I thought the exhibits ugly, for they seemed crude and unrealistic. The bodies were distorted, the colours drab. In some of the paintings there were bungalows and skyscrapers, whereas I had expected to find lions, giraffes, the verdant green foliage of Tarzan movies. This was not the Africa I had imagined. One object did, however, catch my eye. This was a carved wooden figure of Christ on the cross, propped upright on a pedestal. It was an unusual work: firstly the figure, although it sported the usual paraphernalia of crown and thorns and pensive eyes, was black. Secondly, it displayed the most enormous penis which it wielded between its legs like a club. Our teacher tactfully avoided commenting on this artefact, though of course we all noticed it, and throughout the visit my eyes kept wandering back to the strange, crudely carved figure. The light in the ceiling above its head was, I saw, circular, like a halo.

It was such an odd thing, so unlike anything I had seen before, and I immediately wanted it. Was it for sale, I wondered? Before I could ask, we were called on to the next room. I lingered, the last in our group to leave and then, as the others disappeared, hurried to catch them.

In the other rooms were more exhibits, but none of them as flagrantly interesting. I dawdled, then, when scolded for this tardiness, feigned a rapt and deliberately irritating curiosity towards all the pieces on display. This interest was only real, however, when we stopped to eat in the museum café which aspired towards a cosmopolitan atmosphere but which could still only muster up a milky, sweet coffee substitute and day-after pastries which had the bland heaviness characterising all the food available during the war.

This done, we prepared to return home. On the minibus, before leaving, I admitted to a sudden and inexplicable need to go to the toilet and, excused, rushed back into the museum where the exhibit stood, unattended.

The carving slipped easily beneath my jacket. It was such an obvious action, and I knew I was doing wrong, fully expecting attendants to leap out of nowhere, or for hidden alarms to ring out shrilly. But there was nothing.

It was a hot day and, walking back, I kept on imagining people staring at me, speculating on the reason for my zipped-up jacket. As perhaps they were: the figure protruded beneath the cloth at all sorts of odd angles. In school it remained in my desk then, once I arrived home, I tried to hide it beneath my bed. Fearing this was too obvious a place, it eventually ended up among a mound of dolls I never played with.

That night I was unable to sleep and instead lay awake, longing for the following day to come. In my mind I kept on returning to the moment I had stolen the carving from its pedestal, wondering if anyone had seen, or if I would be found out in some other way. I clutched my body and almost cried with fear. At the same time I anticipated my father's certain delight. His smile flashed close up out of an almost-dream.

It was because of my father that I had stolen the figure. Two days previously his birthday had passed and in a fit of spite I had given him nothing, spending the money my mother had pressed into my hand on black market sweets and fizzy drinks. His expression of hurt on discovering this was unmistakable, and I had felt guilty ever since. Now I imagined his look of surprise and delight as he was presented with the black Christ. There were depictions of the crucifixion hanging from the walls of virtually every inhabited room in the house, but none resembled the one I had taken. Stupidly, I imagined he collected these figures, much as one would collect model railways or antiques. I wanted him to exclaim with pleasure and hug me with the great hams of arms: I could not remember a time when he had ever given me such a direct display of affection.

The following day was a Saturday but I rose early. Everyone else in the house was still asleep, so in an effort to awaken them I clattered about, opening and closing windows, doors. From the street came the sound of birdsong, the whine of a milk float. My mother called down from the bedroom, telling me to make less noise. In repentance I closed the windows, but turned on the television with the sound up loud to watch the Saturday morning cartoons. Already the day seemed to stretch on forever. Bored, I switched channels, but that was even worse because it was all news about the war. I tried to go out into the garden, but the door was locked, and I was unable to reach the uppermost bolts. Instead, I read a comic, then read it again. The ink came away on my fingers. Finally, sounds of movement came from upstairs. In anticipation, I ran up to my room and retrieved the statuette from its hiding place. Hanging above my bed was another figure of Christ, and I showed it the black carving I held.

"Hello," said Jesus pinned above the bed. "I haven't seen anyone like you before. Why are you black?" And he frowned.

"I'm from Africa," said the African Christ. "Everyone's black in my country. Maybe you can go with me there one day." And he smiled.

"I'd like that," said the white Christ. Then, frowning again, he added, "Is your blood black too?"

"Yes," replied black Christ, "That's why you can't see it on my body."

White Christ: "Mine's red, it's all over me."

Black Christ: "I can see."

At which I pushed the figure's penis into the white Christ's side, pretending it was the Roman pushing in the spear.

On the stairs I met Martin. When he saw the carving I carried, he burst out laughing but would not explain why. "What are you going to do with that?" he asked, but I would not tell him, instead carrying it downstairs to place it on the breakfast table, propping it up against the vase standing there. Martin followed me.

"It's a present for daddy," I confided, and when I told him that, he laughed even more.

"If it's a present," he said, "then you should wrap it up properly." Rummaging in a drawer, he emerged with a length of yellow ribbon which he tied around the figure's phallus. Our father's heavy footsteps could be heard descending. "Ssh. Here he comes now."

I waited in anticipation.

At first he noticed nothing. As he emerged through the doorway, his head was bent over the newspaper he carried, reading the headlines. Pulling out a chair, he sat down at the table, waiting for our mother to come and serve the breakfast. The paper rustled as it pressed against the table. His foot tapped a silent rhythm. He turned a page, then another. The excitement inside me swelled, threatening to burst out of my mouth. At last I could bear it no longer and cried out, "Daddy." And again, "Daddy, don't you see?"

Then he did look, glancing up to find himself staring directly at the carving with its vast, erect penis. At first he said nothing, but then his face flushed, it roared red. Even the bald patch on top of his head coloured.

"Who did that? Who was it?" He grabbed Martin by the arm and shook him. "Was it you? It was, wasn't it?"

His voice was so loud, I was frightened. I had never seen him so angry before. Perhaps he knew the figure was stolen. By now Martin was prised up against the table, sending cutlery spinning, clattering to the floor. Seizing a fork, he brandished it ineffectually at my father, who in turn knocked it from his hand.

"You'd do that to me too, wouldn't you? Yes, you would." He punched Martin in the stomach so he doubled over, white and gasping.

That was when I shouted. I cried, "No it wasn't him. It was me. It was me. Let him go daddy, it was me." I pulled at his arm, trying to claw his grip on Martin free. I bit his hand. He slapped me in the face, hard, so I was knocked down between the chairs and the tables. The furniture scraped and clattered. I hit my head and began sobbing. For a moment there seemed to be no other sound, and then our mother appeared, alarmed, asking, "What on earth is going on?"

For the rest of the afternoon we were confined to our rooms. On the day following the incident, our mother appeared, explaining that we must never, ever do anything like that again. The carving had been returned to the gallery, she revealed. There would be nothing more said about it, but we must be very careful what we said and did in front of daddy in the future, and we were to tell nothing of what had happened to anybody. I would not listen though, still white-faced and feeling bitterly angry. My head still hurt and Martin's arm, he showed me, was badly bruised. I hated my father more than ever then. I thought: *Why don't you die?* I thought it and thought it, and imagined if I concentrated hard enough then it would become true. Sounds of his imminent demise did not, however, come. There was only a silence that seemed to engulf the house.

That same night, Martin crept into my room. He knelt down by my bed and whispered, "I'm going to run away. I can't stand living here any more. Are you coming too?"

Of course, I agreed.

Our escape was made the following night. We stole out the kitchen window with a bagful of food and clothing. Although it was late, it was not yet completely dark, and the city was full of harsh noises and excited shrieks. There was a moon in the sky, pale and stretched thin as paper. Martin led the way, telling me, "I've done this before." I wondered when. Our movements were exaggeratedly slow and measured. We spoke in low voices even when we could no longer see our house. My feelings were all in a jumble and the further the distance between us and our home, the more confused they became. I felt fear and I felt excitement. I wanted to return and at the same time I wanted to run and never look back.

The route we followed took us down side streets and alleyways. A light rain let loose the smell of old brick and garbage. It was already dark but it grew darker, until the glow of the moonlight could be seen reflected dimly on the paving stones. The houses we passed seemed dead and empty. If we encountered others on the street, we hid until they passed or set off in another direction. The wet ground began to produce a warm mist. Overhead, faint stars appeared between the clouds in the sky. We took turns in carrying the bag of provisions, but still it was tiring and my arms ached.

Eventually, we stopped to rest in the doorway of a closed-down Chinese takeaway.

"Only for a little while," said Martin. "We'll have to get as far away as possible, while it's still dark."

I dared not complain, but still I felt tired and wanted to sleep. The roads we had travelled seemed endless. Curling up against the door's metal grille, I placed my head on Martin's shoulder, feeling myself slowly drift away from my surroundings.

"Don't sleep now," Martin said. But I did anyway.

When I woke it was abruptly, to the sound of a voice shouting.

"Who's that?" it said. "Don't touch me! Thieves! Robbers! Scum!"

Sitting up, I found myself face-to-face with a filthy old man who emerged from a pile of clothing heaped next to us. He stunk of sweat and alcohol. All this time he had been beside us, and we had failed to notice. I shrieked, and reached for Martin, who was already on his feet.

The vagrant cried, "Away! Away! I tell you I'm armed. I'm ready for you! Coming for me, eh, eh?"

We backed into the corner, staring at the stranger with scared rabbit eyes. The man, meanwhile, was scrabbling amongst his bedding for an item he apparently had difficulty in locating. Martin gasped, "A gun!" and indeed there was an object of some sort grasped in the man's hand. Both of us, I'm ashamed to say, screamed. But I was the one to act: yes, I tensed, I paused, but finally I kicked the old coot in the balls. There was cry of pain, and the object he held went somersaulting through the air before crashing on the pavement. Only a bottle of wine. Fragments of glass and a sharp acid odour. We ran then, carrying our bag between us, while behind the man staggered to his feet screaming, "I'll get you! You hear? I'll get you!" He slurred his words though, and swayed as he stood. When we dared look back, breathless, he was still where we had left him, waving his fist ineffectually in the air.

After that, we were too scared to stop until our destination had been reached. This proved to be the ruins which stood in the outer reaches of the city. It was turning light then, and a mist hovered over the stones.

"We'll hide here until they stop looking for us," said Martin, "then we'll go somewhere I can earn some money."

It did not occur to me to ask who would possibly want to employ a twelve year old, because I trusted my brother implicitly.

We made our way into the ruins. Most of the buildings in this area had been demolished, but a few still stood intact. There were inverted roofs and rubble had sloughed through the floors, collecting in mounds in the lower rooms. There were fallen shafts of wood and charred frames of furniture. Planks burst through ceilings and see-sawed precariously as we walked beneath them. There were shadows colliding everywhere. Spent rain fell and filtered through the rafters. Each room we passed through seemed more desolate than the last. Finally we found one room that remained undamaged. Its original furnishings – chairs, settee, table – remained untouched, but stunk of animal piss and mildew.

"This'll do," Martin said. "We probably won't find anything better and I'm too tired to look just now anyway."

Slumping down on the floor, against one wall, he threw down our baggage with a noisy clatter. Immediately, this set up a great howling and barking just outside the room's main window.

I said, "Wolves!"

My brother smiled, reassuring. "Don't worry, it's only stray dogs. We can close the door and they won't get in."

When we tried this though, the door refused to shut properly, jamming half-way, and as I peered out of the grimed windows, I could see them out there in a pack, barking and snarling.

"They still look like wolves to me, Martin." But he was asleep, unable to reply. Soon I was asleep too, curled up beside him.

I woke to sun streaming into my eyes. The sky was hard and blue. Already Martin had risen, unpacking our belongings and arranging them in a straight line along the floor. It was a very short line, I noticed. He looked up.

"You're awake then. I didn't want to disturb you. Hungry?"

I nodded, but first had to rush outside to urinate, pulling down my pants and feeling exposed. The dogs, I was relieved to see, were nowhere in the area. Breakfast was a handful of biscuits. We had brought cans of food with us (but no tin opener), sausages (but nothing to cook them on) and a loaf of bread, but we did not eat these.

"We've got to keep our food because we might have to stay here longer than we think. The police are probably out now, looking for us."

I nodded, trying to look stoical, but really all I wanted was something to eat. I imagined myself wasted, like the black children on TV.

In the daylight, the room was shown to be less well preserved than it first had seemed. Furniture was gnawed and torn, allowing stuffing to boil out, while several carefully deposited turds lay amongst the cushions. In the ceiling was a jagged hole where the light fixture had been. The carpet was dirtily sodden, and when I pulled back one of the corners, insects scurried away from the light.

"Can we find somewhere better? I don't want to stay here, it's horrible. Please." I heard a petulant tone creeping into my voice and hated myself for it.

"Maybe later," my brother replied. "It's only for a few days after all, and we don't have to stay inside all the time. Come on, help me collect some firewood. If it gets cold later on, we can build a fire. It'll be something to do."

Outside, the sun was directly above us and blistering. Hauling off my clothes, I ran about nearly-naked, shrieking as I hopped over burning stones. "Come catch me," I would say, and Martin would chase me for brief periods, but it was too tiring, and he always ended up sitting in the shade, wiping the sweat from his forehead and wheezing. I would dance away then, shouting, "I'm faster than you now. I am! I am!" but not even this calculated aggravation would raise him. "You go on," he would call, "I'll catch up later." It was the sort of thing an adult would say and, looking at him then, I caught a glimpse of the grown-up in him, in his spindly body and his face that was losing its softness and turning into something harder. This frightened me somehow, and I raced on ahead. "Don't forget the firewood," he reminded me, but I barely heard.

There was stone everywhere, but hardly any usable wood. Most of what was there proved too large and clumsy to carry. Unenthusiastic, I lifted half-a-dozen sticks then dropped them again. It was too hot. The air warped to a blue shimmer. In the distance Martin was reduced to a shrunken smudge. The sun, glancing off the stones, was white and blinding. As I walked, flies flew up underfoot, furious and buzzing, attracted by my sweat and resisting attempts to shoo them away. I held my hand over my mouth and nose, so as not to breathe them in.

Martin was rising and waving, but he was so far away that it was like a dream. All the buzzing grew louder, it sounded like a babble of voices. I thought of being caught in the midst of a great, chattering crowd. Martin pulled off his shirt and wrapped it around one wrist where it swung like a beacon. Walking backwards, I watched his movements. The landscape was reduced to a vast flatness of earth and sky, divided into white and blue, and he stepped between the two, walking out of the shimmer. Flies crawling, tickling on my skin. A buzzing getting louder. Somewhere, a ripe sickly smell…

I tripped and fell. A choking cloud of flies rose. I had fallen backwards onto something that was both soft and hard. Stone banged against my head, cut my elbow, my calf. I bit my lip. The sky seemed to range down on me, swimming. I cried out with pain and shock, but the breath had gone from my body and there was no sound. For a while I lay there with eyes closed, gulping lungfuls of air. Then, when I opened them again, it took a moment for the objects around me to fix into focus. There were rings of light. The light turned into a face. I was looking at a face. There was a softness beneath me. I was lying on a body. Flies were crawling all over. It had a stench of rotten meat. Without rising, I clambered away, pulling myself over the stones. This time it was the fear that had stolen my voice. "MMM," I went, "MMM," as though I were mute.

Martin came running. His feet kicked clouds of dust from the ground, he called out, "Are you all right?" and "What's wrong?" But I was too busy looking at the body to reply.

The body face down on the ground with one arm stretched out and the other beneath its chest. It was a man. His legs were crumpled together. He was missing a shoe. He wore were khaki green clothing smeared with dirt. Later, I realised the dirt was really dried blood. Where the skin was exposed, it was ripped and raw. Flies massed black and noisy around the wounds. I was horrified. I was curious. Experimentally, I nudged the body with my toes. The skin was warm and puffy. The head lolled back to reveal a gaping mouth and strange milky eyes. The features resembled Martin's. At that I let it fall, and there was a sudden release of a sweet, sickening odour.

I collided with Martin, and for the first time realised he had been standing there the whole time, watching.

"Who is it?" he asked.

"I don't know. A man," I replied.

"Stay here, I'll look."

He walked over to the body but remained at a safe distance. Using one of the sticks I had dropped, he prodded its limbs. Flies flew up in a cloud then settled again. When he knelt to the ground, I thought he was saying a prayer, but when he came back I realised he had been sick. There was no colour in his face at all.

"Let's go," he said, "We can't stay here any longer."

Walking back the way we had come, we barely spoke. It was hotter than ever, and I asked, "Didn't you bring anything to drink?" but there was no reply. My brother walked so fast, it was hard to keep up. His hands were balled into fists. Our feet clattered over the stones. In the distance the sun glinted off a million windows in the city. Carried on a freak wind, I heard police sirens and wondered if they were looking for us. Briefly there was the clamour of traffic, the shriek of a whistle, and those few stray sounds made me feel alone and unhappy. Martin seemed preoccupied, staring unfocussed into the empty space before him. I thought about the body, but the image had lost its sharpness, and the wounds seemed less vivid in retrospect. I was hungry again too.

When we reached the building in which our belongings had been stored, we found the dogs had returned. They massed immediately outside the door in a mongrel pack, all sizes, yapping and snarling amongst themselves. They were thin, pitiful things, wild with malnutrition and covered with sores. At our approach some began to fight with each other, while others skulked forward on their bellies, baring their fangs and snapping the air before returning again. We retreated, stepping backwards. I had been told not to run away from dogs, because they could sense their victim's fear and would follow. I picked up stones for protection, intending to throw them if any of them came too near. The fighting, I noticed, had turned into a mass rutting, but then just as quickly degenerated into violence again. When a tangle-haired spaniel-thing broke free and came bounding towards me, yapping, I brained it with a brick and it collapsed, making cycling movements in the air before it was still. Another came over to sniff at the body and I prepared to hit it too, before Martin stopped me.

"If you miss them, it'll only make them angrier."

In letting the stones slip from my fingers, one dashed from my foot, but I did not dare yell.

"Get around the back," he whispered, "we'll get in the house that way."

We shuffled sideways, like crabs.

"There, climb in that window."

Before we could do this, a further two dogs burst out the front doorway, carrying the string of sausages we had brought between them. The rest of the pack immediately threw themselves on the food, and there was a flurry of biting and snarling. I cried out, "That's ours!" and for a moment all the dogs looked up at once. I was afraid they would attack, but they returned to their battle, too preoccupied now to bother with us any longer.

We entered through a side window and landed on the broken remains of a toilet bowl. My foot left a bloody imprint on the cracked ceramic.

"What if there are more of them in there?" I asked.

"There won't be. And if there are, just remember, they're more frightened of us than we are of them."

I was not convinced, and lifted a rotten shard of wood for protection. The planks beneath our feet shifted and rasped. I tried to listen for other sounds of movement in the house, but it was difficult to tell with the frantic activity going on outside. As we neared the living room doorway, I raised the wood above my head, brandishing it like a club. My arms were weak though, and they trembled.

But there was nothing there, the room was empty, and only evidence of the dogs' intrusion remained. The food that had been neatly stacked in one corner now lay scattered around the floor: half-eaten slices of bread, gnawed cans, ravaged biscuit packets. A plastic bottle lay with a gash on its side, contents spilling into a muddy pool on the carpet. There were dusty paw marks everywhere, even up on the walls. Our clothes lay in a roiled trail along the centre of the room, ending with a shirt of my own before my feet. When I lifted it up there were jagged teeth marks along the collar.

We tidied the room in silence, but both knew we would have to return home. Outside, the dogs had grown quieter, and I kept looking at the half-opened door, afraid they would return. The body of the man we had found, had the dogs located him too? I kept remembering how his clothes had been torn. The way his head had lolled back to reveal a face like Martin's. Shining through the window, the sun looked sharp and cruel. My mouth felt very dry and I was hot but shivering. Martin paced the room, anxious, looking out the window. Both hands leaning on the window frame. "Returning home like the prodigal," he said, and all the dogs began to howl at once, as though they knew it.

When, years later, I returned to the ruins, they seemed virtually unchanged. Some of the buildings had collapsed in on themselves, and the stone had been bleached a paler colour, but that was all. It looked smaller from an adult's perspective, not the vast wasteland I had imagined as a child. A white, concrete munitions factory had been built nearby, windowless, and surrounded by a high barbed-wire fence. All day long I would hear the sound of its tireless machinery.

This was some time after Martin's arrest. I had only learned of it recently and, fearing he would name names – or, more specifically *my* name – I had fled. Prepared this time, I took food and money secure in a rucksack. This time, there were no dogs. Probably they had died, and their descendents moved off to other areas with more lucrative pickings. Poor, skinny things, they seemed wretched in retrospect. Still, that first night I lay awake listening for signs of their approach – a stray howl, a panting of doggy breath. When none came, I slept fitfully, dreaming of my escape.

I was, admittedly, paranoid. I had brought dark glasses and a badly-fitting blonde wig, wearing these on the underground while other passengers stared past me or through me, or diverted attention to the newspapers they carried. When I looked through the train windows, watching the blue, sparking cables, a strange cheap-looking blonde gazed back at me.

Frequently I changed stations, sometimes heading away from my intended destination, and avoiding all contact with officials or anyone who looked as though they might be in a position of authority. If someone approached to ask for directions, I pretended not to understand and walked brusquely away. It took time to reach the ruins, my progress hampered by the large rucksack I had taken with me. The close proximity of the munitions factory was frightening at first, but then the audacity of the idea hit me: who would look for me here? I found a room that was relatively undamaged, and set up my belongings there. Where the window had been there was now only an empty space, but I covered this with a sheet of clear plastic. When the wind rose, it flexed in and out with a crackling, puckering sound.

For the first few days, I barely left the room, squatting on the floor and poring over newspaper headlines. I looked for some mention of Martin or, worse yet, of myself, but naturally there was nothing. At night I lay staring at the sky through the inky warp of the window, listening to the noise from the factory. It pounded continually, like the beating of a great, metallic heart. I fell asleep to the sound of these machines, and then in the morning they were there to wake me. Rising, I would wash myself at a shallow stream that passed by the house. Bubbling up through rubble, it ran for a short distance before disappearing again, and sometimes birds and small animals came there to drink. I assumed its source was a leak in one of the pipelines that led to the factory because the ruins were everywhere else as dusty and dry and bare as ever. The water was clean, but tasted of iron.

So I would wash then, and read, but the days still dragged, they seemed endless. I had taken a diary to fill up the long hours, but the pages remained blank because only this seemed an accurate reflection of the days themselves. Then too, I longed for human company. If I caught myself speaking aloud, my voice sounded loud and unnatural. When the wind gusted, buffeting in and out of the empty rooms, it was easy to imagine other voices, or the echo of voices among them, but I knew better. Here, the only other sound of human habitation came from the factory, whose sights and sounds were sometimes enough to draw me out of hiding.

It was a blank, featureless building surrounded by a high wire fence and situated on bare dirt ground. Morning and night, workers came and went, filing their way in straggly lines through the metal gates. There were guards everywhere, and some of them carried guns. I had always hated uniforms and hated guns, but I spent all my time watching them through a pair of binoculars I had brought. I wondered if they would see the glint of the sun on the glass. Theirs seemed a boring life, standing around aimlessly all day, only occasionally occupied by the sudden influx of workers, or by vehicles bringing supplies. The factory workers themselves seemed happier, although when they left, the tedium of their work had etched itself onto their faces. Most of them were women, but there was also a smattering of men, presumably the usual mixture of pacifists and homosexuals. Some of them looked familiar, but at this distance it was difficult to be sure. After the factory doors opened and closed, there was a moment's delay and then the odour of acid and metal would hit me, carried by the breeze.

At the times when I felt brave enough I would venture nearer, darting through the ruins and crawling the remaining distance like a snake, on my belly, over the stones. When I had gone as close as I dared, I lay there, just watching, letting my attraction and dislike grow. My hair would rise on my scalp and neck, shivering. Then a sudden noise or someone glancing in my direction would send me scrambling back the way I had come, into the room where I slept, and there I curled, trembling, hoping I had not been seen.

Here, among my belongings, I kept a small transistor radio that I listened to on nights when sleep would not come. Half-drained batteries and poor reception reduced the signal to a whispering crackle filtered over the airways. Sometimes there was soft, jazzy music punctuated by news that described events so far away that they had the quality of make-believe. Often the voices would become many voices, talking in many languages.

One day, the voice foretold an Indian summer. This was at a time when the days were cool – even a little cold – and it seemed unlikely. A wind was flapping the window, a cold wind, and it made me shiver. Yet two days later I woke to a clambering heat and a sun that burnt away all the clouds in the sky. The house smelt old and dusty and dry: pieces of plaster fell from cracks in the wall when I passed. Outside, the stream at which I usually washed was reduced to a thin film that laced its way though worn-down stones. To drink, it was necessary to kneel down and lap like a dog. Nearby, birds had flown up at my approach to perch on old wood, watching with their hard, unforgiving eyes. It was so hot, it seemed the world was on fire. I splashed some of the water on my face. The skin burned at my touch. I thought, *You're ill girl, you've got a fever.* I drank again, but the thirst remained, and added to this was a bitter aftertaste. Something in the water. Soaking the tail of my shirt, I pressed it to my forehead. The heat of my skin raged through the cloth.

Inside it was better, in the shade, but the air was parched and dusty. I gulped down a fizzy drink and then brought it up again. *Maybe I'm not ill. Maybe it's the heat*, but I knew I was fooling myself. The sound of the factory seemed louder and nearer. For a while, I slept.

Waking was like swimming up through a tropical sea with heavy limbs and vision blurred. Did the world really tilt? The floor tipped unsteadily; the roof seemed to seesaw down. Sun shone in at warped angles. I stood then floated across the room and my body, bursting with heat, seemed to expand and fill the smallest corner. Then I found myself standing by the window looking out. Pounding noises rolled in waves across the stones. The sun's light, reflected, was intense and dazzling.

A figure moved below me. He wore a heavy coat that reached to his toes and a scarf wound tight around his neck and mouth. As I watched, he prised large stones loose from the ground, letting them fall with a heavy thump. The sun was so bright it lit his hair up in a halo, it was like a dark fire. Sudden movements of his head sent it flaring. The warped plastic of the window lent his body a rainbow haze. Hunkered down, he looked like one of those hungry black crows picking amongst the ruins. From beneath the raised stones he excavated useless things: rusted bedsprings and wood that crumbled between his fingers. He worked in a circle and

163

spread outwards, methodical, lifting the stones then replacing them as he went. The heat seemed to have no affect on him, because he worked ceaselessly, only once stopping to piss copiously. Flies in hiding bloomed in a cloud. He seemed to sway a little then, until I realised the movement I attributed to him was in fact my own. Pressing my forehead against the window's plastic covering, I thought it would be cool like glass, but it was hot and soft and clung to my skin. When I closed my eyes, zigzags of colour folded out of the darkness, and there was the sensation of falling. To steady myself, I reached out to lean against the wall but what I touched was only thin plastic that tore and billowed free from the pressure. Only the window frame prevented me from following, slamming into my stomach and stealing all my breath. Framed for a moment by the falling square of plastic, the figure below paused, looked up, and then took to his heels. I tried to call out, but what had stolen my breath had also stolen my voice. The tongue flapping in my mouth felt like an alien thing.

Darkness then and after I was crawling on my hands and knees, first on wooden boards and then on stone that burnt to the touch. At the dwindling stream I knelt and let water run into my mouth. Then there was stone again, there was wood, there was trembling, and sour, watery vomit thrown up from my gut. Several times I called out, but there was no-one to hear.

*

In winter, at the height of the coldness that made everything hard and grey, summer seemed so distant that it felt as if it would never come around again. Our flimsy cotton clothes – those flags – had been traded in for heavy woollens and gloves and thick-soled boots. Breath came in clouds; patterns of frost formed around the corners of shop windows, while icicles grew from the overhangs of buildings. The weather was always violent, with screaming winds that carried wet, lashing snow. Mostly we remained indoors. Our father disliked noise and demanded we talk in almost-whispers. Except for news programmes, he would not permit television in his presence and on the rare occasions we dared listen to the radio, it was always with the sound reduced to a murmur, and never turned to a music station. Restless, we would stare out of the window, pace the rooms, or read each other's comics. The chiming of the clocks broke the day up into neverending moments.

Every winter was bad, but the one which followed the summer in which we found the body was the worst. In the intervening months, something had changed in the relationship with my brother. It was subtle, but it was there: Martin grew more reserved and distant, and would abandon our talk to take part in our parent's infrequent discussions. The games we had played were neglected, and there were times he would lock himself into his room, ignoring my repeated hammerings on the door.

Resenting this unexpected manifestation of privacy, I took to having explosive tantrums that gained me nothing more than an empty stomach and a throbbing ear. Furious, I stomped up and down the corridors, fists clenched and making as much noise as possible. Martin never responded to these devices, much to my distaste, and instead my father would materialise from nowhere, looming black and grim, instructing me to go to my room and not to come out again until I was prepared to behave.

In my room I lay in bed, looking out the window where the snow rushed and the street was deserted. The gardens had turned nude and white and I tried to imagine how they looked in the summer, but it was difficult. Instead I found myself remembering the body we had found, and in my mind I grafted my father's face onto the corpse's. It fitted surprisingly well.

The secret of the body was the knowledge that kept the bond I had with my brother from fraying further. We never spoke about it, but it was always there, in the meeting of our eyes, or underlying innocent conversation. I wondered how long it would take the body to rot and whether there was time to see it again. Sometimes I tried to raise the subject of the ruins with Martin, but he would seize the topic and twist the words so they never led in the direction I intended.

Boredom and isolation forced the creation of new pastimes. One of these was the destruction of my father's books. He had a study full of them, leather-bound, gilt spines lined in long rows running the length of one wall. In the evenings he shut himself in there, closing the door, to read. Each morning, a new volume could be glimpsed on his desk. There would be blackened coals in the hearth, and the room stunk of pipe smoke.

Normally a room such as this would have struck me as uninteresting, even forgettable, but this one was my father's, and he had declared it out of bounds. Consequently, my intrusions came to seem both dangerous and exciting to me.

Some mornings I stole nervously in, glancing all about, as though caught mid-traffic. My father was upstairs then, and my mother in another part of the house, cleaning. Above me, on the shelves, the books were lined in uniform editions. Their spines were red or black or brown, and when I prised one down it was accompanied by a scattering of dust and the need to cough. The volume I held was always chosen at random; and I would open it at random, and where it had been opened I would tear out a page, then another. Where these pages had been, there remained a row like jagged teeth. Then I replaced the book and repeated the process with a different volume. If I found one that had already been defaced, I ripped more pages out anyway. Afterwards, feeling foolhardy and frightened at the same time, I would rush out again, twisting the pages into a knotted strand before disposing them in the kitchen wastepaper bin.

Although these intrusions were not regular, they took place more frequently as Martin and I pulled apart. Often I felt very alone. Once, upset, and not caring of the consequences, I had pulled pages free from the book that lay on my father's desk. It was a copy of Great Expectations and the flyleaf had been inscribed

To Alexander with my love. Tom. I felt guilty then, at the thought of defacing what had clearly been a gift, but then I tore the last page out anyway. I wondered too who the book was from – I had never heard my father talk about this person. But then he seldom talked anyway.

After, I lay on my bed dreaming, remoulding my life into new shapes. In these fantasies my father was banished and my mother reduced to a dim figure that flitted about the background. I was queen of the house then, and Martin was king. We had servants and toys and television played loudly all day. When I ran these dreams around my head, they became as real as the room surrounding me. On days when he had fallen from my favour, Martin was cast in the role of a servant, and I imagined inviting all my friends around to fantastically successful parties, of the type I imagined adults held. Sipping tea and nibbling on cucumber sandwiches, we would listen to rock music blasting from the radio. Sometimes an announcer interrupted with a special news bulletin: my father was dead, hit by a bomb dropped from a passing fighter plane. Hearing this, there would be a moment's silence, and then everyone would rise to their feet clapping and cheering.

The friends that populated these fantasies were not the slight acquaintances I knew at school or encountered on the street, but were mostly invented faces of the type of person I imagined I would like to know. Generally they were older than me, and always good looking, the sort of faces that could be seen in television advertisements and pin-up magazines. A few were based on people that Martin knew, reduced to a skeleton of basic features from the scant details I remembered from our brief meetings. Mostly I did not know their names. I knew Lorraine though. She was black and pretty and lived in an unbearable slum neighbourhood.

The first time I met her, she was hanging around a half-wit boy who smiled incessantly beneath the cover of a pudding bowl haircut. He was unable to speak more than a few words, and when he did it was with a mewling sound like a cat. I liked Lorraine and resented this stupid boy who occupied so much of her attention: when she was not looking, I would spit in his face or trip him up. Then he would lie on the street with a grazed knee, looking up at me, still smiling, and in my guilt I disliked him even more. Rushing to his aid, Lorraine would mutter sympathies with her almost-city-but-not-quite voice and her teeth flashed bright against her skin. I liked that mixture, the light and dark when she smiled. Martin liked her too, I could tell, acting awkward and foolish, spouting interminable nonsense. In my fantasies, Lorraine came to my party dressed in rags, but later surprised everyone by dishing out gifts of money, gold coins in money bags. At the times when Martin had been reduced to the role of a butler, I elevated her to the position he had previously occupied.

There were moments when my mother, worried by the lack of sound, would shout up to my room, saying, "What are you doing?" To which I would reply, "Nothing." There would be a pause then and another shout, "How can you be doing nothing? Come and help me with this." Then I would have to help her in the kitchen, or tidying up the house. It was a problem, I noticed, that Martin never had.

This was particularly annoying as Martin, when he went to his room, not only ignored my parents but me as well. I would stand knocking on his door until my knuckles hurt, calling his name, but there was never any reply. Even a muttered growl to go away would have been welcome. Later, cornering him, I would ask, "What were you doing in there?" and he would say "None of your business. I don't need to tell you anything."

This, of course, only increased my curiosity.

One day I lay in wait. This was a wild day, with the wind blowing sleet askance on the windows. Both unwilling and unable to go out, I was restless and chose to wait out the tedium by hiding below my brother's bed. It was a low bed, placed in a corner up by a radiator, so that it was hot and dark in there. In that place, adding to the lack of comfort, boxes of junk had been pushed under and forgotten, and I had to manoeuvre between them, afraid of altering their position too much. It was very uncomfortable. A long wooden handle kept on nudging me in the ribs. The carpet was hard and gritty with dirt. Above my head, a cobweb had been woven between the bedsprings and I had a terror that somehow the spider, which could not be seen, had landed in my hair. I longed to move but instead the heat made me drowsy and sent me to sleep.

The motion of the bed woke me. Metal springs bit into my back and my face had gained a coating of dust.

The whole room seemed to shake with a continuous movement. I couldn't imagine what was happening. Crawling out on my hands and knees, I shouted out: "What are you doing? I'll tell!"

Martin was aghast. His hand snapped out from beneath the band of his trousers. A flush spread over his entire face. Around him on the bedcover were several magazines displaying women naked, in a variety of athletic positions. The skin of the women was pink and airbrushed and looked like half-cooked meat.

Victorious, I stood up, feigning indignation. "Where did you get those? You're not allowed. I'll tell. I will!" And I stamped my buckled feet and shook my baby-fat fist.

At which point he hit me.

"If you tell, I'll hit you again. And I've seen you in the study as well, with those books. Don't think I haven't."

I fled then. My brother had become something alien. I felt my skin roaring red, and I trembled with anger and fear. The pain of the slap had only been temporary, but I lived in terror of my father finding out that I had been responsible for the defacement of the books. When had Martin seen me? And how often? And how dare he hit me?

In my room I lay on the bed and buried my face in the covers. I was unable to stop shaking: I felt sick. All the time I imagined my father's footsteps coming along the passageway. Shocked, clutching the sheets, I made up my mind to run away, and hide among the ruins. It would serve everybody right if I died of exposure. Imagining their grief was a great consolation.

There was a blizzard blowing. It howled and gusted, spattering snow onto the windowpanes until any view was entirely obliterated. Opening the window latch, I tumbled outside. It was a long fall, but I was cushioned by the snow. The world was transformed to grey and white. Redundant streetlights stood sentry to a city hidden in blackness. There was a streak of yellow dog piss beside the spot where I had fallen. As I had only taken a thin jacket which the wind puffed up and howled through, I often had to stop, sheltering behind walls and down alleyways, gasping, trying to regain the breath the wind had stolen. Beneath my clotted clothes, I was unable to stop shivering. Looking down, I found I had forgotten my shoes and had emerged instead in my slippers. By now they were entirely sodden and I could feel nothing below my ankles.

Soon I realised I was lost. The snow made everything look the same. Standing by the roadside, I tried to read the street names and felt ready to cry. Just then, car headlights appeared at the end of the road. They glowed yellow. An old-fashioned car, the kind they made in the 1920s, drove up. The driver stuck his head out the window, shouting, "Do you want a lift?" I nodded gratefully, and got inside. "And where are you off to on a night like this, m'dear?" the driver asked.

"To the ruins." My voice was just a whisper, it was raw.

"Well then, I'll just drop you off if you want, save you the trouble."

The journey was shorter than I remembered, and we were there in minutes. When the driver dropped me off, I kissed him goodbye on the cheek and he blushed.

There was no blizzard in the ruins. Everything was cold and blue and still. A full moon was chiselled in the sky. I had not noticed it before. I wore a thick jacket and new boots which the driver had fetched from the back seat. "This'll keep you warm," he had said.

The snow here was soft and powdery, and as I walked it was thrown up in flurries, glittering. I moulded the snow into balls between my hands – oh, I had forgotten, the driver had also given me gloves – but when I hurled them into the air, they fell apart and showered down soft and white on my head. I laughed, and my voice echoed among the ruined buildings. They looked eerie in the snow and the moon's light. They looked as though they were carved out of bones.

In one of the buildings I found an old rag doll caught beneath one of the rafters. I freed it and it spoke to me, it said, "Hello, I'm Lorraine. Can I be your friend?"

Normally I did not like the many dolls that were given to me as gifts, but I liked this one, and so I said, "Of course you can. You can keep me company here."

We set off together through the snow. It was so quiet my footsteps seemed as loud as a giant's. All the time I was looking for the body, but was unable to remember where it had lain.

"Why don't you try this way?" suggested Lorraine, and then I realised she was right because it was in that direction we had found it before.

A pack of wolves broke free from the cover of the darkness. I could see they were wolves, I had been right the first time. They were silver grey and they bounded through the snow in great, leaping arcs. When they howled, they all howled together, as a pack. Wolves have long memories and, recognising me, they began their chase. I was fast though, faster than them, and when I looked back they were only blurs in the distance, silver blurs.

Something tripped me up. I think it was my own feet. Suddenly the wolves were very near. They had pink, hot mouths and bedraggled fur. They had a dirty smell. I had a twisted ankle and was unable to move but *(Lorraine helped you up)* Lorraine helped me up. Her hand had the texture of cloth. She had wool for hair. Even holding my hand she could run faster than the wind. Soon the wolves were out of sight.

By chance, we arrived at the very spot where the body lay. It seemed to have remained undisturbed since the last time I had seen it, but now all that was left was a lattice of bones, a few tatters of flesh over which lay a coating of snow. I brushed it free with my hand. There was still a matting of hair over the skull. When I pulled at this dirty tangle, the skull came free in my hand. Hanging, its features spun towards me, then away, then back again. All skulls grin, but this one looked mournful. It reminded me of my father. Then of Martin. Then of my father. I let it fall. Striking a slab of concrete that protruded through the snow, it shattered. The shards of bone glittered and spun in the moonlight. I heard laughter and, turning, saw Lorraine was the source of the sound. Her breath, I noticed, did not plume as mine did in the cold air. I clasped her body. It was soft and warm, a doll's warmth and —

- and then I was rising from my bed and smiling and worrying about the books and my father all at once. My mother was calling from downstairs. My name. This time I helped her with the chores without even being asked.

*

The fever was a strange one, it came and went. On some days I was well enough to eat, stinging my lips on segments of tinned orange and strips of dried meat. Then I staggered down to the water source which was sometimes dry, sometimes not. The air warped and shimmered, making everything look smoky and unreal. On these expeditions, tottering around on a new foal's limbs, I had to stop and rest, lying down on the uneven stone, skin prickling with the heat, listening to the sound of the factory whose machines were the only thing the sun had not beaten into submission. When at last I felt able to move, my body left a dark stain of sweat where I had lain. Back in the building, I cooked on a primus stove, forcing down food that seemed to take forever to swallow, while the fever returned in rushes, controlling my limbs which seemed unwieldy and distorted. Then I would shiver in silence for a few more days.

In my fever I had many dreams. Some of these concerned my father who returned not as the grey, frail figure he had been at the last, but as the stern and aloof man who frightened me as a child. He was in a dark, metallic room that I took to be part of the factory, with dirty, antiquated machinery lined along the walls. At first there was silence, but then he spoke and when he spoke it was with a hell-and-damnation voice I had never heard him use before. Spittle flew from his lips. His hands waved crazily. He used specific, accusing words I would never later remember but which always stung me awake, riddled with guilt and crying. I would be unable to sleep then but could never get up, rising a little from the floor then falling, the sun piercing the room sharp and irritating. Running my hands through my hair, my skin slick, shouting, "No! No!" head mechanically turning side to side and legs weakly kicking. In those moments I longed for death, just for it to be over and so the memories and fury would drain away and allow peace to come at last, at least that.

Naturally it never arrived. Once I awoke, opened my eyes and sat up, thinking *I've escaped from hell.* My temperature had fallen and I felt stronger. The weather had changed too, clouds heavy and clustering around the sky. It was still hot, but it was a different sort of heat, clammy and threatening. I rose and drank and ate. On the floor lay a newspaper that the sun had turned yellow and ancient. I wondered what the date was, how long the fever had claimed me.

Outside, a cracking of stones. Someone there. Once, I would have hidden, but the sound now was the sound of a saviour. Staggering to the window, I hoped to gain a glimpse of a human face, but it was only the strange figure in the coat and scarf again, wandering aimlessly though the rubble.

"Hello," I shouted, "are you back here again?" He looked up then, he saw me, I swear he did. His did his frightened rabbit scamper and was gone in seconds. I laughed and laughed at that, but it was a hysterical sort of laughter, full of pain. That moment when he had looked up, I knew him but did not know him, at the same time.

That same night, both my fever and the dreams of my father returned. The fever was less that it had been, but it brought strange visions. In these my father was younger and slimmer than I had ever seen him, the way he appeared in early photos. Again he was in the factory, in the darkened room, on an old brass bedstead. He was entirely naked. In the darkness another body pressed to his. It was a man's body. I was unable to see a face, but the movement of the bodies together was slow and sexual. Their skin was pink, lurid, and their rhythm turned quick and slow. My father looked up then, suddenly, directly into my eyes. He said, "I'll burn in hell for this." Then there was the sudden image of paper bursting into flame, crackling.

I rose. Around me objects wavered, drifted in and out of focus. I knew where I had to go. Outside, in the remains of the stream, I washed my face, I slicked back my hair. Was I presentable? The clothes I wore stunk, mottled with dirt and sweat. There was dried vomit on my sleeve. Salt had creased white into the uppers of my shoes. I thought I looked normal enough.

Creeping near to the factory, I hid by an outcrop of stones. The stones retained the day's heat and were warm. I slept. Then I woke and there were voices and the humming of car engines. Workers clustered together, passing through the factory gates. I was amongst them. Nobody looked at me. It was as though I were a ghost. The guards did not even appear to see me.

Inside, it was neon lit and stunk of metal and oil. It was brighter and cleaner than I had imagined. There were assembly lines below and staircases above that led to darker, less accessible rooms with peeling metal doors. There were rows of metal tanks sandwiched together in a long room where the harsh, acid air caught at my throat.

People never stopped me, no matter where I went. It was as if I had been so wasted by fever they saw right through me. I passed between two white-coated individuals who were talking, but their conversation did not even falter.

Another time I squeezed through a group of people I clearly knew, faces that came back from my childhood and, later, from the time of the riots. Some of them smiled at me, others apologised and moved to let me past (they were crowded together in a passageway). One of them handed me a canister of paraffin, another a box of matches. I thanked them and hurried on.

There were stairs. I climbed them. The clatter and hum was louder here, and there were brief, unexpected passages of warm air. The steps were metal and counted out the fall of my footsteps.

At the head of the stairs was a corridor where sound did not enter. There was a bitter chemical smell and the doors that lined the corridor had windows tinted brown. One of the doors, when opened, revealed a deserted room. Dusty bottles were lined up on an old wooden desk and brittle, faded paper curled in the desk's centre. There was a light switch fitted but the bulb had blown.

It was here, in the darkness, that I soaked my clothes in paraffin and set them ablaze. Naked, I watched the flames spread, floating and leaping along the walls. As they travelled, the flames began to change colour, turning orange, yellow, purple. When they crept alongside my feet, I fled, leaving the door of the room ajar. The floor here was wood over metal and the trail of flames followed me as I ran.

At the sound of someone's approach, I hid in a toilet until they had passed but by then the fire alarm had begun to ring anyway. Workers began to file through the corridors, laughing nervously, making brittle jokes, and I weaved, ducking in and out amongst them. Nobody seemed to notice my state of undress. At the exit, there was a crush as, panicking, several people simultaneously tried to press through the doorway. The smell of smoke was strong by then.

Outside, it was raining. It drummed off the ground. People gathered in clusters and I was alone, but they were too busy watching the fire to see me make my escape. As I ran, I thought of my father who I imagined melting like an old plastic doll. There would be intense white flames and black, black smoke. The body would burst outwards, revealing a hollow interior, and then would cave in again. All of it was mixed up in my head: the fever, the factory, the rain and the roaring flames. There was thunder overhead that sounded like someone trundling a huge object from one end of the sky to the other. For seconds everything would burst into focus with a flash of lightning. There was the smell of smoke and ozone.

My run had become a stumble and after some time I became aware of someone following, footsteps echoing my own, clattering over rocks. At first I was unsure who it was. Who had seen me leave? I kept on wiping the rain from my eyes. It tasted of soot. Who? My father? No. Only the figure in the long coat. This time he had abandoned his scarf and his coat was undone. It flapped behind his back and twisted around his legs. He was shouting. He was running towards me and waving his arms. He was calling my name. How did he know my name? The voice sounded familiar but in the drone of the rainfall it was hard to place. I stood, hesitant, unsure whether to stay or go. An acrid smell. Smoke in the distance. Voices mingled with the downpour. Then: light burning up the whole sky, forking down, stealing the sight from my eyes. The rain hammered louder, louder. There was the sound of sirens.

I had seen him fall. There was no movement but still I suspected a trap. I edged closer and closer and there was the smell of burnt flesh.

The figure lay face down. His clothes were smouldering. Holes had been burst in the soles of his shoes. On the skull, part of the hair was burnt away. The lightning had struck him there, I supposed. The skin was a strange yellow colour that had the odour of charred pork. Blood seeped from the tips of his fingers. The earth around about was black and friable.

I tipped the body with my foot. Even before I saw, I somehow knew. Something in the air. Pieces of blackened cloth fell away in flakes. The flesh crackled. The rain drummed remorselessly down, on and on. Dead earth smell released from the soil. I stood there looking, seeing but hardly believing. Because I was looking at the face, the face on the body, and it was his face, it was his body, it was Martin, it was my brother.

TWO

My! How he cried, that child, when she hit him. That red rummeled face all folds and laminated, looking like nothing I'd ever imagined, hanging upside down from one foot while the other flapped free, and the midwife, this big, brutal woman, slapping him – whoomph – on the back so he let out this cry that filled the whole house, you could hear it outside even: my neighbour, she heard it, she looked up, she said, "It's born then."

That was the first, that was Martin. He came easily, as though it was all he could do to prevent himself from emerging earlier, he just slid out, and all these fantasies, well they seemed like premonitions. I'd be standing there in a supermarket with this trolley full of groceries in front of me, belly pushed hard against the handle, and I'd think: My God, what if it happened here? What if I looked down and there was this red and bloody mess lying at my feet? And then I'd imagine this squalling, kicking thing that resembled some baby seen on the street or in a magazine, and I'd have to lift him up and hold him under the harshness of the supermarket light with all the other shoppers looking on, aghast or jeering. Nobody had told me what strange things being pregnant could do to your mind.

Emily came later, but I was prepared then. Nothing teaches you like experience, that's what my mother used to say, and it was true. All the articles, all the books couldn't say what it was like to have your belly balloon before you, and your body to jitter its hormonal out-of-balance. In any case, it was easier the second time. More of a tiresome routine that stretched long overdue and ended in a fierce burst of pain.

The name Emily wasn't my choice. That was her father's decision, and while I'd much rather have had something more modern, the sort of smartly anonymous name you'd find all the other girls in the area with, I didn't dare argue. We'd chosen our son's name together but he chose our daughter's name himself: that was the way our marriage had become. I know that later she hated the name, oh just hated it, she said it was like a throwback to another world. You could tell it was her father's choice: he'd turned so formal, so Victorian, that it was true he could have come from another time. It could be seen in his speech, the insistence on silence he carried from room to room like a sharp, cold air. I don't think he remembered really, what it was like to be young. All the time he'd stifle his children's movements with that excessive formality of his, trying to shape them, if not in his own image, then at least of the image he held of them. Maybe it would work for a little while, but it was like trying to hold down a spring the whole time, and just when you weren't expecting it, they'd shoot off in some other direction

It wasn't always like that. At one time, I remember that wherever he went, storms were sure to follow. It didn't matter, there could be blue skies and sun, no trace of cloud at all, but the day after it was certain to be overcast and clammy, a denseness that eventually turned to rain and then to storm. We'd see him often, usually just travelling through, but sometimes walking door to door and carrying those Bibles of his with their black leather covers and the gold gilt lettering that came off in your fingers when you handled it.

If they answered at all, most people wouldn't invite him in, because there was no time for religion our way, it was all hard, dreary practicalities that left no opportunity for anything else. Some would go the church maybe, but there was nothing, no great faith to bind us all together. So there'd be those who'd shut the door in his face, while others would leave him standing on the doorstep, usually in the rain, while he recited that litany of his that was all faith and redemption and which he hoped would end in a transaction. With the storm behind him and dressed in an oversized suit that was black and creased, he must have scared them a little. After a while the door would close, and they'd have given him a few coins, maybe a note if he was lucky, and he'd go away. I wondered why he bothered.

The thing was, he may have been odd, but he was also very good-looking. Most days I'd hang around with my girl friends on the street, slouching under lampposts and exchanging gossip or smoking cigarettes, and if we'd see him we'd whistle and catcall because he had the features of an old-fashioned filmstar, one of those matinee idols, all slicked-back hair and sculpted cheekbones. When he didn't reply or even look our way, we'd laugh, telling ourselves he was queer, and we'd invent lewd fantasies about what we'd do if we ever got hold of him.

It was an unusual event to encounter a Bible salesman. Mormons were common enough, or Jehovah's Witnesses, but Bible salesmen were something you associated with a past age, and even then with America, or maybe Ireland. I wondered if he was mad, but he looked normal enough. There wasn't any drooling at the mouth or bloodshot eyes, anyway.

There was that day he came to our house, knocking on the door and spilling out that prepared little speech of his to my mother, who answered. We lived in a run-down area of the city, our house a granite-bricked, walled-in place that had clearly seen better times, so maybe he thought he could sell us a sap for our souls, I don't know. So many people thought the poor would take anything that was offered and that choice was for the rich. It was a common enough idea back then. In any case he was invited in, out of sympathy I think, and given tea and biscuits while he wheeled out all these stories of damnation. It was quite impressive, the way he'd live them out, his face turning red and sweaty and his voice rising and falling in peaks. I stopped listening after a while to what he was saying and just stared, he was so good to look at, his face and body, the way he'd move, and I'd feel these sharp spasms of excitement inside, these tremors. All that staring, it was a wonder he didn't notice, but then maybe he was used to it, that constant attention. His hands were soft and shaped like a pampered woman's and looked odd holding that ornate, heavy Bible. Only after he had finished did he tell us his name (it was Alexander) and then he left without selling anything, but took a pound note from my mother and my own ill-disguised admiration. I rushed upstairs then, just so I could see the top of his head disappearing down the street. Afterwards, when

I'd tell people how we'd first met, they'd talk about love, but it wasn't love at all, just lust. That, and a great desire for freedom.

You have to understand, I'd lived in that place all of my life. It was a council estate that would have been a good place to stay in once, but it had been neglected in recent years, it had a tired look, with broken windows boarded up and layers of hewn-out graffiti over the walls and fences. Nobody wanted to live there if they could help it, but then they didn't have the choice. People would stay in the same houses in which they'd been born, never having risen above the dead-end jobs they'd worked in all their lives, if they had a job at all. I desperately wanted to escape that trap. It seemed to me the worst possible thing that maybe you'd reach seventy and look back to discover all that had happened in your life was that you'd got older, frailer and poorer.

It was impossible to be free of those sorts of thoughts. Since my infancy my mother had suffered a series of debilitating illnesses that left her looking thin and tired, with a permanent limp. My father was seldom unemployed, but the jobs he could find were tedious and menial, often making him suffer from depression. I loved him a great deal and can still remember the calluses on his hands and the tobacco smell on his breath when he lifted me to bed and kissed me goodnight. Sometimes, joking, he'd say it was just as well I was an only child, because how could they afford to keep another? He didn't mean anything by it, naturally, but those occasional remarks left me feeling guilty enough to leave school from the moment I was old enough, even though others told me I should stay on, I was clever.

You can't blame me then for taking whatever I could, even a shabby Bible salesman with even less of a future than my own and no belongings beyond a stack of Bibles and the clothes he wore. Thinking about it now, it could have been a lot worse if things hadn't changed the way they did. At sixteen though, you can make anything seem attractive, and to me he was like someone out of one of those romance novels I was addicted to even then, addicted to even though I understood their worthlessness, and there'd be days I'd just dream and dream about some dark, brooding figure come to steal me away, dreaming even when I was working, so even drudgery was transformed into a false promise.

Of course, he wasn't like that at all and I suppose there was some part of me that knew it even then. The poverty of his situation was always apparent, what with his suits too large and beginning to fray. He was thin too, not at all like the intimidating portly figure he'd become. At the time of our second meeting, just a few days after he'd been to our house, he looked like a real down-and-out, just some drifter on his way from town to town, which turned out not to be so far from the truth after all.

It was raining, I recall, so he was sheltering in the doorway while the rain fell down in long, heavy sweeps, making a noise like sheets cracking in the wind, shattering over windowpanes and the old walls with their new graffiti, the sodium light reflected in the water that pooled and ran corrugated down the gutters. It was impulse that made me join him, made me hurry down the pavement to where he stood, a bag of groceries pushed under my coat making me look like a pregnant woman. So we huddled in the doorway of a closed-down arcade, shivering with the cold (it was winter), clothes sodden and dripping, and saying nothing, not even hello, to each other. I supposed he didn't recognise me while, after my initial boldness, I was too embarrassed to speak to him. Or maybe I sensed even then how much he valued silence, like a craving. It was difficult to know what to say in any case. I wanted to ask: *How many souls have you saved anyway?* But I'd only to have to look at that face and the question would have died on my lips. Clearing my throat, I tapped my feet, I gazed with unusual curiosity at the scuffed toes of my shoes, I tried to read the headlines of a sodden newspaper trampled into the pavement. Finally he left, before I did, in the downpour, and I watched him hurry down the street, with his suit jacket pulled tight around his body. I hoped he'd look back, I hoped so hard: but naturally he didn't.

Are there patterns in life? Sometimes it seems that way, with all the pieces fitting so neatly together you think: *There's something behind this, it was meant to happen.* After meeting Alexander I began to think about these things for the first time, but I never reached any sort of conclusion. Instead, all the answers just led to other questions. A few times I even tried to read the Bible, but it was too boring, people seemed to spend all their time begetting and doing nothing else. I only wanted to read it to impress Alexander anyway, imagining myself in conversation with him, dropping obscure references and quoting chapter and verse, the way I'd seen him do. That always seemed such an intellectual thing to do somehow, and when I thought about him, dreaming, I always imagined him to be sharp and clever, despite the evidence I had seen to the contrary. Somehow, I didn't doubt we'd meet again.

Eventually we did. It happened a few weeks after we'd sheltered in the doorway, as I was leaving the house, going to work. He was standing on the other side of the street - it was early, he was the only other person there - and I could see him watching, not directly, but following me first with his eyes, then with his feet. It was a cold day and I found myself wishing I hadn't worn so many clothes, knowing that from a distance I'd look fat and frumpy. At that time of the morning there were so few people about I didn't think that he'd have any problem seeing where I was going, but just to be sure I'd stop now and again, tying my shoelace or looking into a shop window, then sneaking a look to make sure he was still there. When I sidestepped into a café, one of those rundown corner affairs with circular tables and plastic chairs, I just sat there, waiting. A few minutes later he came in, as I knew he would, ordering a coffee, pulling up a chair alongside mine, exchanging a few words, nothing special, just banalities.

A year later we were married.

Would I have taken anyone? Maybe. At that age you're so confused you'll grasp onto anything and tell yourself it's better than what you already have. To tell the truth there were even times I didn't like him much, he could be so humourless and dour, and if we went out somewhere he'd just sit, looking. Maybe, I told myself, it was different with religious people. He was older than I was too, twenty seven, almost ten years between us, and older people had a separate way of seeing things, they'd different attitudes. So maybe that was it. I couldn't say I loved him, and if later a fondness developed, it was because he was there all the time, this familiar presence.

Nobody said it might be a mistake, even though there was age and religion between us. As it was, I think my parents were glad in a way to be rid of me, to be done of the responsibility of marrying me off early on. It was still the accepted thing then, a route you followed, getting married, having children, accumulating everything that was needed for the house before you became too old or sick to afford it any more.

Ours was a small wedding in a church where I wore a hand-me-down gown, and after that there was a torturous three months where I stayed with his parents in a small, miserable village that lived off the trade of passing tourists. Alexander was away then, and his parents were humourless, miserly people who made it seem as though my visit lasted forever. It was three months of strained, brittle silence. When my husband returned from his travels that time, he brought an old brown saloon with him, larger than the car he'd traded it in for, and we lived in the back of that, all our clothes and bedding heaped in the back seat. My life began to revolve around motorways, petrol pumps and cheap motorside cafes.

Looking back on those days now, our plight seems more appealing than it really was. It's taken on a ramshackle quality, the way you think maybe of the Depression, but it wasn't like that at all. Those were grey, disheartening times when people would see Alexander coming to the door and not bother to answer, lifting the corner of the curtain and watching until he had gone. Most days he wasn't making any money at all, and if I sometimes hadn't managed to get a job waitressing or cleaning when we were staying in one place for any length of time, we simply couldn't have survived.

The talk of another war was just beginning then, and far from the sense of camaraderie, of pulling together I'd always imagined there would be at that time, people become hard and mean, seeming to wrap an air of isolation around themselves. It could be seen from the way they'd walk along the streets, pulling their long coats tight and bowing their heads, pushing their separate ways and not speaking to anybody. You'd have thought they'd be anxious to speak, to know what was going on, but no, that seemed to be exactly what they were afraid of. I probably knew more than they did because the days were long and I'd read the newspapers from cover to cover, memorising everything that was happening, or at least as much as the government chose to reveal.

A greater abundance of flags began to appear in the towns we passed through, limp, multi-coloured things that flapped miserably in the cold winds. More noticeably, recruitment for the army seemed to be on the increase: everywhere you looked there were posters pasted on telegraph poles, fences, on walls. For a time, even Alexander talked about joining but, less timid in those days, I argued against it, and by that time we'd travelled to the north of the country where the signs of patriotism were much less tangible. In these surroundings, the impulse seemed to leave him. I often wondered if it was just an excuse to leave me anyway, an escape from the responsibilities he'd taken on.

He was an odd man, Alexander, so strict in his attitudes, almost puritanical, the sort of person who gave you the impression he'd been born that way. It struck me as being strange because his parents, for all their dislikeable traits, weren't like that at all. He was quiet, but his silence had a stern quality about it that reminded you of a schoolmaster or something like that. It was only when he preached - he'd do that on occasion, in the street – that there was any real sign of animation, the way his voice would soar and dip and his whole body would tremble, there was something sexual in the way it shook. Alone, we'd never talk about religion at all and I was grateful for that. Even when I made a joke once, about how he should have been born in the Bible Belt, there was this feeling of intrusion, as if I'd said something I shouldn't. He took it the wrong way anyway, like it was a serious comment or something, and ended up agreeing. It was times like that I'd think: *If he smiles, his face will crack.*

The same reserve made it more bearable though, travelling up and down those long roads that ran past grey buildings all alike, watching them at night when they'd become these long columns of light, feeling it then, all the time, how we didn't have a home. Or we'd follow the roads that veered and curved, their trails of cat's eyes glittering, always just ahead of a storm. Trying to outrace the clouds that hunched on the horizon, listening expectantly for the first sounds of rain or the dislocated wrench of thunder. On reaching our destination, Alexander would carry that big Bible of his from door to door while I'd haunt the restaurants or corner shops to see if they needed any short-term help. If they didn't, I'd go back to the car, winding down the windows and sprawling in the front two seats to listen to the radio or read some second-hand romance picked up for near to nothing at an out-of-the-way bookstore. I'd read these so often the spines would crack and the pages slide free, so I'd constantly have to put them back in order. Sometimes they'd get mixed up from book to book, but it didn't make any difference and I'd read them again anyway. When Alexander returned, all hot and short-tempered from the heat, we'd eat at the cheapest café that could be found, fat-saturated foods that were the staple of long-distance truckers and travelling salesmen.

Every few months, the money would simply dry up and we'd have to return to Alexander's parents, living in their house and eating their food. It was an arrangement they resented and all the time, at every opportunity, they would choose to remind us of our dependence. "Taking the food out of our mouths," they'd stage-whisper. Still, it meant a chance to rest, although I always carried the momentum of the journey with me and it was difficult to settle, I was always pacing. At night, when I lay down to sleep, the bed would seem to lurch like the forward motion of a car and I'd dream of empty motorways that seemed to stretch on forever. It was better though than the daytime which was spent bickering with his parents, an endless squabbling that left me desperate for the time we would take off again in the brown saloon, familiar now with the weather's pattern, the way the air would clench hot, stifling, then drop suddenly in the aftermath of a storm. It made for more dramatic impact, Alexander said, to arrive in that way, with the dense cloud cracked open by lightning. It's the only comment he ever made about what he did, and revealed an awareness about the image he presented I thought him incapable of. Me, I just wondered how long it would be before we had travelled every road, called at every house, finally reaching the point where all the doors, every one, had been shut in my husband's face. Always I worried about money, wondering how much longer we could go on this way, scrimping and saving and homeless. If I'd known what was ahead, perhaps those times would have been more bearable. Just thinking about it now, about how different it could have been, there's this fist of anxiety in my stomach. Silly, really, how worked up you can get about the past, all those dead things.

From the first he wanted children. He made that plain, but I told him it was stupid, we couldn't rear them in the back of the car or feed them on beans and chips. Still, he made every effort, not pulling out when I asked him to, and I'd be forced to stop at the nearest toilets, washing myself with a primitive douche of soap, as if there wasn't such a thing as contraception. I wouldn't have dared to have gone on the pill: he wouldn't have approved, and there were few secrets that could be kept when we lived in such close proximity. In time I learned the secret of making him come when he wasn't expecting it, in other parts of my body, but still there were mistakes. In the second year of our marriage I became pregnant with Martin.

At the same time, it became evident the threat of war that had for so long hung around us was moving to the inevitable. The newspapers we found discarded around the streets were full of staunchly patriotic headlines while the radio played brash, militaristic music. The atmosphere in the towns we passed through was an odd mixture of fervour and tension, and at night when we slept in the car, the air was full of drunken cries and singing tinged with desperation.

We never stayed long, but the mood was still contagious, it couldn't help but infect. All the time I worried about the war, about the child that grew in my womb, and the money I'd count each night in copper and silver: wondering how far it would go. Sitting in the car each day was no help either, it was just time that turned to worry, and the worry had no end, it was as tireless as the roads we travelled.

One day all of that changed. It was late, another one of those airless, claustrophobic evenings to which I'd become accustomed, clouds bleeding on the horizon. Alexander was later than usual and, from where the car was parked in a lay-by, I waited for his approach, expecting all the time to see his wasted, black-clothed figure trudging up the road. It had been a long, empty day. That morning I had been sick for the first time, a horrid acid bile. After that I had been unable to move, I could only sit and stare. All day long I'd watched the comings and goings at a roadside petrol station. Two men in overalls were arguing, arms waving. Then it began raining and there was nothing to be seen any more, just the flashing headlights of cars and trees at the road's edge that had turned to blurs of green. It was very hot, I remember, and the windowpanes had steamed up on the inside, there was this distant roar, it was the rain but it sounded like the sea. Something dreamy and unreal about that sound. Lying there, tired, I curled up in the seat and I must have dozed in a worried, fitful way, because suddenly there was banging, a blast of rain-flecked wind and then Alexander was beside me, sodden and shivering and spilling a brown sheaf of notes over my lap.

I'd never seen him like that before, with that sort of sharp alertness in his face, the darting eyes lifting the scattered money and the laughter that fell uncontrolled from his mouth. For a moment there, half-asleep, I thought there was a big black crow beside me. Then I thought: *he's stolen it, he's hurt somebody for the money.* But that wasn't it at all.

That night we slept in a hotel. On the way there, he pointed at the house he'd visited and described the man who lived there, gloomily wealthy, wasting from some sort of inner disease and worried for his soul. It had been a grand building once, a formal Victorian construction, but now it had fallen into disrepair. I wondered, guiltily, if the man had given Alexander all he had, his life savings or something. There'd been nearly four hundred pounds in that roll of notes he'd clasped into my husband's hands.

Oh, I slept well though, like I'd fallen into this great, dark pit that went on forever. There were no dreams, there was no surfacing in the night with worries stirring around in my head. When I woke to a morning that was cloudless and full of sun, I felt like I'd wished all the storms away.

Alexander was gone by then, but the space in the bed beside me was still warm. I lay there a bit longer, then ate breakfast in a dining room that was almost empty: it was later than I'd imagined. From time to time I'd think of the previous night when the money had fallen around me like dirty snow, and I'd wonder where Alexander was now, but it really didn't seem to matter.

At noon he returned, bundled me into the car and drove me to his parents, hardly speaking along the way. The nervous agitation of the day before was gone, and he just drove with his eyes on the road. On our arrival he dropped me by the roadside along with my suitcase, then left me standing there while he drove back in the direction from which we had come. "I won't be long," was all he had to say.

After that, I didn't hear from him again for nearly three months. There were no letters, no telephone calls, nothing. In his absence my belly began to swell, and even small tasks began to feel tiring. I wondered what it would be like when I grew like other women I'd see, with their protruding bellies and backs arched forward and their rounded faces.

The thought of a grandchild seemed to please Alexander's parents, and their criticisms became muted, but I avoided them anyway. They lived near the coast line, so I'd spend the day looking out of the bedroom window to the grey-blue skies, listening to the wind which gusted ceaselessly and sent window frames and dustbin lids clattering. In the moments when contact became unavoidable, such as at mealtimes, I carried past hurts with me, and our conversation was reduced to brief, formal exchanges, punctuated by the sound of knives, forks, scraping on plates. When the television went on it was a relief, and we'd sit there in the dark, mute, with the blue light that shifted over the walls. Either that or I'd visit the old-style pavilion nearby, standing outside in the cold and watching people come and go, listening to the music, all waltzes, stuff like that. Occasionally I'd talk to the doorman, broad and bow-tied, who'd tell me, "It's less and less every year, love. It's only the wrinklies that come, and they're dying off now, seems every week there's another face gone." And I'd touch my belly at that, like it was a charm to ward off evil. When the pavilion closed for the end of the season, it was for the last time and I felt lonelier, more isolated than ever.

Then one day there were big black clouds stacked high on the horizon, dense and heavy with rain, and I thought: *He's coming home.*

He came with money. You could see it in his walk, that moneyed swagger, and you could tell from the way he talked: when he opened his mouth you expected coins to fall out. The clothes were new and fitted his frame and he arrived on the first-class carriage of the train, stepping out on the platform to the accompaniment of a loud peal of thunder. He brought nothing else with him, not even his Bible. For a moment there he didn't even look like the man I'd married. We travelled back to his parents under a sky full of wind and rain and birds that the storm had startled from the trees. All my questions were turned aside: he just sat staring at the taxi driver's back, but I could see the need to reply bubbling out of him, if I could only find the right words to set it free.

That night we made love and his body was tainted by a strange, unfamiliar scent. You know what it is, I thought, it's the smell of money. Only it wasn't that at all. I knew that from the fading marks around his back and neck. I slept and dreamt of many strange and dangerous things.

In a week we were gone. The storm followed and I first saw our new house in rain that turned its brick a muddy brown and made its windows dark and impenetrable. It took me some days before I realised where I had seen it before. Its garden was overgrown, lush and green, while other buildings in the area were full of light and the shadows of moving figures. I looked at it and thought it would never seem like a home, but I live there still, and it's grown as familiar as my body. On those nights when I'm anxious and alone, I think back to how it was then, when we first arrived, all empty and draughty and cold, and I look around now to its light and warmth, and I tell myself, *You haven't done so bad.*

That was where Martin was born, the way he kicked and fought his way out of my womb, it's where the sky was full of lights and planes and distant, frightening noises. I lie on the same bed on which my husband died, and there's still the hint of him on one side, where the bedsprings sag and make a small ridge under the sheets. I couldn't have guessed any of those things then, I was only twenty, and it seemed terrible that we so suddenly had so much, and all from a dead man's fears. Now I'm mercenary and think: *Better you should have it than any other.*

I have the copy of the will somewhere, in a box mixed up with all the other papers, but it still hurts to look at it, it stirs up all these memories. At first I'd lie in bed at night, wondering how anyone could have so much guilt, and sometimes I'd say to Alexander, "But what had he done? I don't understand. Tell me about him." But he'd only purse his lips and shake his head as if to say, *No, I'm not telling you, not ever.* There something else too, some expression that showed briefly on his face and then was hidden again. I never found out what it was. We owed that dying man so much, and all I can remember now is his first name: Tom.

Alexander wasn't the same after that though, it was as if he'd traded in one type of life for another. He stopped talking about religion – but wouldn't say why – and all the worst aspects of his personality, the strictness, the coldness, became more and more pronounced as the years went by. I often wonder: why did he do it? Was it love? Was it greed? Was it practicality? Because he was happy before, in his way.

When the war began, I think he even welcomed it, for the distraction. Martin was only three months old then. All those newspaper headlines, the speeches, the people who would stop you in the street and pin little union jacks to your clothes, they were of precious little use at the moment when the face appeared on the TV screen and read out a prepared little speech, looking very grim and patriotic, while you felt small and scared. When it was done, I took Martin up to my bedroom and sat there and cried. A little later Alexander came in. He didn't say anything: we just held each other while we listened to the silence, the awful deadening silence that rose up from the streets.

Sleep never came easily after that. In a few years time, the nights were often punctuated by cracks and flashes that would bring the children into our room to find refuge beneath the bed covers, fitting their thin bodies between our own, and somehow I would feel safer too when they were there, the warmth of their skin pressed to mine. In those times, listening to the sirens became a sort of unconscious decision, the sort of thing that was no more thought about than breathing – you'd listen and there'd be a moment of two of suspense before the bombs fell, usually in some other part of the city, and you knew then you were safe, at least for a little while. If we turned off the lights and opened the blackout curtains, the searchlights could be seen, the way they panned the skyline, lighting up the rooftops or the oblong shapes of barrage balloons, their tautened guylines. Sometimes corners of the city were lit with a raging glow that sent sparks into the air, along with black clouds of smoke that would fall the next day as dark smudges of rain.

Safety was something distant then, something so far off you forgot it ever existed. Always there were sounds – explosions, voices – to remind you how fragile everything was, and how easily it could collapse without warning. I'd look at our house with its solid walls, its firm roof, the stone grimed with age, and tell myself it was ageless, but even it was no protection against the falling apart, the collapsing I'd see each day from the window. Once I'd been able to view the distant outlines of a park from our home, and the rising dome of the cathedral, but the cathedral was gone now, it was just rubble, and the trees in the park were blackened and bare.

Did I dream of leaving? Of course I did. Once I had that habit, it kept on returning, like a craving. I dreamt of a country house with green fields and tall trees and twisted chains of roses that clung around the door. A place like that probably never existed in the idyllic form I imagined, but that didn't stop me from hoping, longing for it so much it became like an ache inside.

When that feeling came, I'd ask, I'd beg Alexander to move away, but he wouldn't listen, he always ignored those sorts of suggestions. It was as though he'd spent so long travelling that he couldn't bear to leave this place he'd found, that he could call his own.

I felt that too, along with the need to escape, the two emotions becoming mixed together. It was strange how familiar it had become, those rooms, that furniture, the smell you'd get of smoke and polish, the stains and knocks you'd come to know like marks on your own skin. When it grew windy, all the timbers they'd shift and strain, the same as if you were in some big ship, and any moment you'd expect it to lurch, the furniture to slide around the rooms. I'd close my eyes and think of that, just sailing, but then I'd open them again and it was all still there, the same street, the same houses, the same lack of people.

It felt like being stranded at times, when you'd look and see all the darkened buildings, the overgrown gardens, the signs to show they were for sale. When the war began, one household after another had moved away, until there was one family at one end, a group of squatters at the other, ourselves, not many others. People coming through here must have thought it was like a ghost town or one of those places that had been evacuated because of unexploded bombs.

A life like that wasn't normal. How could it be, when everyone had to exist like that? It was seldom said, it was all reserve around there, and you could only guess at what was happening. Those sort of secrets only seeped out in rumour and gossip, and it was hard to tell what was truth and what was lies.

We had our secrets too. Martin would have these nightmares – not always, but sometimes – and they'd leave him shaking and crying, all huddled down in bed with the sheets and blankets tangled around his body. Catching him crying, I'd lift him and his skin would be hot, feverish, and he'd have wet the bed. "What's upset you?" I'd ask, but he wouldn't say, he'd just shake his head, all wet and mottled with sweat. The fear then, you could feel it coming through his skin.

That was when he was younger. Children get scared of anything, and it's worse when they can't see it, when it's out there in the dark. I grew afraid myself, hearing the shriek and cry of the bombs, the way they dropped, seeing the fires, the way they burned. You can't imagine if you haven't lived through it yourself. Alexander always told me, "Don't worry, he'll grow out of it," and he did. Only, then he started to sleepwalk. Each night there'd be a stirring, the slap of feet on the floorboards, doors opening and closing, their soft sighs, one after the other. In time it grew familiar, something you'd come to expect, but at first it wasn't like that at all. I woke in the night and thought, *My God – it's a burglar!* Break-ins were common then, even more so than now, and when an object came onto the black market, there was forever the suspicion that this was how it had been obtained. Buying always left a smear of guilt.

That first time I heard movement, I was so afraid that I wormed stupidly down under the bedcovers, as though that would make the source of the sound go away. Waking to a situation like that seemed so unreal and I wondered, as you do at those times, if I was dreaming. All sorts of odd thoughts. The sound of my breath seemed amplified, like a roar. If I moved eventually, it was because of the thought of the children's safety rather than some great reserve of courage: slipping from between the sheets so as not to make a noise, brandishing an upturned table lamp and treading down the stairs feeling both frightened and ridiculous. I don't know why I didn't wake Alexander. Neither did I know what I would find. Certainly I didn't imagine it would be Martin, pyjama'd and senseless, with his face squashed all misshapen to the wooden panels of the front door, his hand ineffectually turning the door handle, that rattle. At first I couldn't imagine what he was doing, but then I saw the half-closed eyes, and the slack, dopey expression and that was when I understood.

I led him to his bedroom like a lost dog, careful not to disturb him because I'd heard you mustn't wake sleepwalkers. In my hand I still held the table lamp, I remember, and it was only then I saw how it shook. In a situation like that, the fear doesn't hit you until later, and then it pours out and you can't make it stop, it goes on and on. When I lay him on the mattress and he curled tight into a ball, he looked so odd and faraway in his sleep that it was difficult to leave him. I just sat there in a chair, watching the curve of his body beneath the blankets, listening to his breathing, the sound it made. Then I slept too - after which it was morning, with the light just beginning to creep through the window.

The following times it became easier, something you learned to expect each night, lying there and listening for sounds of movement in other parts of the house. If they came he'd always be there by the door, trying to get out, sometimes hammering on the wood. As a precaution I had another lock fitted, and another bolt. It became familiar, a routine, and it made me realise: you could get used to anything in time. I wondered if that was what had happened with me and Alexander.

Since we'd married, I used to worry all the time about what people had been saying, the sort of stories that had gone around before our arrival. I wondered what they knew and whether they talked in condescending tones about this Bible salesman and his wife that were coming, you knew the sort. Sometimes I wondered that myself, what right we had to move into a dead man's house, to take his money, to live in this street of Victorian houses with their perfect gardens and their owners with their proper accents. It was possible that Alexander had even knocked on their doors at some point, quoting from the Bible in that demanding voice of his, until it was silenced with a hurriedly-offered note and a muttered goodbye. I always looked for signs of disapproval in their eyes, some less agreeable emotion behind their smiles. It was difficult to tell because everyone around was so polite and proper, just exchanging a few words before withdrawing into their gardens or houses where they'd watch you with these distant, unreadable expressions. Soon most of them were gone, but I still worried anyway.

The thing was, I never had security or untroubled love, just lust and loneliness and then a husband and children. They followed one after the other, as though they were inevitable, and I suppose I followed, not knowing any better. Always I hoped things would improve somehow, and then it seemed they did: but the truth was that they had just become familiar enough to be tolerable. It's only now when I can look at the past without any real involvement that I realise how odd and awkward things had become. I tell myself, *If that happened now, I'd behave differently, it wouldn't be the same*, but probably it would: it's easy to be brave from a distance.

And it's hard to be brave in the face of strangeness. When Martin's nightmares began, I thought, *He's got them from his father,* as though it was something that could be passed through the genes like hair colour or build or the shape of the face. Because he had them too, Alexander, although less frequently, the same dreams that would leave him trembling and sweating with fear. When we'd married, I couldn't imagine him being scared of anything, but now it was there, it surfaced at night in those dreams and their accompanying mumblings, words you could never quite make out. Then, too, sometimes during the day I'd catch him sitting alone, unawares, with this unfamiliar emotion splayed all over his face. What was it he feared? I never asked. Was it the money? It fed us and clothed us and brought us the house, but there was this impression, he gave it sometimes, that it wasn't good money, that it had been marked by the past somehow. It wasn't just imagination, I'm sure. I'd this theory I told myself sometimes that Tom, the man we'd inherited this money from, was some sort of criminal, his fortune illegally made and, knowing this, Alexander also felt as though he'd inherited the burden of sin. Although I didn't know much about sin, this seemed a perfectly reasonable idea. I bought a Bible for the children, one of those big, illustrated ones, and began to read through it with them. I thought I might find clues, pointers to the way Alexander felt, but it didn't really help any.

Then there was his sudden fetish for hanging up these figures of Christ on the cross: every room had at least one, all of them coloured gold, all of them hanging bleeding, those sad-dog eyes that seemed to follow you everywhere. They were (I imagined) expensive, but looked cheap, they had all the tackiness of a toy you'd find in a funfair. All the time I expected to find signs of discolouration, the green among the gold, or to find it peeling like old paint, but it never did. When you looked closely at the faces they disappeared into a crudely painted crisscross of lines, but from a distance they all had the same anguished expression. Some of them were covered in so much blood it looked as though they'd been involved in a motorcycle accident. It was stupid, but I was too scared to even dust them, forever passing them by, until a thin grime had collected on those golden bodies, and cobwebs had been formed and abandoned between the intersections of the cross. This only made them look more realistic somehow, and it times it would seem they followed me everywhere, watching everything I did. Maybe that was what they were for.

There was even one on the roof. He must have spent a fortune on having it made especially, a lightning rod in the shape of a cross, with this featureless, crudely-shaped figure hanging limp from it. The way it was positioned made it clearly visible from a distance, fitting there among the chimney pots and TV aerials: once a couple even came to the door to ask if our house was a church of some sort. On nights when the city was burning, the cross seemed to fill up with light, sending this pool of flame around the roof, as though it was burning too, and full of fire.

I tell you, his guilt swelled him up like a balloon, it wasn't only dreams and obsessions it created, with his belly sticking out before him in a great paunch, his arms thickening, face becoming round and anonymous, his beauty lost between folds of fat. He grew a beard, and if we kissed, it was like pressing my lips to steel wool. But then I seldom kissed him any longer anyway. Sometimes, looking at him, it was like looking at a stranger, not the person I'd married at all but someone older, odder, and slightly repulsive. The coldness and distance he inspired became all the greater, like his intolerance, his dislike of unpunctuality, his love of discipline, and to the children he must have resembled some fearsome old schoolmaster, the kind I'd known in my own schooldays. If they were late for their meals they went without: I'd feed them later, in secret, if he wasn't watching. Similarly any noise, the sort all children make, was forbidden so the house trembled with the silence, and even if the three of us, the children and myself, listened to the radio, we had to huddle around it, like it was some sort of fire, like it gave off some sort of heat, and listen with the volume turned down.

Growing up like that, it was a wonder they were even remotely happy: I could never have imagined living that way when I was young. The war, their father – they'd none of the freedoms I had.

Martin was my favourite of the two, even though I tried not to make those sorts of distinctions. Perhaps it was because he was the first-born, or maybe it was just as I'd been told, boys got on better with their mothers, girls with their fathers. If I look back, it's my father I think of, it's true, but then my mother was such a wretched, thin thing, always wracked with pain, that it was difficult to get to know her. I think of her now with compassion but never with love, because that's an emotion she was never able to show to me. There's this picture I have of her in my mind, seated in front of the dressing table and combing her thin, greying hair, sitting awkward in the way she holds the comb, a stiffness in her fingers and the corner of her mouth set, as always, in a slight grimace of discomfort. It chased everything else away, that feeling. In that respect at least, I'd proved myself better. I couldn't help but love because raising the children took all of my time, every bit of it, demanding in a way I'd never imagined. So they had all my love, but also all my hate, my frustration, my fear, my compassion, it was all directed at them, even when they were unable to understand or even comprehend my moods. When as an infant, Martin would stand, I'd be filled with delight: but also fear, because he was always reckless, always headstrong, trying to run before he could even properly walk, and inevitably falling in the process. I was so afraid he'd develop bow legs, running that way.

With Emily it was different, because I knew by then something of what to expect. Still, she was a strange, wayward child, secretive where Martin was forthcoming. When she spoke it was in a whisper, shielding her mouth with her hands as if she wasn't the person responsible. "Don't do that," I'd say, "it's not nice manners," and I'd pull her hands away, but she'd keep on doing it anyway. That was her other side, the stubbornness, the refusal to do as she was told unless she felt like it. It was difficult to tell which was the real Emily, the shy one or the stubborn, or if they were both disguises, something she hid behind. Then again, those were her father's qualities, that opaqueness, so it shouldn't have been surprising. Some of it had to rub off.

Maybe all that would have changed if there hadn't been a war. Oh, it affected everything. People lived on hand-me-downs and ration books, and you'd get the daily newspaper that would be printed on thick pulpy paper with uncut edges. There were power cuts, the water supplies would reduce to a trickle and the television would go off the air for days at a time, there'd just be this grey static hiss. Outside, you'd hear the bombs drop, the high shriek and then the explosion that would sometimes send tremors through the house, all the glass and ornaments rattling. If they came close enough, Alexander would gather us all together and pray in a tone of voice somewhere between pleading and demand. I could never concentrate though, listening instead to the bombs, the gutter of voices that rose from the streets. If a window was open, smoke would enter to catch at your throat.

That was why I didn't like the children going out on the street: I was always afraid they wouldn't return. There'd be other girls and boys out there playing, come to the quiet of this area, and they never seemed to come to much harm, but I always thought, I always told myself: *I'd rather have them cooped up than dead.* Above all, there was the worry they'd go to the slum areas, the poor parts of the city where all the munitions factories had been built, because that's where the bombs fell most often. Every day there'd be reports, official and unofficial, of more dead.

Imagine how I felt then when they began to run away. It was a phase they went through together, because the difference in age wasn't great, and they'd goad each other on. Just by watching them you could tell they'd something planned.

One time they went, it was one of the worst nights of the war, when the whole sky was lit up with great bursts of light. It must have been exciting to escape out into that world with its noise and heat, knowing nobody would pay attention. There would be no need to hide, because all that confusion would shift and shape itself around you. That time, the first time, Alexander went out to look for them, disappearing down the unlit street – I can see it still – with the wind blowing his clothes all twisted, a storm wind, and houses, whole streets, burning in the distance, their spit and roar drowning out his voice which came in gasps or not at all. Me, I stood watching, waiting by the window, seeing these little darts of fire racing past, sparks that carried even here, like messages from the other side of the city. There, in that house with its collection of shadows and its smell of woodsmoke, it was easy to be frightened and to feel isolated. I was afraid they wouldn't come back, not any of them, and that feeling, that feeling of isolation, was the worst of all. Once, I tried to phone the police, but the lines were down, like the lights had gone, and it could have been a dead world out there.

The source of that fear wasn't just the war, although that was bad enough. A number of children had disappeared that year, in circumstances never fully explained. There was never anything in the papers or on the radio, but you'd catch snippets of conversation down in the street, in the shops, and you'd learn it all there, how somebody's son had gone missing last week, or this other person's daughter just yesterday afternoon, and nobody knew where. Although it was never said, it was assumed child molesters were responsible. Sometimes, remembering these reports, I'd try to catch the eyes of people who passed on the street, trying to read whatever secrets they held, only I never could.

There was this one old man who used to sleep down at the railway station, he was dirty and smelled bad. In the daytime, he'd hang around the street corners begging money, and I was forever afraid he'd come near me, stinking with his street smells and his teeth all rotten. Money, it makes you forget what it's like to be poor, and there's be times I'd be on the verge of contacting the police, convinced he was the one responsible for the abduction of children. I don't know what held me back. Then one morning they found him dead, frozen on the sidewalk, it was winter and he was lying there like those corpses of birds you find fallen at your feet, or how there'd sometimes be a cat all stiff and bloody. When they took him away, I didn't worry so much, but the children kept on disappearing anyway. That was how it was.

So you can understand why I was afraid for them. The dark it hides so much, it lets people do what they want to. So stupid to worry like that, I know: it's all out of your hands what happens, a fitting together in ways you can't imagine. When Alexander returned with the children that night, it was like something fated – no other reason for their arrival out of that wind and heat – the children's faces blasted with dirt, their expressions tired and frightened, one on either side of their father, tucked beneath his arms. It looked like some weird ritual that scene, and I close my eyes and I can still see them there, approaching, coming out of the darkness, framed by the window, the three of them, sheltered beneath the shivering branches of an avenue of heavy trees.

Let me tell you about madness. I was mad once, not so long ago, the sort of madness where the walls seem to creep and twine themselves around you, and every noise seems loud and sharp. Where my husband grew fat and distant, I grew thin and nervous, pale from seldom going outdoors. If it was quiet (and it was always quiet),

I'd drop a plate, an ornament, just to hear the sound, the splintering that was like the falling of bombs, the cracking of wood, the crying of voices. Night became full of heavy, whispering things, doubts that pricked at my ears like needles. Oh, I was mad then, very mad, but it was such a long time before anyone noticed I can't help wondering if anyone was sane then, anyone at all.

I don't remember the beginning: there's no line to point at and say, *There, that's where it started*, because it wasn't like a switch, one moment sane, and one moment not. Instead it crept up gradually, in degrees, stealing my sense away piece by piece. I think of my madness as a thief, slipping in and out like a shadow, thin and wily with a lean weasel face. A mask and swagger bag and a black and red striped shirt. Fingers slim as a pianists. When he smiles, there's sharp rodent teeth.

One afternoon, when we took the children to a carnival, I met someone like that. Imagine! Multi-coloured lights and tireless crowds, music floating tinnily from worn speakers, all those old songs I'd forgotten, while a Ferris wheel spun tilted and crazy with these cries just falling free. Amongst it was a freak show – the children pleaded but we wouldn't let them see inside – with the ticket seller, my weasel thief, seated behind a wooden booth sucking at a cigarette, his tweed suit too small, and his eyes, the sort that pierce, following me through the crowd. Eyes that undress, because I knew, yes even then, that I still had my looks, the heads would turn, following, most times not even conscious of what they were doing. I gathered the children around me, Alexander, strangers, but I still felt them, those eyes.

That was one of the happiest times, all the same. You can get drunk on the scent of a carnival, its sticky candy-floss and popcorn odours, the unforced laughter, all those men on leave so handsome. That noise, it kept the war temporarily at bay. There was a roller coaster studded with lights and when it dipped we screamed, clinging onto the handles of our seats. Afterwards I kissed Alexander and he went around the rest of the evening with this smear of pink lipstick on his cheek. Oh that was love, it was, but it was like the carnival, one night and it was over, it was a flimsy sort of emotion, and you suspected it was a happiness that was only bought by money. After that there was only the trace of love, this memory. We went out so seldom.

At home that evening, a summer's night at the time of year when the night scarcely has time to intrude, I could still hear the carnival. By then the laughter had a drunken ring, there were shouts and whoops mixed in with the music, car horns were blaring. Those sounds, they made me feel young again. I'd married early, it was true, and I had so seldom experienced nights like that, the sort that filled you with a reckless feeling. It could be detected in the voices I heard, the edge they had. Listening to them, there was no war, and I couldn't resist them, they made me pace around the house, spying on Alexander in his study, the children asleep, or looking out on the streets which were black and empty but were full of sound. I kept on thinking of the ticket seller.

It was late when I left. I didn't say I was going, I just stepped out into this world of blackness and stars, even a touch of frost scuffed on the streets. The cars that passed had fogged-up screens and muffled headlights so the passengers inside were just these vague shapes, these smears of colour lost in their speeding car world. My footsteps sounded very loud. Where were they taking me? I told myself I didn't know, but of course I knew all along, it was just that I didn't want to admit it.

The carnival was empty by the time I arrived. No-one was around to see me stepping through the empty wrappers and cracked cardboard cups, that tangle of taffeta and kiss-me-quick hats. It could have been the remains of some party, the way it looked, all punctured balloons and bobs of fallen candy floss. All the stalls were closed. Caravans were set amongst them, most of them silent, although sometimes there'd be the sound of a television, some late-night talk show, or there'd a be a radio, music playing, From a distance they looked ghostly, but up close they were just shabby, long past their best, all their blemishes revealed. The attractions were the same, with their paint faded or peeled, boarded up for the night, padlocked, no movement at all: it was like the cold air had frozen them. At night the place was so different you couldn't believe. I wandered between the caravans, the closed-down stalls, and there'd be these brief sparks of memory, of pushing through the crowds earlier in the evening, only now there were just lines of strung-out washing all stiff and frosted What brought me here? Down among the oil smells and litter, the dirty tent with the board in front that read AMAZING COLLECTION OF CURIOSITIES INSIDE!; and when I did go inside, slipping through that limp tent flap, there wasn't anything but empty cages lined with straw, a raw grass floor hardened into mud. Nothing of interest there. All around the place was a dirty animal stench, strong and sour, and it frightened me to think that people, even carnival people, could stink that way. On each of the cages there were plaques, but it was too dark to read them, to imagine what they might have held. I moved up closer. When I lit a match, light and shadows went flurrying around the tent, so everything was revealed for brief seconds.

The ticket seller was watching me. He was standing in the far corner of the tent, behind the cages: I saw his wired body for those few seconds of illumination. When it was dark again, I was too afraid to move. I had no idea where he was and I wondered again why I had come here. Then he lit a cigarette. He said, "Are you looking for something? Maybe I can help you." He said this in a tone of breathy insincerity. I watched the little coal of his cigarette, cupped in hand, come closer towards me. His face was shown for brief seconds with each inhalation. Its light made his face a sickly yellow. I felt a terrible longing, mixed with revulsion. He reached for me. He touched my wrist, and his other hand pressed my breasts, moved down. We kissed. He had a sour, oniony taste. It was repulsive and attractive at the same time. He pushed me up against a cage which opened, and inside we fell, onto the straw.

I didn't say anything as I left. Once I was through the flap of the tent, I ran. The carnival grounds were still and empty but nevertheless I kept on banging into all these objects hidden in the dark: ropes, gas canisters, things like that. It was horror at what I'd done. *Is that why I came here?* I thought. I was like an animal. And then there'd be the memory of his touch, his arm tight around my waist. The next morning there'd still be marks where his nails had dug into my skin.

The city that night was so quiet you'd have thought it was dead, all its life used up at the carnival. Earlier there'd been music and voices spilling out everywhere, but now the only thing that could be heard was the sound of my footfalls, running, and the rush of traffic around main roads, far away. Their muted headlights played off the sides of buildings but barely penetrated the darkness. I followed the back streets which looked sad and faded with their run-down and bombed-out corner stores. All along the pavement sacks of refuse had been put out for collection, and when I passed they would give this old whore's sag, it was like they were talking to me, whispering. Some of the buildings were nothing but ruins, and I'd think about the people who'd lived there, their belongings that could still be seen in remnants through the remaining brick and plaster, and it was like stepping into a graveyard, it had that sense of intrusion. There were dogs sometimes who would hear your approach and snarl, they'd bark, they'd gone wild, I could tell, and I'd go back, turning in my tracks down some alleyway or other. In the dark like that, afraid like that, it's easy to lose direction and imagine you're lost in a maze. Whatever mood had led me on, that fearlessness, it was gone by then.

Our house, when it came into view, was just one shadow among many. Where there was an absence of stars, I could make out the shape of the gables, the chimney pots, the lightning rod in the shape of a cross. How late was it? Perhaps everyone was asleep – I'd no idea how long I'd been away – and I suddenly wanted to steal back into the house and crawl into bed without anyone wanting to know where I'd been, or what I'd been doing. I wanted that very much. All the time my body kept on trembling, shaking in great spasms, but I wasn't sure if this was from shock or cold. I could only stand there shivering, thinking about going into the house, but not moving at all.

Somewhere up on the rooftops, something moved. There was a scuffling, a scrabbling, a flash of white over the roof tiles. One of the upstairs windows had been opened: I could see the raised frame and hear the dull flapping of the curtains where they had been sucked through the gap. Again, the flash of white and something moving, blocking out the sky, a great blackness of bulk like some huge beast: or else something small and timorous, because the size seemed to vary from moment to moment. It was difficult to tell up there among the shadows, the rows of chimney pots. It moved in precise concentration, the way a tightrope walker does, right along the ridge, momentarily disappearing – it was the way the light fell or maybe the figure had ducked low – before reappearing, stepping out of the blackness but seeming to drag the darkness with it, so it fell in drifts around the body. Only after did I realise this was due to the looseness of the clothing. It was so quiet I could hear the slap of feet across the tiles. A thief's walk. Near to the centre of the roof it stopped, bent down, arms clasped around a chimney stack showing now and thin. How diminutive it seemed then. A face moved out of the shadows, and I knew then, oh yes, I knew.

I called out. I don't remember what, not the words, there was just the noise, it was like vomiting it out, that sound. On the roof the figure halted, frozen. In the house, the curtains in my bedroom were pulled back, there was this sharp beam of light, violating blackout. In the light, Alexander's bulk, swimming towards the window. On the roof, one hand still holding onto the chimney pots, Martin was caught half-naked with his pyjama jacket flapping open, one trouser leg bunched up to his knee. His eyes reflected in the light shone like a cat's. What did he see? Not me. Not the roof he stitched along. Not his father leaning out of the window and catching the reflection of his son in the levered glass. And when Martin began to move again, to waver his way along the rooftop, I was afraid to call out, to disturb him, because he was asleep you see, this walk was a sleepwalk, and I had this vision of him waking up and slipping: I could see his fall.

What happened next I saw alone: Alexander had also gone, I later learned, to the skylight. I think I remember now the skylight glinting and rising. Above, between the columns of brick and the television aerial, Martin reached for the lightning rod, a sleepwalker's lurch, like he was blind, clinging with his arms and legs all wrapped around the metal, pressing his face against that cold, gold head so that later there'd be the imprint, yes the very imprint of those thorns on his skin. Then he rose, holding on to the cross, lifting himself up with those pale, thin arms, more strength there than you'd imagine, stretching above the lightning rod like a gymnast, quivering... and then falling... It was deliberate, I saw, the dropping of the body onto the cross, piercing his stomach, but he didn't even cry out, not a sound, and then the cross was falling too, spinning down into the street, landing there with this great metallic clatter. Martin remained on the roof, lying there, slumped over tiles and the blood glittering black down the rooftop, spreading. Then there was a stouter body, Alexander's, lifting him, panicking, sliding on the frosty roof so at last I was able to shout, "Don't! Don't fall!" while all down the street, in the last of the occupied houses, lights were going on, voices joined my own.

After that, the doors were bolted, the windows padlocked, and it became more like a prison than ever. Was it any wonder I went mad? Martin, it seemed, was the least affected of us all. There were times I'd catch him standing by the window with his shirt pulled up to his chest, grinning, displaying his scar to passers-by in the street, turning so they could see the way it ran from his belly right round to his armpit. At the base of the scar was a small gnarled knot where a sliver of metal remained, lost somewhere between muscle and intestine. I found it distressing to remember, but he wore his injury like an emblem, he wore it with pride. Things like that reminded you how strange life could be. If I look out the window, the same window he clambered out then, it comes back in every detail: the night, the roof, the same clumsy sleepwalk. It comes like a dream, from that first moment at the carnival to the conclusion that seems so inevitable now. At times it's like a closed world I can't escape: it's a lot like madness in that respect.

The asylum, when I went there, was all high walls and locked doors, the sort that looked as though they would never open for you again. Inside, it was as if the war had failed to happen, beyond the meanness of food and clothing you found everywhere: if there were any troubles outside these walls, we never came to hear of it except when visitors came, and even then it seemed distant and faraway, not anything to feel concerned about. I suppose I was happy following that routine, waking up in the morning to light filtering through the curtains, and outside a thin mist hanging over the lawns, the trees bending wet and heavy, sounds emerging from other rooms. There would be nurses, stiff-uniformed, and doctors with questions that made you give confused, contradictory answers. Mealtimes were for picking at food, talking to people or ignoring them. It was easy to talk: we all had our madness in common. When visitors came, there was always this barrier between you and them, because you always knew: they were sane and you weren't.

Still, I looked forward to them, those visits. Mostly it was Martin who came, sometimes Emily, and Alexander hardly at all. Each time they looked different: older, mostly, and it always came as a shock because in that place you forgot about time, the way there wasn't enough of it, and how cruel it could be. The children grew up into more mature versions of themselves, and time was good to them, but Alexander seemed so frail, so drawn into himself that at each meeting I'd think, Is that me? Is that what I look like? When he stopped coming altogether, it was a relief in a way. Sometimes I'd ask Martin or Emily about him, how he was, but they'd grow elusive, the subject would always change somehow, and I'd never really learn. It was only after he'd gone that I learned about his illness, and I wished then I'd known, so I could have gone to visit him or something. I owed him that much. Martin and Emily couldn't fill all the gaps he left because there were parts of my life I'd never let them see, not even in that place in which I found myself and which caused everything else to be revealed.

The visits were brief anyway, and filled with news of people and events I couldn't relate to any longer. The rest of the time I was left in the company of the other patients in the hospital, most of them lonely and a bit afraid, like myself.

Mostly the loneliness took two forms: there was the type of person that would come and sit beside you, uninvited, filling up the air with talk, any sort of talk, just so long as the sound of their voice could be heard. The second group were the very opposite, barely speaking at all, and even if you spoke to them they'd only mutter, if that, looking at their feet or hands or the ground, any place at all, as long as it wasn't at your face. Some would swing between those two extremes, depending on their mood.

Mary was like that. I never found out her second name, because when I asked she'd laugh and reply, "Mary Magdalene," then change the subject like it was some big secret that should never be told. She was a great, fat olive-skinned woman who could only wear smocks large as canopies and who had a cartoon character's high-pitched voice. For all her size though, there was a grace to her movements, a daintiness almost, something you would never guess if you only saw her sitting or lying down (as was frequently the case: she was also very lazy). Some days she'd sit beside me and talk about her son in London, or recite a made-up poem, or sing some song she'd heard that morning on the radio. Then she'd laugh and I'd watch fascinated at the way her very flesh on her body seemed to laugh with her, the way it trembled. Other times though, she'd just hide, not wanting to speak at all, and then her entire form would sag with unhappiness, not responding to anything you could say to lessen that burden. I couldn't understand why she'd ended up that way, because her whole life up to the time of her breakdown seemed to have been composed of good things, all the things I had and more: all the things I wanted too.

Still, there was an oddness about her I couldn't quite define, something quite apart from her often evident depressions. Once, screwing up her ovoid face, she leaned over and told me she had the gift of second sight, that the whole future would roll out for her to see, like it was some long scroll. I smiled politely at that, as I often did, because declarations of being in some way *special* were common enough in there, and the subject had gone no further. To tell the truth, I forgot about it. It was easy to forget these things because this was a place where the present was obliterated, and the past took precedence, dragged out by the doctors and your own guilt so it was always returning to you, like scenes from an old movie.

After this revelation, just a few weeks later, I found her upset, sitting alone on a garden bench, twisting her long black hair into knots. Such an odd mood, quite different from her usual depressions, something dreamy and faraway in her eyes. When I asked what was wrong, there was no reply, not even a recognition I was there. It was late summer then, and I can remember her seated in the afternoon light with a drizzle begun. All the grass wet and shining and the bench turned a different sort of green. There was birdsong and that slight roar you get when the rain sifts through the trees. She looked the least alive thing there really, it wasn't like her at all. "Come on," I said, "You'll get wet," and this time she did move, with an invalid's shuffle, I was holding her by the shoulders urging her on, and all this time the rain was getting heavier and heavier, the whole land filling up with this beating noise, this rattle that rose up into the air, the ground trembling. That was when she turned to me, grasping the wet folds of my dress and staring right into my eyes. I remember the noise of the birds, so loud. Her added weight was making me slip on the already-sodden grass. When she opened her mouth, at first nothing came out. But then she told me about her vision of Martin, and in it she'd seen him die, and she told me how he would die. There, in that place, in the wet, you could believe it was true. There were strings of spittle around her mouth. Her hand, grasping, left a weal on my shoulder. I avoided her for a long time after that; but it proved to be true what she said, every word of it.

That night, in bed, the darkness seemed to hold all these fears. It seems cruel, but I would rather the prediction had been about Emily, not Martin. It wasn't often that she came to visit me, and when she did it was someone distant, a stranger, some woman I barely knew at all. She still had that same way of smiling though, the way her face hid behind her hand. Always she was secretive. Martin wasn't like that, it seemed he'd stay the same forever, and I thought, *I could lose a stranger, but I couldn't lose a son.* Then these ideas would make me ashamed and I'd tell myself it was the madness talking, that hysterical voice I'd come to know so well, but it wasn't that at all. I always thought myself capable of love. Just lying there, the whole world would seem to whirl around and around, this blur of colour and speed racing through my head, it was all those roads and maps speeded up, like a film on fast forward. Then when I woke and rose, there was a stillness that seemed to have frozen everything into this one moment of doubt that would never end. I'd always imagined the mad would be rowdy, but theirs is a drugged sleep, all silences, worse than any clamour. Looking out there into the garden, all leafy and damp and green, it seemed like a lost world, a dead world, and I was this lost, dead person with all these useless dead thoughts dragging around my brain. But that was the depression setting in, it always came like that, a crushing weight.

When you're young, you don't imagine these things will come, because the future doesn't exist then at all. "What do you want to be when you grow up?" people would ask, and I'd reply, "I want to be a nurse," because I had this nurse outfit and a plastic play kit with its toy scissors and black eyepatch and pink coloured syringe. Only I didn't want to be a nurse, it was just the sort of answer you'd give that grown-ups seemed pleased with. Those days and evenings spent among the streets and buildings of my childhood, they never seemed to end, all smoky light and brickwork dying, falling down. You get older though and time passes more quickly, it races past so fast you can't catch it, and only the pockets of loneliness and fear make you realise what time was, those moments when you could move around it like a vast playground. There was once this bird I caught, you could hear its heart beating, the danger in its eyes, but I couldn't hold it, it just flew away.

I remember the last time I saw Martin. It was when I'd started to go out again, into that other world that lay outside the hospital walls. You forget how cold and noisy it is out there, and how unpredictable.

We went down to the docks that day. It was winter then, and freezing, there were flurries of snow everywhere. I stood on the footpath of the bridge that overlooked the water. Peering over its crisscrossed metalwork to the river below, watching the rushing brown current, its boats and moored ships. Martin lagged behind, silent for once, his hands rammed deep into his pockets and shunting from one foot to the next with the cold. At first I thought he didn't want to interfere on this, my first day out, but the distracted expression on his face, the way he would only half-answer my questions suggested some preoccupation, something I didn't know about. Maybe if I'd asked what was wrong, the thing I can only guess at now, it would have made a difference. I was too excited then though, and nervous to be out in the city again. I'd forgotten how it was out among that great light and noise, where crossing the road was like travelling a huge gulf and the city seemed as though it had become this strange, alien thing, all clamour and cars and smog that drafted down over the tower blocks. Standing there on the bridge felt safer, just watching. There was some sort of demonstration going on in the docks, a strike or something, but it was difficult to tell, the voices that rose up drowned out by the rush of the traffic, its long roar. Seeing that, we didn't go any further, just stood there like a pair of tourists come to see the sights, not speaking at all. It was such a wasted opportunity: the last time I'd see him, and there was all this static, this noise, just interference. So loud that there was no room for anything else at all.

When I think of him now, I see him as a passenger on a train pulling away from its station. He's in the carriage in the end, standing with his face pressed to the window, hands against the glass and steam rising from the tracks, the way it drifts and stirs. There's a look on his face I can't quite place, partially because the window is clouded over with condensation but also because it's that sort of look: impenetrable. All along the platform there are people waving, they're relatives, lovers, friends, I don't know what, but the handkerchiefs are out, the hands are making these great swipes, there are whistles and cries and handfuls of tossed confetti. Every one of these people, they're celebrating or lamenting, but they've come, and the faces that line the windows know they've come. When the train pulls away with its rattle and heavy gusting, his mouth opens, his hand splays out against the glass and there's this scream, a thin, long drawn-out cry that's heard above all the other noise, that great, chattering crowd noise, and it's my scream that's heard, endless, as the train pulls further and further into the distance, roaring, clattering, spewing out its great bursts of steam, until finally it's gone, it can't be seen at all.

THREE

Well of course I broke him. What else was there to do? If it hadn't been me it would have been someone further down the line. That man used women like Kleenex.

Even now there's anger. I keep his photograph on my dresser, simply to remind myself how angry I can be. The manner in which he preens towards the camera is a constant source of irritation. Each afternoon the sun catches the frame in its path and the picture fades by degrees, the porcelain face seeming to age; by the time it has become nothing more than a pastel blur, I tell myself my anger will have vanished too.

The picture is not the only the only thing he has left behind. Frequently, when I least expect it, some object will turn up hidden in the back of a drawer or buried in the bottom of the wardrobe. I keep them all: a pair of socks, a blunt razor, a paperback with a broken spine, a reel of tickertape with his name printed over and over: MARTINMARTINMARTINMARTIN. These items are deposited in a box under my bed which I will occasionally pull out, examining each object in turn, not knowing why I look or what I feel. Each time there is a memory or a spark of memory and I'll catch myself smiling, scowling, reliving a past event as I'm kneeling there holding a box of relics that should have been disposed of long ago. When men occupy my bed, near-strangers, it's there even in the heat of touching, a sensation I'd forgotten, brought back from the past. In sleep I grow confused, calling out, "Martin!" But then I'll wake to find another body beside me, a stranger's scent on my skin.

The truth is this: even when my flat is deserted, I am never alone now. All over there are secret markings of his passage, in a code decipherable only to me. Just the other day I made the discovery of an old newspaper, with the crossword half-completed in handwriting not my own. Now it is in the box too, along with all the other mementos.

The objects mount, the photograph fades, my fury grows. There are moments when it burns so deeply I cannot bear to look at his features any longer and I have to turn his picture face towards the wall. The emotion is so bitter I can taste it on my tongue. These are the longest days, sitting by the window, sewing, dressed in black. If I look for him on the street, he's never there: but of course he wouldn't be.

Nina brought him to me. Nina, who is a riot of colour and who has a laugh like a parrot's screech. We would sit in the living room drinking tea, nibbling biscuits, and she'd be dressed in red, blue, orange to compare with my black, telling stories of a life so far removed from my own that I never knew whether they were true. "Katherine," she would say, "Katherine, I really must tell you what happened to me today," and she'd speak about a famous person she'd met, or a place she'd visited on the spur of the moment and "Inside it was like nothing you've ever seen! I tell you, Katherine, you'd dream of living in a place like that." Throughout the dialogue her hands would wave, words mattering less than the shapes she pulled from the air. When she was done, I'd sit there drained as if I had been living through these things with her. My forehead would be slick with sweat. When it was time for Nina to leave, light would burst through the opened door so brightly it was like being woken from a dream.

Nobody could have been less similar than we two. Hers was a life so full that it was difficult to imagine how there was time to experience it all. If anybody mentioned her name, I thought of exploding fireworks. Pedestrians passing her on the street would ask, "Who's that?" without fail. "Don't you know? That's Nina." Who could not notice her? When she came to visit, I never wanted her to go.

In contrast, I seldom left my flat. It was small, dark, full of shadows, and with patches of damp on the walls. Even when the sun entered it seemed drained of colour. When a person has lived in a place like that for as long as I have, some of its drabness seems to rub off on them. That was another reason why it was so good when Nina came, because she in turn left some of her brightness behind.

Her initial description of Martin made him sound beautiful but fragile, as though he were a doll that would smash if it were dropped. Immediately I wanted him. Yet when she mentioned that she would bring him around sometime, I began to feel guilty.

There is no need to feel guilt now. My husband has been dead for long enough. Still I wear black. How many years before it's possible to tear it off, crying "Enough! No more!" without having to deal with disapproving glances? Not until the war is over, I'm sure. Throughout the city are widows like me, sitting by the window, sewing. Waiting. Probably Martin has known them all.

At times I'll be holding a cup of tea and my hand trembles so much its contents go spilling over the floor. Age has crept up so quickly on me. I grow tired so easily too: by the time the afternoon comes, passers-by in the street have turned featureless, and the stitches I make grow subtly crooked. That's the best time to sleep, sinking back into the chair to let the pain eat its way out of me. I wake when Martin approaches in my dreams.

On other occasions I dream of Christian who comes to me naked, full of light, back from the dead. After I embrace him, holding him to me, I come away with hands covered with blood.

As I watch the crowds in the street, from the window, they seem far away, as though they are images on the television screen when the sound has been turned down low. There are faces I've come to know so well that I wonder what has happened when they pass by.

On the television, when pictures are shown of the place where he died, I see nothing worth dying for. It's a barren rock where exotic creatures drape themselves in the sun. The waters are so clear the reef below can be easily seen, along with sea plants that wave in long, coloured trenches. That is where he is now, Christian, my husband, or what is left of him. I cannot say there is a vast, aching gap in my life now that the space he occupied has been vacated, but still I miss him. If I try to picture him, it's difficult to remember what he looks like, and there are times when it's Martin's face that comes to me instead.

At night it's hardest, especially in summer, when I'll sit on the doorstep and watch teenagers parading past, looking so strange. That's when it comes, a huge unfocussed longing no amount of work or mindless activity can fill. Black looks so absurd in the sunlight, even if it's dying sunlight.

The youths that go past – it's difficult to place ages any more – often laugh at me sitting there, a premature shroud, but it no longer hurts. Instead it is I that laugh at their absurd hairstyles, their endless confidence, the way they strut around in defiance of what is around them. The music they listen to sounds alien, as though it has come from another planet, and knowing this they turn the volume up loud enough for the entire street to hear. Noisy, full of laughter: I was like that too when I was young. Now I look at them and wonder, *What do they think, what do they feel?* They travel in groups, talking in a secret language it's barely possible to decipher, all slang, exclamations, wildly waving hands. It's not this wrecked, smoky city they live in, but a dream city that's written between the lines in invisible ink. When they pass by, it's almost possible to smell the scent of change.

Perhaps that's what made Martin appear so attractive. Nina would tell me stories so bizarre I never knew whether to be thrilled or appalled. Nevertheless, the more I discovered, the more I wanted to learn, until it seemed inevitable that I would meet him, and be added to the fabric of his story.

His conquests, I was told, were innumerable. Many of them were widows because he had once allegedly vowed to seduce each and every widow in the city, regardless of their age, colour or size. Naturally, in time this would lead him to me. Before me there were many others. Down the rows of terraced houses he would go, one after the other, peering through the windows. Here he would encounter his own reflection, an empty room, or perhaps a house full of people. If he was fortunate though, there would be a solitary figure sitting in the half-light, shadowed, the way others must see me when they pass, and then he would stop, he would look and know. His boldness was legendary.

It may be that he doesn't recall the name of the first. I remember it for him. Marian. Poor, timid woman, prematurely drawn. He must have charmed her so that she clung to him like a limpet. A bad choice: he left her within a week.

Think of him prowling around like a thief or devil, all of his victims willingly offered. No-one could have resisted those looks or the charm he could exude so effortlessly. Certainly not poor, lonely women who could never have imagined the sort of person he truly was. In the face of adoration his beauty would visibly increase, but inside he grew blacker, more corrupt all the time. If he'd been cut open I'm sure there would have been found a substance darker than the night, accompanied by the rotting odour of brimstone.

At first Nina said I exaggerated and that, besides, those women knew exactly what they were getting into: she accused me of being patronising. I countered with evidence of his corrupting touch, his smile, and now he has gone she agrees with me. I warn you: never trust anyone who has the looks of an angel.

The second and third came together. Lily and Suzy, two sisters who owned and worked in a Chinese restaurant and lived in the flat overhead. At night the restaurant would fill with soft, dimmed light, with tinkling elevator music, while customers drifted in and out, spending what little money there was to be gained.

Upstairs, the flat was cold and mildewed, heated by electric radiators whose warmth escaped through the building's thin shell. Pictures of their parents' homeland had been torn from the colour supplements then plastered to the walls. The rooms were exclusively lit by candles: wax that had fallen, molten, formed slippery ridges on the floorboards. They slept on blankets spread over newspapers while a wind whistled though badly-fitting windows. It was the sort of place that looked as if it had wafted in from somebody else's bad dreams. He told me that much himself. I'd have thought he would have been shocked because he had never known anything other than the safety of his home, but all he did was complain of the discomfort.

What were women to him? They were toys, they were dolls, objects to play with then throw aside when they had been broken. The sisters curl up beside him like divided Siamese twins, unaware of each other's activities *(but however did he manage…)* smiling their stereotypically inscrutable Chinese smiles which no doubt cracked simultaneously when he left them for another woman who had fallen for those perfect looks, those charming manners, that grin that would thaw the coldest heart.

A week after he left them, both flat and restaurant burnt down. Could that have been coincidence alone?

Some chemicals need only be exposed to air before they burst into flame.

Who was the fourth? So many lovers: Mary, Linda, Martine, Yasmin, Jean, Roshi, others whose names evade, their stories merging into one.

Valerie died, but it is the sisters who haunt me.

At night I pull out his belongings and look at them one by one, over and over.

Nina brought Martin to me on an afternoon so silent it seemed as if all the sound had been sucked out of the air. Few pedestrians on the street, only the echo of traffic, and the atmosphere heavy. Even she seemed subdued, having lost some of the light she would normally generate. I suspect he absorbed it into himself, like a sponge. Hearing the tread of her feet on the steps, I wasn't sure at first who it was as the sound lacked its usual buoyancy, while another followed behind, slightly out of sync.

My first thought was that he had eyes you could fall into and never get out of again. Beside him, Nina appeared insignificant, even drab, a witless something that followed him about like a shadow. I had expected that, however and indeed the myths I had built around him in my head would have tolerated nothing less. But I had also anticipated him to be brash, overconfident, whereas he seemed reserved, almost formal. When he walked it was with a slight limp, and when he talked, he fingered the buttons of his shirt nervously. I liked him more for these imperfections which made him less of the characterless object the beautiful are in danger of becoming, but later I found he feigned these traits in order to gain sympathy. Often I think he was so aware of himself that others hardly existed for him at all, and then only as a mirror in which he could be defined more clearly.

I assumed he has a draft-dodger, as so many of his age were. It was impossible to imagine that unworn body of his involved in manual activity, submitting itself to the danger of imperfection. Moreover, there was an element of determination in his movements that said: no he had not been broken. To imagine him in such any mundane situation was unthinkable. It was proof to see him in our company, uncomfortable, fidgeting, attempting to disguise this with formality but still stirring like a trapped insect. He appeared to be wondering why he had come at all.

To be honest, I was at first a little disappointed. Instead of the dangerous figure I had imagined, he had allowed himself to become the object of curiosity in a tea party populated by two middle-aged women where polite speech was interspersed with the sharp clatter of cups on saucers. Only the night before, I had lain awake in bed, trying to imagine what he would be like, and letting odd, sexual fantasies creep around my mind. Now though, it was as if I was trying to view an object through a refracted pane of glass where each movement threw the outline into a different definition.

That night, the night I first met him, terrible driving rains flooded the roads, making them run like rivers. In the morning the world seemed to have died a little overnight.

It was a Sunday of blue skies and cut-out sun, the sort that often follows a summer storm, and there were children's voices shrill in the street. I lay in bed with the covers thrown back, listening, the tension gone from my body. The sound of pealing bells made me dream of childhood, of growing up in a place like this, but at a time when the city was whole, not broken the way it is today. If I saw a uniform then, it was a cause of excitement, an excuse to fawn and giggle, not the object of remorse it became.

I regularly went to church at one time. My parents were both strict Protestants who brought me up to believe a show of emotion was almost a sin, certainly something to be frowned upon. During adolescence I walked around feeling as though I'd been tied up inside with wires.

Martin's father had been a Bible salesman and preacher, or so Nina once told me. Not the meek, preoccupied English sort either, but the real hell-and damnation type that seem to exclusively inhabit park corners or out-of-the way sections of the street. That's the sort of person who talks with such conviction, then undercuts it with the irrational glint in their eyes. It was difficult to imagine that Martin, who was so anarchic, could have come from a background of that sort. He never made any mention of it, but that type of upbringing is impossible to escape: I knew, because at times a need for redemption would come to me, a tremendous need like a terrible hunger.

That day though, I felt none of that, so the reason for my visit to the church remains a mystery even to me.

I rose late and then, as was customary, sat by the window sewing, peering at the stitching with eyes prematurely deteriorated. This done, I stood, dressed in my best clothes (still black), then went out into streets full of people walking at a lazy pace. I confess, I did not know even then where I was going. When eventually I returned I found the door standing open wide.

So perhaps I was caught up in the dream everyone seemed to share that afternoon. The sky, shimmering, seemed to make the very pavements I travelled liquid. Others I encountered wore gaudy shorts, T-shirts, bright yellow dresses, while the children ran around almost naked. I crawled past in black.

Understand this: I had never been in a church since the day of Christian's funeral. Yet that was where I found myself then, an old, stripped-down building with coloured glass windows and smog-dirty walls. One corner of the roof had recently been repaired, the tiles unevenly applied and of a lighter shade than those around about. Through the bars of a high iron fence flaking green, grass grew untidy and wild. At first the church appeared deserted, but then through the door standing ajar I saw movement.

Pushed open, the gate shred rust. Inside the building it was bare but filled with the scent of old wood. My feet made small, hard sounds on the bare floor. The interior was split by sunlight into strips of light then dark, and I chose to sit in the darkness, on a pew, with my head bowed low. I have no idea of what I intended to do.

Distant sounds of laughter filtered in, tinnily. Putting my hands to my face, I discovered my cheeks wet. The inside of the church seemed blurred. Looking down, I found my feet were bare.

Then. He approached from behind: I think I knew he was there all along. When he placed his hand on mine, it was cold, as though he had come from the grave. I wondered how long he had been waiting there, in the shadows. When I looked up, his eyes seemed to glow like a cat's.

Still grasping my wrist, Martin slid alongside me in the pew saying, "I thought you were never coming." At first I thought he had mistaken me for someone else. "Katherine," he said, "my black tulip." From his pocket he drew a bead necklace, pressing it into my hand; then as I held it he pulled one end taut so the string snapped and the beads cracked, bounced, clattered over the floor. "Everything falls apart eventually. It's a matter of knowing when." There, in that light, or lack of light, it didn't look like the same person I had seen the previous afternoon at all. Even his voice had changed, it had an animal's purr. His breath had the fragrant odour of tropical fruit.

I knew then what he was after, looking as if he would eat me up and afterwards spit me out. In a church, no less. I curled myself tight, in a ball. "Tell me Katherine, don't you ever get tired of being a widow? Six, seven, eight years. Soon you'll be old, and your skin will wrinkle and sag and you'll look ancient and ageless, all at once. That's what comes of wearing black."

He traced a finger down my nose, my lips, then swept back my hair to the top of my head, allowing my face and neck to appear naked, unframed. "An unblemished face. A voice like raw silk." And although that description had no basis in reality, still I was flattered. He'd chosen his victim well, because a desire had begun to grow inside me, a need that swirled, tangled, in my stomach.

"The first time I saw you, I said to myself, I know that woman inside out. I've known her all my life." He hooked his leg around my own.. "Tell me something – anything – I don't about you already." Life in a straightjacket, pining in a closed-off room.

I had the image of the string of beads pulled tight, snapping, flying off in all directions.

His arm went down my shoulder. The light in the church immediately diminished, causing the pictures in the windows to return to fragmented jumbles of colour. I tried and tried but was unable to think of anything to say, paralysed instead, aware of his arm's progress, his hand grasping my waist: the movements of his body, the tang of his breath. There is a film I have seen of rabbits frozen by weasels, birds by snakes. When the wind blows, the trees shiver with excitement.

Both of his arms were clasped against my back then, his face against mine, as though it were a slow dance, rising, steering me through the narrow space of the pew, feet treading clumsily alongside my own. When we reached the end, he pressed me into a sitting position once more, up against the pew's wooden arm rest so I was prevented from moving any further. I looked around and wondered, *Where could I go?*

What I did not expect, however, was to be pushed down suddenly as I was, so forcefully I slid from the seat onto the floor, knees banging on the worn wood. Then Martin was alongside, levering me down beneath the long seats while he slithered alongside, atavistic, on his stomach. When I began, involuntarily, to moan, his hand clamped over my mouth and he whispered in my ear, telling me to be quiet.

It was then I saw the feet stepping past: sober black shoes, the trailing of a cassock. I imagined for a moment they would stop, that their owner would bend down, peering, and catch us where we lay. But instead they carried on, moving from range of sight. There was the sound of a door opening, closing again. After that, only silence, the sound of our breathing.

I rose. The upper half of my dress fell away, unclasped at the back, straps sliding down the front. When had that happened? I couldn't remember. Hurriedly, firmly, I pulled it back into place, and I shivered. Martin hung around me, seeming to have lost some of that irresistible grace, clumsy in the wake of the unexpected interruption. His kiss, when it came, was like a schoolboy's first. Was that deliberate too? Even now there are things I am unsure of.

Each time he kissed me, it was as if I had left something of myself behind. On some nights when it was stormy, I'd wake, slipping out of bed while he lay asleep, to stand by the window with the rain whipped dark across the glass, able only to see my own reflection and through it the faint image of the street. A wildness of movement. The person I saw mirrored then, nearly-naked, dark-eyed, looked like a stranger. Those were the moments when I wanted most of all to leave all of my belongings behind, to become faceless in the street where crowds would brush by, never looking, not caring. It was difficult to live in close contact after such a long time alone.

From the moment he arrived, he seldom left the flat. There was a natural indolence to him that manifested itself when he lay in bed, tangled among the covers, cajoling me to join him, or reading old magazines, listening to the radio. I'd sit sewing until the light fell and then I'd join him beneath the sheets where we'd couple with slow, deliberate movements.

That was when he'd tell me, "Monica was fat but you're so slim. Judith was stupid but you're so smart. Alexandra was neurotic but you're so stable. What we have is going to last forever." Fool that I was, I believed him. Usually I am not so gullible: I have been accused of being cold, uncaring, but never of abandoning myself to the raw rush of emotion. In photographs I resemble an object hard and chiselled, a statue.

Martin had a body that tasted of butter. Along his side and reaching around his stomach was a scar, jagged, raised like Braille, that he would not let me examine, squirming away from the touch of my fingers. When asked, he told me it was the result of an accident when he was younger, but would not elaborate. Whenever I tried to pin him down, it was inevitably the same, he would become evasive, deliberately forgetful. The only time I ever discovered anything about his past was when other people told me. Each time, learning a new fact was like discovering a dead skin unobtrusively shed among the litter of his past deeds.

The room is full of these ghosts wherever I turn. I wonder if this is how the others felt. Lily and Suzy living deluded in a cold run-down flat, brass chimes singing each time the wind sneaked through the doors and window frames, yellowed newspapers plastered over the floor rustling, old iron heaters releasing loose packets of warmth, the smell of burning. Suzy sitting hunched in a broken-backed wooden chair, listening to pop music from a transistor radio, Lily in the kitchen, at the sink, and the thought of Martin hovering unseen between them.

How they could not know? One slept in the main room, the other in a bedroom the size of a cupboard, living quarters so confined it was impossible to move without stumbling over each other. How could he come and go without being seen? There was a hint of the supernatural about it, that silence of movement.

Nina told me how he would wait under the streetlights, impatient for the restaurant's brightness to dim, hopeful when the scent of cooking came wafting onto the street each time the door was opened. There would be short bursts of laughter, the sisters standing giggling at the counter, chattering in Chinese. Each time they would take it in turns to come sneaking down the stairs to let him in.

What he got out of it: a headful of vanity, perhaps a perverse sort of pleasure. The feeling of being wanted, the sense of superiority that came when he grew tired and discarded them one after the other. The days and months he had spent with them counted for nothing when countered by his bored, facile whim. There may have been other reasons too, but he kept them hidden.

There are times when I dream about the sisters' house, crackling brilliantly as it burns to the ground.

Then when I wake trembling, there's a cold thread inside me that threatens to freeze, to crack.

What he got from me: my money, my emotion, my time. What he left behind: anger, fear, uncertainty, memories played so often they've become warped, ghostly, like archive film.

There are some days when his photograph seems to fade more quickly than others.

During those months together, we hardly let anyone into the room. Often people came knocking and only if they were insistent would I answer, finding a pretext to send them away again. Martin would be behind me then, slipped half-naked from the bed, his arm around my waist, hands probing sensitive areas. I would have my head peering through the cracked-open door, disembodied, barely succeeding in keeping my voice level, my expression even, until they'd gone. Then we'd collapse boneless, rigid, to the carpet, fluttering hands and tongues, our passion drowning out the noise of the television, the radio. Even now it doesn't seem like hollow emotion.

Behind it all, however, was fear, a dread the callers had come not for me but for Martin. It was the time of the purges and people lived in a state of constant worry, guilty or not. How greater then when that worry was justified. It was never said, never spoken about, but a sense of complicity bound us together.

At other times I felt the need to get away. The room constantly had the ghosts of stale sweat, of dead sex lingering, so it was a relief to escape outdoors, with the freshness of its confusion, the air cold and unforgiving. I didn't know what he did then. I thought it was nothing, because when I'd return he'd be sitting in the same place, doing the same things. I thought I had him domesticated, you see.

I spent those occasions visiting Nina, meeting her in cafes, or in the park if the weather was good. Exposed to the open, she seemed different, distracted. Perhaps it was boredom because all I could talk about was Martin, using every topic as an opportunity to return to that one, obsessive point of conversation. Finally she began to issue warnings about the consequences of drifting so unconcernedly into the dark tides of a relationship, a place where so many had lost their footing, and these questions were obviously directed at me. I think she regretted bringing him to me, and I began to wonder about the events that had led to the circumstances of that first meeting. This was the start of the time I became aware of other movements, other forces shifting subtly beneath the surface of things, leaving traces so fine that only in retrospect did it become apparent they were there.

She told me about Valerie. As soon as Nina described her to me, I knew who she was talking about. A girl, in her early twenties perhaps, with hair dyed the blackest of black, with clothes also in black, all to contrast her features which were leeched of every trace of health by a thick application of makeup. Piercings in her nose, her lips, her eyebrows, her ears – and those only the places I could see. She was a friend of Martin's, I knew. I had seen them more than once, out talking, in the twilight, the time of day that seemed to suit her most, as though she were the type of nocturnal creature she seemed so desperate to imitate. He and Valerie were very close, Nina intimated. "How close?" I wanted to ask, but that would have been a sign of defeat, an admission of the subtle tussle of wills that was going on. "She's not right in the head you know. The doctor, he keeps her on tranquillisers all of the time. You watch her: she walks like she's dreaming."

Here is a bloodied razor. Here are the scars still fresh along her wrists.

All along he must have known what he was doing. Clinging around the layers of her skirts, dog-hungry for sex, sifting the impossibilities that were her dreams, saying exactly the right thing to tease her. There, in her flat, with its accumulation of discarded cigarette packets, bottles of pills opened then forgotten, the house neglected with its tin cans ranked along the sink top, fly-blown in the summer heat, a sweet, high smell that filled the chaotic rooms. Floating along on an ocean of sloth:

what else could she do but cling to the only person available, Martin, that useless anchor? I see it now, oracle-like, at night when I lie in bed. It was money he wanted me for, the money he never managed to keep, all of it spun away, clattering on the run of chance, a life coded in colours, numbers, moving so quickly it became a rattling blur. His sole possessions amount to a bagful of clothing which he brought to me the day he moved in. All of it was unwashed.

I'll admit that at the time I questioned Nina's motives in hinting at what in retrospect is so evident. I had finally managed to grasp some of the glamour she had accumulated around her life and she was jealous! The image I had at the time was of a jackdaw, intent on stealing bright and shining objects. Oh, the things that you can imagine at a moment like that. Now I see she was only being a friend, telling me what she knew in the manner that would be least painful to me.

Did the makeup Valerie wore hide bruises? Was there a side to him so hidden from me that an entire part of his personality had never been revealed? In the church, it was true, the darkness had clung to him like clothing, his tones had become animal, but that was the sort of place in which even the innocent cast shadows. Would it stretch as far as flesh beating against flesh, that vicious extension of love? I imagined all sorts of things. Imagine all sorts of things. Even now the story is incomplete.

When I returned home after I had met Nina, Martin would look up from his book and ask, "Where have you been? What have you been doing?" so the secrets I'd heard must have shown on my face. "I was meeting, Nina, that's all," I'd reply.

"What was she saying then? You could bring her here, you know."

But if I did that, then she wouldn't be able to talk freely, he must have realised that. He must have suspected. He must have suspected that I suspected. What did he do when I was gone, I wanted to know, but I never asked – I was too afraid of the answer. Then, silence would replace our conversation, and when I wasn't bent over sewing, snapping at threads with my teeth, I'd drink endless cups of tea, that intrusion of crockery that always sounded so loud. It always ended with us together in bed somehow, an apology made with our bodies, and afterwards it would be difficult to sleep, our unspoken thoughts keeping us awake but mute. Once, I fell asleep to dream of a room with the walls tinted red, and populated with people with voices like chewed, screeching metal.

I rose, stalked the room, drank some more tea. Martin lay, pretending to be asleep as he earlier had pretended to read. I opened the window to let in the night air and small insects on the wing. The curtains clattered anxiously on the rails. Through the window a figure hovered pale out of my eye's line of vision. It was never there when I turned to catch it in view, but at one point I was certain there had been a figure, wide-eyed, standing a little down the street, looking at me.

After that, sleep was impossible in any case, because I was too anxious, nerves wired, the clock showing three a.m., the time when the body, even waking, slips into a dream world of anxiety where the smallest problems inflate, hovering almost tangibly before you.

"Martin," I'd whisper, "are you awake?" And then again, "Are you awake?" but he was past hearing, the tension in the air replaced by more private fears, grey stretches of loneliness from which I was excluded. I listened closely to his talk in his sleep, the crushed words that fell from his lips, but there was never the word I waited for, the single name: Valerie.

During the following days we acted out a pretence of normality that eventually gave way to the real thing. My suspicions faded, and if I had to leave the flat, I avoided Nina, in this way too avoiding confronting the memory of the stories she had told me.

Those were the days of the most terrible storms. Winds blew angrily, dominant, litter scattering, uprooted vegetation whipped past raggedly, windows flexing inwards, trees uprooted from gardens, telegraph wires stretched taut and then snapping. For long hours we would be left in darkness, able only to see by candles that left the room reeking of black tallow smoke. With the warmth chased away we would crawl into bed, under the blankets, doing nothing, seldom speaking, simply holding onto each other for protection, skin against skin. "The first time I saw you," Martin said, "it was like coming across somebody who'd been waiting for me all their life." With his arms clasped across my stomach, his legs crooked into the back of mine, he'd add, "You felt it too, I could tell." And I'd feel the warmth of that memory, the truth of what he'd described, the feeling that we'd spun towards a new centre of gravity, helpless, each moment binding us closer together. Even asleep there was the sensation nothing could prise us apart.

One night I woke from this sensation to the sound of sirens. It had been so long they had last been heard that I thought I was sleeping still: sound coming in waves, beating in and out of the wind. Martin stirred, eyes straining awake while he extricated himself from the sheets, his years regressing in seconds like my own: six years or more. Down the street, lights were coming on, faces poked from opened windows, expectant. I watched for flames, listened for their drone, but there were only the usual night noises. Chequering with light, the city spread off in the distance, brought to life by the sirens, their continual howl, when they should have remained in darkness.

We waited, but nothing came. The waiting continued to cut through from the past. Sitting in the still, dark room, I draped my arm around Martin who had gone quiet, all colour drained away. "I thought it was over," he said, "but it never is, is it?" There was a shivering, hot along his skin. I led him to bed, folded him beneath the blankets, but he only turned face to the wall, curled up tight in a ball. I think that was the start of it, his instability. When there was a knock at the door, not my door, but the house alongside, he bunched even tighter, seeming to sink beneath the covers, not emerging until the voices that sounded in the corridor receded, the door slammed, the door clicked shut. It was the war that had come to haunt him: he had thought himself safe here, but of course there is no safety, not from your own paranoia.

The following day there was a report about the air raid warning in the paper. Apparently there had been a faulty circuit, a microchip gone awry; something like that. The small paragraph printed seemed inadequate after the anxiety caused. People talked of nothing else all day.

The sirens marked the end of the storms. I began to venture out of doors again and tried to persuade Martin to come with me. "Maybe later," he said. "I don't feel like it just now." Of course, now I realise it wasn't just the purges that worried him, the rounding up of draft-dodgers and anti-war protestors, it was also the thought of all the women he had left behind, frightened they would come after him like vengeful ghosts. From the past they'd race, one hundred widows, burning with an interior fire. I know that's how they felt because that's how I feel too.

That was the day Valerie came. She must have been waiting for me to go out, hiding somewhere in the street or even the garden, until she saw me pass. Perhaps it was a pre-arranged rendezvous, perhaps not. I don't know what to believe, even now. The important thing is that she came, and she came with the intent of seeing Martin.

I was not gone long. I bought a few provisions, such as they were, because even then the shops were poorly stocked. I did not hurry back, however, because there was no premonition, no vision of the scene that would greet me hovering mirage-like before my eyes. Even after the warnings I had been given, I suspected nothing. It was a fine day, I remember that. I remember talking to a neighbour on the way to the house. I remember laughing and joking with him. How quickly that disappeared when I saw Valerie leaving. She was impossible to miss: the only person dressed more dourly than I. She ran, and she was crying, and she bumped into me as she ran down the street, not even seeing me, even then. What had happened? Something terrible, I had no doubt.

Martin would not open the door, and I had to fumble with my keys. How violently my hand shook! Inside, it was dark. He had drawn the curtains and had retreated into a corner, as if afraid of what he had done. I could smell it, you see, the spillage, the aftermath of sex. He looked like a child that has been caught with his hand in his mother's purse. How plainly the guilt was there to see.

I did not speak to him. Perhaps he could have talked me around, charmed me with excuses, all the things I wanted to hear. Instead, I passed him, and went to my bedroom, slamming the door behind me. How brittle the silence after that, the absence of sound that indicated the gulf that had opened between us. It was worse by far than any commotion we could have caused.

At that point I knew there were only two options: either he would stay or go. Or at least those were the only two that presented themselves to me, although many more have since occurred. In any event, I did not reach any decision, curling on the floor as though I were a squatter in my own house, its discomfort a welcome distraction. Covered with an old overcoat, I lay on the carpet which had worn to a mottled hardness, trying to rest, but kept awake by the activity of my mind which spun too quickly. I wondered what Martin was doing. The cold, climbing up from the floor, seemed to work its way into my bones.

Eventually, I slept. The sleep was so heavy it felt like being sucked to the bottom of a deep, deep pool. Strange, dark thoughts swirled around in the sediment of my dreams. Christian came to me and said, "Don't cry," and while my reply was, "I'm not crying," I found that when I put my hand to my face, tears had worn grooves into my cheek. There was a cry like machinery running backwards while a voice, whispering said, "Just like the church."

When I woke, Martin was no longer there. The bedroom door stood open, the few clothes he had owned were gone. In the living room I could see the mark of his body where it had lain on the settee. The scent of his skin still clung to the sheets. I placed my body into the outline of his own, pressing my face into the cushions. There was a sense of sadness, I'll admit, because I had been deceived, like all the others.

Why then did I go in search of him? That's one more question that I'm unable to answer. Some force more primal that reason made me leave the house and trawl the neighbourhood, the adjoining neighbourhood, places I have never been before, nor will be again.

People were hurrying to work, that inevitable pull. Women mostly and old mostly, because the war had taken so may of the young away. Those who evaded conscription could be seen hanging around the shopping precinct in their second-hand clothes, baggy pullovers, too-big trousers crumpled around their ankles. On the occasions when the authorities would pursue them, they were never to be seen: word spread quickly, it was an invisible code. In any case, it was impossible to do more than temporarily diffuse their numbers. They ran in packs, street-hungry children, flitting from one squat to another, somehow staying free. I wondered, now that he was no longer with me, would he be out with them? Curious, I hung around the vicinity of these groups, picking out faces, anyone that seemed familiar, but I was too old to cross the gulf into their world. Martin could have done it though, he'd turn faceless among their numbers. Continually I kept returning to that moment in the Church, the day after I had first met him, the moment when the beads had been pulled taut and then scattered. "Everything flies apart eventually," he had said. "it's just a matter of knowing when."

In my dream the voice told me: "Just like in the church."

Eventually I went in search of Valerie. I had been delaying this moment because, when you came down to it, wasn't that where he was most likely to be? Even now I don't know what I intended to do, or say, when I found her. When I found them. It would be *them*, I was sure.

I called Nina from a phone box. She told me where Valerie lived. In fairness, she did not gloat but there was a hint of validation in her tone.

She directed me to a block of flats, in an area of the city that normally I would not have dared to enter, such was its reputation. It had the look and even the scent of deprivation. A rotten orange peel odour mixed with the dampness and decrepitude of its interior. The stairwell was concrete, cold, and entirely unwelcoming. Its sentries were the hostile children who took delight in terrorizing me with their antagonistic gazes. I tried not to show fear – as with the attack of an aggressive animal, you mustn't show fear. Don't make eye contact. Just keep on walking. Keep on walking. Don't look back. How uncertain life must be in a place like that.

The doors I passed were all identical, and many unnumbered. She lived in 617b. It seemed such a long way to climb.

There was nothing about the door of her flat to distinguish it from any of the others. It had no window, no peephole, no doorbell or knocker. Its purpose was to keep people out, not let them in. I'll admit I hesitated for some time, afraid to knock, and more afraid still as to who might answer. Then I thought, *his hand knocked here before me*, and I rapped, loudly, loud enough for even the neighbours to hear.

There was no reply. I listened for any sounds of activity, voices in hushed tones, hurried footsteps, anything like that. I knocked again. And again.

The door clicked open. At first I thought someone had answered, but it appeared to have opened of its own accord. Again I hesitated; then I entered.

There was no evidence of anybody inside. The flat was sparse and furnished with third-hand furniture. On the wall was a photograph of Martin in a gold-coloured frame. This in itself should have been enough to confirm my suspicions, but still I wanted more. A picture was nothing, it was not evidence of infidelity, or so I told myself. I think really I was curious. I wanted an excuse to go further into the flat.

In the kitchen a cat leapt out and began to mew frantically for food. It looked famished, the poor thing. I looked for food, but there appeared to be none, just a loaf of bread that had begun to go mouldy. Instead, I put out a saucer of water which it lapped at gratefully. "Poor puss," I said and rubbed her ears, which caused her to purr so loudly I could still hear her even when I went to the next room, which proved to be the bathroom. The bathroom too was empty.

I had saved the bedroom until the last. I almost expected to find them there, lying side by side, listening to my approach, with Martin whispering, "They've come for me. Don't let them know I'm here."

There was none of that though. I had expected cries, expressions of fear and then anger, but the only cry was my own.

Valerie lay on the bed. She was naked and her wrists were cut. Blood had soaked into the sheets and had congealed. When I touched her skin, it was cold, and blue. Dead. For how long? Long enough. Long enough. Hours perhaps, long past any hope of redemption.

I had seen death before and it did not scare me. Quietly, I closed the bedroom and made to leave the flat. She had been a pretty girl, up close, under all of that make up. I wondered what had made her do it, but of course really I knew. Martin. It was always Martin. Before I left, I scooped the cat up and buried her under my coat, hiding her later in the old shed that stood at the back of my nominal, shared garden. Remember that when you call me hard, when you hear what I did next. The helpless always bring out the protector in me.

No one saw me leave, except for the children. They watched me with the same inflexible expression they had before, and I thought if they'd had beaks, if they'd been crows, they'd have pecked my eyes out.

I travelled back around the dirty buildings, through streets full of people with ugly voices, in a heavy fall of rain. The rain was dark and tasted of metal. At the corner of one street, an old man had slipped on the wet pavement. He lay on the ground, covered with a stranger's jacket, muttering a polyglot's curses and expressions of pain while waiting for an ambulance to come. His eyes rolled as if they were independent creatures, displaying their whites. In the wet, the streets had turned monochrome. The memory came to me of broken glass and blood.

On arriving home, I found Martin had returned. He lay asleep, face down on the bed, still fully clothed, hair tangled and wet. Not knowing what to do then, I sat silently, watching him. Asleep, he did not look guilty.

No, he did not look like a murderer of women. How deceptive looks can be.

Later that evening, I pretended I had seen nothing, that all was forgiven, that everything had returned to the way it once had been. Even after all I had seen, I was tempted, believe me, to let it remain that way.

"I just couldn't stay away – there were things to take care of," Martin had said, a cat's purr in his voice. "You will forgive me?" He had his arm wrapped around my waist as he said that.

"Of course I will," I said, "I'd forgive you anything." How well I adopted his habit of lying.

Through the open window, sounds of children playing entered. *Make the most of it while you can*, I thought, *It only gets more difficult as you get older.* Martin lay back, listening. He said, "The sun's shining. It's a lovely day."

I excused myself and went to the kitchen to pour a glass of lemonade. "Do you want some?" I asked, trying to act as nonchalant as possible.

"I wouldn't mind," came the reply.

When my husband had been killed, I had been prescribed sleeping tablets. I put two of these in Martin's glass. It was home-made lemonade, the kind with sediment that stirs around the bottom, sweet and bitter at the same time. He wouldn't notice. When he drank it all down with a smile, I almost felt guilty.

I left when he was sleeping.

It only took a single phone call. Down a line that hissed, that crackled, I told the most terrible lies. A voice at the other end kept demanding, "Who is this please?" I spoke with a handkerchief over my mouth, and refused to answer. Repeatedly I made reference to anarchists, and political unrest. I mentioned the address several times. When I hung up, I turned to face a small queue of people that had formed waiting to get into the kiosk. They looked at me with curiosity, but I pretended nothing untoward had happened.

Overnight, I stayed with Nina. I did not say why I had come and I suppose she imagined there must have been some sort of falling out between myself and Martin. "I won't pry," she said, "and it's nice to have you here anyway". We watched the black and white fuzz of images on television and chatted, and went for a stroll down into the park, just as the sun was setting. I pretended I was having a good time.

The next day, when I returned to flat, he was gone, together with his belongings. There was no sign of a struggle. Perhaps he had left before they had come, warned by friends of friends who could obtain information of this sort through the dissenters' grapevine. Maybe he had gone voluntarily, resigned to his fate. Or perhaps he had left of his own accord, and they had not come for him at all. I tried not to care. Really, I tried. How empty the house seemed without him though. It was difficult to tell he had ever been there: that would take days of sifting, hunting out items. Accumulating evidence.

At night, when I am lying half-asleep, the ghosts of the widows crowd into my room, mourning. They're wearing black but it's for themselves, not Martin. "You did the right thing," they say, "you set us all free." I'm not so sure. There's still anger inside, bitter, acid, and it hurts. The Chinese sisters walk past, and then there is a tinkling of wind chimes. Valerie sits at the end of my bed, but she's still drawn, still sad. I know I'm in there too, but I can never see quite where among that crowd of faces. When the dreams start they're chased away, every one, and I feel lonely and near to tears.

His photograph still stands in the window. The picture is sharper if it is taken out from under the glass, but even then it can be seen how the colour has wasted. Those definite features are beginning to lose their identity, becoming smooth, uniform. In my mind his face has begun to take on similar properties. Sometimes I'll think of him and another face will come. At other times I sit in the evening for hours on end. A wind blows through the house, hot in summer, cold in winter. It's forever windy now, the way the climate is changing. The windows grow so dirty they're impossible to see through. Even the light finds it hard to enter.

Always I fall asleep and wait for him in my dreams.

FOUR

On my sixteenth birthday I was told, "Lorraine, you get involved with men, you use one of these," and with that my mum pulled out this square, foil packet with a magician's flourish. "You use a condom, you got that, girl?" But I'd already met Martin, so this particular form of contraception was already highly familiar to me. Looking away, I pretended to be coy and embarrassed, and maybe even managed the faintest of blushes. She was smart though, my mum, and she must have seen through this display of mock modesty. God knows, by that time she'd few enough illusions about me already.

There's a photo taken of me around the same period. In it I'm swinging around the pedestal of a huge marble statue – all you can see of it is a horse's rear legs – and I've one foot planted on the pedestal itself, one arm wrapped around the horse's great hewn-out hooves, while my remaining limbs are stretched straight out, freefall and waving. The picture's blurred, but still I look a sight: afro partially bleached, cheap plastic shades, an outsized white T-shirt and obscenely large flares. On my feet is a pair of platforms so hideously ugly it's a wonder I wasn't arrested for indecent exposure.

Something like that is a useful reminder of humility. If I'm at a party and there's a lull in the conversation, all I need to do is produce this photograph and there'll be shrieks of laughter, and everybody will start reminiscing about the way it was back then, how we looked and behaved.

I keep it for another reason too. In the background of the picture, right in the corner, lifting his head so he's neatly decapitated by the photo's edge, is Martin. It's the only picture I have of him and we were, among other things, good friends.

The first time I met him was in the slums. That's not how I thought of them then, but in retrospect that's how they appear. Grey, damp buildings that were slowly toppling down. The gutters of the streets were crowded with litter while the air was harsh and smelt of sulphur. People lived on top of each other in cluttered pokey-hole flats, hanging their washing out from the windows and listening to conversations that leaked from above, from below, from either side. The stairways that led to each flat were covered with spraypaint graffiti and always smelt of puke and piss. At night, voices carried up through iron and concrete, loud and threatening. Everyone knew everyone else, even if they wished they didn't.

That's how I knew Martin wasn't from around there. That and his accent and his clothes that spoke of money. The first time we met he'd his sister in tow, while I was with Joe, who was simple.

People who grow up poor have an instinctive distrust of those who are rich, and at first Martin seemed to combine all the elements I disliked most. He appeared on the street looking as though he'd walked right out of an advertisement for a high-class department store while we stood around in our hand-me-down and make-dos, feeling inferior. So I loathed him for that straight away. I hated that and I hated his accent, and most of all I hated the way he came across so brash and arrogant, telling everyone what to do and putting them down whenever they'd a suggestion to make of their own. Naturally I invited him to fight, but he refused, saying, "I don't fight girls, it's not right." I fought him anyway and won, so he went home dusty and bloody with his fancy clothes torn. His sister, a girl who wore a permanent, irritating half-grin, followed him like a forlorn puppy.

I thought that would be the end of it. Another intruder repelled and the neighbourhood our own once more. But he returned the next day, no more or less than he had been before, the arrogance flashing out of him, and you'd have thought it had never happened, that I'd never had his face pressed down to the ground with my knee until he was almost blubbing with fear. I learned later that money does that, it gives you an insulation against the world because you can't accept everything can't be bought and sold, you don't believe the world's such a cruel, hard place. Talk about self-denial: the rich have their whole lives built around it.

I didn't know that then and I respected him, or despised him, I don't know which, for turning up again. Certainly he wasn't afraid, that was something. That attitude demanded respect in our part of the city. Maybe because of that, I left them alone and limited my aggression to taunts they seemed unaware of, or were unaffected by.

Besides, they were a novelty. I'd hardly spoken to rich kids before and I circled them for the best part of an afternoon, sending up their accents and asking sharp, probing questions. I grew to like them, in an odd sort of way, although it may just have been the sort of cruel fascination children have for the exotic, the way you would catch a butterfly and examine its beauty, before crushing it to death.

I led them through the dirty streets with their half-dried puddles you'd skid through and their abandoned dogs that yapped and snarled at your feet. There was only me, the two of them, and Joe, which maybe explained why I was less antagonistic: there was less to prove without an audience.

When it began to get dark, I took them to a place levelled by bombs and subsequently adopted as a permanent residence by the homeless who constructed unstable shanties out of the fallen timbers and who built bonfires out of the ruined furniture to keep themselves warm. We danced, giggling, in front of flames that lit our faces red and sent knots of sparks into the sky. An old man told us about when he was a boy, how different everything was then. His clothes were stiff and stunk of sweat. Joe said, "You smell," and started laughing, but the man didn't notice, or pretended not to. It must have seemed like another world to Martin and Emily but they acted blasé, like it was something they came across every day. Maybe they looked on it as part of a great adventure: Martin confided to me that they had run away from home more than once. That was when I learned that even the rich can be unhappy.

Other things revealed themselves to me that night too. It was the first time I became aware of the war as something other than a distorted, angry jangle in the background of my life. Martin and Emily didn't see things the way I did, staring at things I'd always taken for granted, like the way tower blocks stood among heaps of rubble, or the wounded who brushed past us, clumsily bound with bandages and patches. I thought, *Don't they have anything like that where they come from?* Now I know they did, only it was so much more carefully concealed. So much circles around that moment when I began to see things through their eyes, it's hard to imagine what life would be like otherwise. One moment I was content, the next I wasn't.

So I did the teenage thing and rebelled. Not a focussed, controlled revolt - I didn't understand what I was protesting about yet - but a screaming tantrum where I lashed out at everything around me. Those were the days of the dyed afro and the shades and platform shoes. God, I thought I looked so cool. I changed my friends. I abandoned all ambitions. Life seemed to revolve around nights and weekends when we'd stalk the pavements in a bullying mass, drinking cheap bottles of cider stashed beneath our jackets, swearing at passers-by or embarrassing them by shouting lewd comments. "Hey mister," I'd call out to some innocent bystander, "want to feel my tits?" and the men would always hang their heads and skulk away, humiliated. Not all of it was undeserved, though, because nothing was more loathsome than some dirty old man peeling me naked from a distance.

Sometimes we were joined by Martin and Emily. At first the others only tolerated them for my sake and only later accepted they shared our sense of undirected frustration. "They're all right for posh kids," I'd say, though in reality they never seemed to have more money than we did. Sometimes they'd bring wine, which we would drink with a grimace, unfamiliar with its taste, but which we endured for its undeniable potency. Those nights I'd reel into the house on a string of slurred excuses and then collapse, boneless, onto the floor. "I hope you've learned your lesson," I'd be told the next morning. Curled up, dying, I'd promise I had; but then it wouldn't be long before the same thing happened again.

Christ, I remember how one time we got drunk and broke into a corner shop, the kind that stays open until the smallest hours, because it's an off-licence. I don't know what time it was by then, it's a night that comes and goes in fragments of shameful remembrance, but it must have been late, dawn or almost-dawn, maybe. We'd clambered though a back window – these were the days before burglar alarms or security systems were widely used – tearing our clothes on the shattered glass. It was so dark that at first no-one could see, but then we found we were in a store room, boxes stacked in pillar formations, and all of them holding the most precious of contraband – alcohol and cigarettes, and even overpriced snacks, the sort you only buy when you're grotesquely drunk and the money parts from you with an easy grace. How many of us were there? Nine in all, I think. Nine, in that cramped space, falling over each other, not even the sense between us to be quiet. We opened bottles of spirits we'd never even heard the names of, much less consumed, more potent than anything we'd been used to. Nobody told me you didn't drink gin in the quantities in which you consumed cider, or beer; or perhaps they did, and I was too drunk by that point even to care. Martin joined me, and we drank measure for measure, sliding into a corner behind the stacks of boxes until at some point coherence and then consciousness disappeared, and all I remember then is rising and being violently sick over my own clothing.

In the morning we were still there. My wake up call was, "Jesus fuck, Philip, would you look at this?" I opened my eyes. I was still where I'd collapsed the night before, behind the boxes, and Martin, who was also awake, was beside me. I noted that he too had been sick during the night, although he'd aimed with more precision than I had, into a half-opened carton of cigarettes. The voice again: "Fucking kids."

At first I thought they were talking about us – which they were of course, in a way – but we were hidden from their view and would remain so, if they didn't examine the corner into which we'd fallen. I remained still, stiller-than-still, in the hope we wouldn't be discovered. Martin, I noticed, was violently resisting the urge to vomit again. The footsteps approached, close enough to catch a glimpse of clothing and the scent of brylcreemed hair, and then they receded. One of them struck a match to light a cigar and the blue wisps of smoke knew where to seek us out, crouched there, in that flimsiest of hiding places. They were silent, listening perhaps, or maybe they were contemplating the cost of the chaos that surrounded them. It's one of the things about being young: you don't have any idea about the consequences of what you're doing, not until you're older and you have to face those consequences yourself.

Eventually one of them sighed, "Well. It's one for the police, I think." I heard him leave, but the other stayed behind. Through the density of boxes it was hard to see, but I thought he stood in front of us, the only obstacle between us and the doorway. Beyond him was the other man, his voice carrying from the shop beyond, as he spoke on the telephone. And after him? Who knew what. A locked door perhaps, or customers arriving, or worse, the police already on their way. There was no escape in that direction.

Martin was looking around and gestured at the window behind us, which remained open. To climb up there though would in turn cause us to be noticed. Around us was the barricade of boxes, big heavy packing cases stacked one on top of the other, and while these formed our protection, they were in turn our prison. It was, I felt, a hopeless situation.

Martin chose that moment to stand up. I made to pull him down, but he had seen what I had not: that the man who made our escape impossible stood with his back to us. He lifted two bottles of whisky and tossed first one and then the other through the gap in the broken window. They crashed down on the other side with a violent shattering. By this time he had ducked down again.

"Dennis? Do you hear that? They're still around the back of the shop." The man went rushing out of the room, and there was the sound of the two of them going to investigate.

"Take off your T-shirt," Martin hissed, "and put my jacket on." I did as he asked, abandoning the vomit-splattered garment. "Now," he said, "we go out into the shop and wait for them to come back. Have you got any money?"

In my pocket I found two pound notes.

"That'll do. Hurry now."

The storeroom led into a passageway and from that into the shop. The door stood open, but there was no-one there.

"We should make a run for it", I said.

"No time," replied Martin and, as if to illustrate this fact the two men chose this moment to re-enter the shop, breathless and arguing. We stood waiting at the counter, quite brazenly, and bought twenty No 6 and a bag of pandrops. They seemed to look at us somewhat strangely, I'll admit, but that may have been my own paranoia at work. Martin even stopped outside the doorway on the way out and asked a passerby for a light. He had no fear, that man, and you got the idea that if he set his mind on it, he could bluff his way into and out of any situation.

I always remembered his actions that day, and after that we were inseparable.

Years later we'd fuck voraciously in the cupboard space I'd call my bedsit. Him on his hands and knees, naked and white, clambering over rumpled bedcovers and around me, the taste of salt sweat on his skin. His fingers, expertly trained, knowing exactly where to fall so that I'd gasp "No," which meant "Yes," and there was such intensity in the way we'd push together that we threatened to swallow each other up.

There was no love there, only friendship and desire. We'd pull apart and then, elastic, snap back together again, murmuring stupid, reassuring phrases in each other's ears. Weather hot or cold outside. Inside, only heat, lust, straining at the boundaries of exhaustion. Listening for footsteps all the time in case any of the others came back and caught us in our ludicrous positions. Those were times of lust and need and fear.

Afterwards, we'd drift in opposite directions, not seeing each other for weeks or even months, our reunions never planned, always the result of chance, and always ending the same way, grunting and groaning on that old, squeaky bed that rocked to the movements of our bodies.

Later we'd go out on the streets still flushed and sweating, and the sun would prickle our skins, or the wind would be cool and would be laced with rain.

There was an old dwarf woman who lived nearby. I'd sometimes see her walking past in clothes that were obviously designed for children, so you had this grotesque contradiction of an old woman who dressed like a teenybopper. When Martin was gone, I'd dream of waking one morning and finding myself small and squat and oversized all at once. Somebody told me her name was Lorraine, the same as me, but later I found it was really Jasmine, or something old-fashioned like that. I wondered if that was why she always wore such cloying perfume: trying to match her name.

In the riots, three people died in our neighbourhood, and she was one of them. By that time there were six of us squeezed into the one bedsit, pooling the money we'd tap passers-by for on the street, living on soup heated in the can over an old primus stove. There was a lot of sympathy for us, squeezing out of authority's reach, living as we could, day to day. People muttered words of encouragement as they handed over their money, but they spoke in whispers, in case anybody else was listening.

People had grown tired of the war. The newspapers were full of the same patriotic headlines, but we'd listen to foreign radio stations to gain a clearer picture about what was happening. The truth could be seen on the street anyway, soldiers returning home blind and maimed, many of them with faces that seemed to have melted and then reset, as wax does on a candle. It was a generation of the disabled that wheeled themselves past, wheezing and coughing, a death rattle stopped short in their lungs. Some of them wore plastic masks over part of their faces, so that looked at from a certain angle they had the characterless look of shop dummies. I'd be standing with the others, talking and joking, when one of them would go by, lurching past on crutches, half-blind, and our talk would grow louder, our laughter forced, to disguise our discomfort. It was better, I suppose, than indifference.

Following the example of others, we called ourselves anarchists but we were really toytown copies, not the real thing. Some days we'd spend standing around on the streets, handing out leaflets to anyone who was interested. The leaflets showed a flagstone pavement, on which photographs of prominent politicians were superimposed, while flowers, representing the resistance to the social order, grew between the cracks. It was laughable, but at the time I thought it poetic. Near to the time of the riots, people even started to read them.

That was a hot summer. The city simmered in the heat. Water was rationed and moods became irritable, violent. During the day everyone slouched around lifelessly, but at night there were shouts and screams and the breaking of glass. I lay almost naked on the floor of my bedsit, listening, somehow knowing what was to come: I could feel the tension coiled tight in the pit of my stomach.

The city had come to resemble hard, baked clay, its buildings and roads turning grey and dusty. The cars that drove past all looked alike with their coating of dirt, and their horns continually sounded in short, angry bursts. Martin and Emily were among those staying with me at the time, and when the police cruised the streets we'd all have to cram into the same small space, getting on each other's nerves. It was like a prison with us all cooped up together, staring at the walls and feeling bored. When they'd gone, we'd rush outside, high enough to make it seem it had been weeks rather than hours since we had last been out. Our political activities may have been not much more than a pose, but we shared the same paranoia that invades every political organisation.

There was one time we were all crowded into the room, sitting on the bed, floor, table, that kind of thing, folding leaflets to hand out on the street. To combat the heat of the day, the window was open, letting in the air, letting out our bravado and bluff and forced good humour. The heat made us irritable, and the work was tedious. I hung out the window and spat onto the heads of passers-by, while reading our latest leaflet which contained quotes from Tagore, Tolstoy and Ghandi. It was a call for peaceful revolution which contained, at last count, at least seven spelling mistakes. One of the others cracked a joke I only half-heard, its punchline lost among a roar of guffaws that suddenly, abruptly, ceased. There was a knock on the door then another and, as I peered through the peephole, the sight of a pair of policemen came into view. I said, "Police!" Someone hissed, "It's your door, you answer."

Opening the door a fraction, I poked my head through.

"Excuse me miss, but I wonder if you recognise…" He handed a photograph to me of a pretty girl, curls, floral dress. At the same time I became distinctly aware of the sweet marijuana odour that escaped past me and out the doorway. I pretended to examine the photograph, none too convincingly, I must say.

"No, I'm sorry I really don't recognise her at all, no really I don't. Sorry about that. Goodbye." And I pushed the door shut, sweating. The police, even on their most innocuous visits, threw us into frenzy. "Panic over," I said, "false alarm." The room's occupants were rigid, white-faced. Something was missing too. "Where are the leaflets?" I said, and the reply: "We threw them out the window."

Looking out, there they could be seen caught on the heat-breeze, fluttering everywhere, drifting through the traffic and angrily swiping pedestrians. I could see police in the streets below, and one of them looked up and pointed to the storm of oversized confetti around about. He caught my eye, I'm sure, then spoke to the other policemen again. I drew back out of their line of sight as casually as was possible under the circumstances, and then we scattered, panicked, too afraid to regroup for the remainder of the day.

It wasn't politics that drew us together, but rather a collective desire to avoid the war. I'd grown up surrounded by its effects – the constant shortages, the torn-down buildings and their invisible population, the overdrawn economy that turned the city grey: and still it seemed unnatural. I loved everything that was loud and bright, summer things, but the war was bleak, like winter. Control seemed fearful to me, or at least when it was left to others. That was what drew me to anarchism.

Martin, on the other hand, had no beliefs, or at least none I could discover. That seemed so odd. I asked him about it once and he told me, "Do you know my father was a preacher? Before he'd got his money I mean. If you ever saw the house I grew up in, you'd be able to tell straight away, even if you didn't meet him. There are these crosses everywhere, even up on the roof. People used to stop outside and wonder if it was a church: it had that look anyway. It wasn't healthy, growing up in that. That's why I ran away all the time, to escape the atmosphere. You don't feel inclined to believe in too much when you've lived that way."

He looked past me, distantly, as if he could see somehow back into his childhood.

"What about Emily?" I asked.

"You can't tell with her. She's all these secrets, and even I don't know what they are. The way you see her smile? It's like she's not smiling with you, but at something you can't see that she finds amusing. What affected me, it must have affected her as well, and she just hides from everything now. No-one really knows what's going on inside that head of hers. I think maybe she's a bit of a fantasist. See, it's true, money can't buy you happiness."

"You still go back to the house sometimes, don't you?"

"Sometimes. Sometimes I do, but it's never pleasant, it's always necessity."

I would have left it at that, but he continued,

"Do you know how he got his money? What I heard? The man that was in our house before, it was him that left all the money to my father. He was dying, just months to live. I don't know what of. My father left my mother and moved in with him. For the money. It must have been the money. Why else would he do it? Do you know how hypocritical that makes me feel, just being associated with someone like that? Is it any wonder the money feels dirty, so that I have to get rid of it?"

"You don't know that's true, I said. People talk, they say anything."

"I believe it though, it's why there was this fear in his eyes sometimes. You could see he saw himself being dragged off to hell. That's what all the crosses were for, warding off evil. You'd have thought he was surrounded by fucking vampires."

"Maybe it wasn't as crass as that," I replied. "It happens, sometimes. The man next door to us, he was married to his wife for thirty years, but he upped and offed with this man, some lodger that had been staying with them for a couple of months. People do strange things, sometimes."

"I've thought about that. And maybe you could imagine it was true, but if you'd known him, you could have told: my father wasn't capable of love."

I didn't know what to say to that, so we both sat in silence. Martin didn't talk about his childhood often, and now I knew why. Later, years later, I saw maybe it was the reason for all his behaviour. He wanted to rip it all down, everything around him, and leave it lying there. It was what gave him his maniacal streak, the recklessness. Yet, oddly, this was the same thing that attracted me to him.

There was the contradiction too: he said he hated the money, but he loved the things it could buy. Frivolous things, admittedly, or maybe hedonistic things would be more a more apt description, because there was never anything to show at the end of it all, not unless you counted the hangover pallor and the exhausted sleep that comes from running on elation for days on end. He drank much of it, he spent it on me or on friends, and the remainder he gambled away in long nights when he was gripped with that white intensity you recognise as an addiction. It wasn't the intellectual thrill - no teasing and bluffing around a poker table for him - but rather he preferred the mindless hold of slot machines, arcade games, things over which he had little or no control.

I'd join him sometimes, on these expeditions down to the amusement arcades. At the time there was a craze for pachinko parlours, but he preferred the old-fashioned kind of slot machines where you levered down the side handle to make the wheels spin and the lights flash and you prayed the symbols would show up all in a row.

These arcades seemed to have been untouched by the recession. People loved to gamble. You could see it by the look in their eyes, that hunger. There was very little conversation: gambling, you see, was hard work.

Martin loved those machines, their randomness. Maybe he saw all of his life like that, something you had to pit against the odds, even knowing that you'd probably fail. Or maybe it was the other way round, it was an escape, a way of avoiding the responsibilities life had to offer you: I could never decide.

Certainly there was enough to rally against or escape from. This was the time of the purges. Whole families sometimes would be rounded up to serve in the factories, the army, or be imprisoned. People were angry, you see. They'd grown tired of the endless war, the way one conflict slid into another. They wanted what I wanted: they wanted fun, they wanted life, they wanted bright, gaudy things that make you feel good with their superficiality. What they got was a greyness, a monotony, a scrimping and saving that made you feel you were scrimping and saving on life. That was what they were fighting against. It wasn't just war, it wasn't just death or the wounded who haunted the streets with their mashed-star eyes and lollipop limbs. But the more we pushed against it, the tighter the controls became, you began to worry about even thinking certain things. Just the rumours about what happened were enough to do it.

I think it sent people a bit mad. Sometimes metaphorically, sometimes literally. Martin maybe, his sister maybe. Certainly Nina, who I knew only through Martin, one of those unstable characters he seemed to attract.. Could you ever imagine anyone more ludicrous? She was this swarthy, stumpy woman who overcompensated by wearing the most outrageous clothes and makeup. You could set stone foundations in the mascara she trowelled onto her face, her dresses were striped red and yellow, they had frills and peacock feathers and everything. "That's lovely, Nina," I'd say. "You've gone for the French whore look." And the thing was, she either had selective hearing, or thought I was simply jealous, whereas really, I was being truthful.

She liked to pretend, did Nina. I think it was a form of protection against what was happening around her. We grew to know her at first because she was unavoidable, obviously, certainly unmistakable. She liked to think herself bohemian, and hung around with all the wasters and down-and-outs - our crowd, basically. We tolerated her, because we'd tolerate anybody. Our standards were very low. Or, as Martin once remarked, "Set your standards low enough and you'll never be disappointed," which was true enough, although most people wouldn't have expressed this philosophy quite as bluntly.

Very quickly, it became apparent that Nina was a fantasist. Delusional. Fucked-up. Completely out of touch with reality. You can maybe say we all were, but hers took the most extreme forms. She was rich. She was famous. She socialised with celebrities. She visited exotic locations. The truth was, she was lonely, and she was sad, but if you didn't know her that well, or if you were as susceptible as she was to self-delusion, then maybe she carried it off successfully enough. I don't know.

I do know Martin seemed taken by her, maybe because here was somebody that carried even more mental baggage than he did. They'd sit and talk together, well into the evening, and afterwards he'd always laugh and he'd shrug, saying it was his good deed for the day, but I knew better: there was a deeper attraction.

It was Nina that introduced him to Katherine. I never liked that woman. She was a widow, one of the sort that's grown morbid with brooding over life's misfortunes. I seldom saw her out, and when she did dare to go outdoors, she'd scurry, like some insect that's suddenly been exposed to sunlight. What did Martin see in her? Well, she was very beautiful. Impossibly, stunningly, breathtaking beautiful, and he was always a sucker for a beautiful woman. She'd the longest, sleekest black hair, and the greenest, greenest eyes. I make her sound like a witch's cat, and maybe there was something of that about her. She certainly bewitched Martin. Seduced him and bewitched him and then took him away from us all so we hardly ever saw him again.

I heard the rumours though. And they were the most outrageous rumours. He'd turned into a serial seducer; a murderer; a stealer of souls. Where did these stories come from? Katherine maybe, or Nina, or both. Sometimes life is outrageous, so you can never tell, but I'm sure they were lies. I can only hope they were lies. If you were to ask me who to trust, Martin or those two, I know who I'd believe.

I did hear though about his arrest some months later, and although the details were scant, I believed that story readily enough. It was unremarkable but inevitable, and you knew it was coming to us all eventually. What happened then? Probably the old tricks of interrogation, the feeding of desperation, and then cannon fodder on a battlefield or, more likely, working in a munitions factory somewhere. That was how they played their games, I'd witnessed it often enough. I know for a certainty that I never saw him again, although once I thought I glimpsed him in the distance, and I hurried to him, excited, anxious, only to find it was someone else entirely.

So what does that leave? The photograph. Memories. A whole mass of contradictions. The usual. Maybe the story isn't ended, maybe there's another chapter for us in the times that lie ahead. I can only guess. In the meantime, he's become rumour and stories passed from one person to the next, and he's building his own myth. That's maybe what we'll all become, maybe that's the real weft of our existence. People will say, "Lorraine? Oh yes, I remember her...."

FIVE

Now she comes down the stairs, rubbing her sleepy blue eyes and yawning, showing a flash of fillings. There's a waft of day-old perfume, mixed in with the scent of last night's sex and she's smiling. Toast on the table hot and buttered, swimming, marmalade in the jar - what my mother used to make, her in her slippers and nightdress, grey-streaked hair, shooing children to and fro - and outside it's raining, colours washed together on the glass, hiss of cars passing in the street sloshing through puddles, a queue at the bus stop, heads bowed, huddled underneath umbrellas. Emily sitting, she's sipping tea. Her hair is ruffled, sticking out at odd angles from her head.

"Morning." Sip of tea. "Shouldn't you be at work?"

But I'm still half-undressed, eyes glued together and sucking greedily on a cigarette. "Phone in and say I'm sick. I'm not in the mood."

Rain drumming on the window, the smell of burnt toast.

"That's the second time this month, you'll end up fired."

I'm pouting, I say, "I don't care." Go over and kiss her on the back of the head. "Go on, it'll be the last time for a while."

When she phones I hide in the kitchen, like they can see me from the other end of the line, listening. "...not well today, it this bug that's going around, I think. Hopefully she'll be back tomorrow. Look, I've got to get to work myself –"

And that's a lie too, because Emily goes nowhere, she's no job, no family ties, housework holds no appeal.

Most days she paces the house, bored out of her mind, listening to the radio and reading glossy magazines I steal for her from clinics and doctor's surgeries. Today we'll be bored in tandem. I suggest the zoo.

"In this weather?"

Naturally, I was only joking. We curl up on the couch, holding each other, feeling the warmth of each other's bodies, safe from the rain that's rattling hard enough to drown out the sound of the traffic – it's indigo rain, it's falling for us –

They'll be in the factory soon, breathing in its acid and metal, the clatter and hiss of machines. Maybe I've a pang of guilt, but it doesn't last long. Emily's face is heavy in my hands. The worry lines are fading, one by one, it's like our bunched sheets unfolding –

Movie montage of calendar pages ripping off one after the other – September August July June May April past –

The ruins smelled of rotted cloth and petrol. Emily's face appeared at a window as I looked out. Our eyes met and there was a flash of recognition –

When I took her home she was an unfamiliar animal, flitting from room to room, cowering from my innocent comments. She slept on the couch with her face pressed down into the cushions, then in the morning there'd be a damp patch where she'd dribbled onto the material –

Those same mornings, rising early for work, I'd wake her, shaking her by the shoulder and she'd uncoil – a great cat – something dredged up deep from the ocean – yawning, stretching limbs. Later she'd wake to a kiss –

All day in the factory there was the hum of wires and pulse of machines, mixed with a ferrous sweat, workers mechanical in overalls, a spray of welder's sparks in the far corner, someone one else as automated as the machinery they operated, peering into cloudy glass screens, sighing. I'd think of her then, how she moved, the way she'd look when she talked – askance, giggling, hand over mouth. I wondered what it would be like to touch her body –

At home, she was asking the same question of me… and the moment came when we peeled off each other's clothing, greedy and excited…

The days when I'm gone, the nights, she stands by the window waiting for my return. The panes are always greasy with her fingerprints, her breath steams the glass. Visitors who come knocking are ignored, they imagine an empty house. Then Emily curls up, frightened, into a corner, throws a blanket over her head. Underneath it's dark and stuffy. Once, I arrived home to find my brother on the doorstep and her inside cowering, making bird noises, involuntary wheeps and whistles. When I told her it was my brother, she got it into her head that it was *her* brother, that it was Martin…

Today it's the anniversary of his death, it's why it's raining. Maybe she doesn't realise yet because I keep on waiting for the tears. Maybe she's like me and keeps them hidden. I smooth her hair, it slips between my fingers –

She's not like her brother at all.

- stuttering and bumbling around the factory floor, workers stopping to look and laugh at him playing the fool – a smattering of applause, because everyone's a rebel in that place, at least until the supervisors appear, when silence swims in drown it. Martin frozen in mid-step, one leg lifted and his body falling…A few weeks later and that spark had gone, ground down by routine. His expression bored, dispassionate, resembling no expression at all, his face a mirror of all our faces, the pattern we all followed, fading smiles as we entered the factory gates which were high and metal, shivering in the wind, dust whipped up through them, lashing. I'd sidle up to him in the queue, risking glances of disapproval, of jealousy.

"It's Ann-Marie," I'd say. "Fancy meeting you here." An exchange of winks, a colour of cheeks, unbidden.

Inside the factory, we changed illicit kisses between the metal vats, those spaces where dust and cigarette butts collected on the floor. He wore hair oil which left greasy swatches on my hands, the collar of my blouse. Then out on the floor my name would be called or his, and we'd slip back separately, flushed and trembling. Flickering eyes watched our return and I'd try to read them for warning or disapproval –

At night we'd go back to his place. He never migrated from a bed-sit lifestyle, everything was reduced to its fundamentals, its keyword being decrepitude. The wiring was faulty and the place lit by a candle moulded into an empty wine bottle, that essential accessory of the impoverished. Our last night's sweat still vivid in the air, I'd pull him on top of me, onto the bed, and the springs would creak, old like everything else in this part of the city.

(the factory spewing out steam in the dead metal light – machinery working intricate, components I've no name for – gaps in the ceiling where the light shows and the damp comes though.)

The acid taste of Martin's body. The feel of his muscles taut beneath his skin. The musk of his penis.

Then an exhausted sticky sleep with the covers thrown back because it's impossible to sleep otherwise in this airless, humid place. He'd call out things in his sleep, odd, disjointed phrases, and I'd whisper soft, stupid things in his ear to quieten him –

When the police came, he said, "I told myself it couldn't really be happening. I'd lived with the fear for so long, but when it occurred I was totally unprepared."

Doors kicked open – ducking down on the floor – the flash of gun metal. Voices barking instructions, "Hands on your head. Don't move." He'd mixed real life up with a movie. I'd have done the same myself.

So many memories tucked away in his head, it wasn't healthy. I'd pluck them out one by one –

"There was one man who used to come and question me all the time. I hated them all, but especially I hated him. His nose had been broken and it was squashed out like a pug's. They'd shine a light in my eyes that was so bright that even when I screwed my eyes shut it still hurt. His breath was unhealthy, it had a creeping death upon it. The questions never stopped. I'd find myself agreeing with them because after a while I couldn't even understand what he was saying any more. That was the worst. That was worse even than the beatings –"

Did they ever really beat him? Did they ever really suspect him of being a terrorist? He said they did. The first time he told me I burst out laughing, it was so ludicrous. He'd all the ferocity of a week-old puppy –

"You're frightened," I'd say. "let it all out, it'll help." His words were like poison. He'd weep though the night and I'd hold him. High summer winds blew outside, rattling fire escapes and lifting tiles, the language of the disenfranchised. It's what we all were.

They tired eventually of the game and sent him to the factory to work. It's the place where all the discarded go, half-prison, half military service. His time in custody had taken its toll anyway – deaf in one ear, a permanent stoop and limp now too, so they couldn't send him to the front line –

Even the factory's no escape. There are guards. There are people who are mentally unwell. There are cripples and queers and conscientious objectors. It's a place where rumours keep us under control, whispered from one person to the next. There's talk of uniforms, of camps, of a regime harsher than the constant surveillance we endure, these being electric eyes that plot our paths, clocks that steal our moments and seconds. There are times when violence threatens to combust from our very surroundings, but as yet it hasn't happened. The threat is there though. On my way home sometimes, I keep on glancing over my shoulder, sure that someone is following.

No matter how hard I wash, the smell of acid remains on my clothes. My hands are scrubbed with soap, but the stench of metal buries its way beneath the skin. First Martin in my bed and then Emily. Often I'm too tired to make love. Electricity dipping in and out the night. A woman's hand on my body when I wake. At first I think it should be a man's... there are times when his face breaks through hers and it's like seeing a ghost...

Consumed with lust, I seduced him in the toilets at work. It was our lunch break. The harsh smell of ammonia to catch at our lungs and floor tiles slippery with a disinfectant wash. In the cubicle I pulled down his boiler suit, and mine, then pressed my fingers against his belly, a landscape of wire hair and skin. I wanted to swallow him whole. I wanted him to slip inside me and wear me like a second skin. We would have fused, if we could. It was messy and we came within seconds. He told me I smelled of honeysuckle, the chancer...

It never changed, that feeling, not in all the time I knew him. Even familiarity, when he moved in with me, did nothing to blunt the urgency.

The house I live in once belonged to my mother. It still has the clutter and atmosphere of another generation. Martin hardly changed that. He came with the spring rains, green things pushing through the soil and rubble. Dirt smells and new leaf. All of his belongings were kept in an old holdall slung around his shoulder. The worn strap, sagging to one side. Inside, a few items of clothing, letters from old lovers read once and never again, some so old the ink had faded to an uneven brown, a photograph or two of him and his family. I must have seen Emily, in those pictures, but I can't remember. It's too late now. Time's so deceptive, it slips by so quickly, and you don't appreciate what you have. If I'd thought about it, I'd have kept more evidence, hoarded mementos, preserved those moments to look back on. You never do though. You always think it's going to last forever.

Instead, we frittered it away, those brittle, fragile moments. Half our time we spent curled up together in bed, our comfort and haven, and come the morning I'd have to haul him out, grabbing his leg or issuing mock threats, such was our comfort.

I think too that for him it was a refuge from danger, that warm, woman-smelling sanctuary we'd created. He'd so many fears. They were hidden in the objects around him, invisible to me, but he was a code breaker, seeing profane messages everywhere. Was it like that before they interrogated him? Not as bad, surely. There were streets he'd avoid (places he'd lived, the haunt of old lovers?) and faces that would throw him into disarray (people he'd known, or imagined he'd known?). On stormy nights, the wind high and whipping rain, he'd pace the house, arms folded, pale and nervous, a tic in his face – waiting for it to pass. When it didn't, I'd lure him to bed, that protective place, and I'd wrap myself around him, arms and legs, and wait for him to fall asleep. My breath and his, in and out of sync. The wind rising and falling. Window frames rattling.

I have fears too but I keep them hidden. Looking at Emily, I can tell she holds secrets just as he did. I worry it will end the same way, these precious moments extinguished. Her sudden gifts of affection, the whisperings of love, the momentary doubts hidden behind a nervous smile. Oh yes, I imagine it coming. It's like the storms that come ever more frequently, the climatic change.

I have never told Emily about Martin. Does she ever suspect? Do I talk in my sleep? That's my greatest fear. *You slept with him and now you sleep with me. Don't you think that's perverse? Is that all you see in me, him?* These are not her words, of course, not her fears. They are my own, the thoughts that come to me in moments of doubt.

We live in a world of secrets. Only Emily knows what she was doing in the ruins. Maybe even she doesn't know. She was wasted then, and parched from the sun. She'd been ill. Dirty. Living on scraps like the wild dogs that lived in that place with her. Winter came, snow coating the stones, plants and trees stripped bare. Her skin so cold… it must have been a terrible fear. She has a small mouth – no secrets will come out – she wears lipstick the colour of berries and blood, she walks barefoot over the linoleumed floor. The little things that together make up the whole. I only know a part of her. It isn't lack of trust, but the way she is. She keeps some things to herself. Does the paranoia of the street, the rumours it generates make her this way? Those images of high stone walls, barbed wire, faces once familiar never seen again…

Martin knew it all. He knew the rumours that turned fear to paranoia. Strange things thrashing out of his dreams. He'd be ravelled in bedclothes, crying out, his voice hoarse from all the calling.

"Ann-Marie," he said. "I want to arrange a code. When you come home, knock six times, all in a row. That way I'll know it's you."

"Who else," I said, "could it be?"

"I don't know. Them – the light – I have dreams."

It took many bribes to make sure we kept on working the same shifts – this being the age of the black market economy –

At night, sleeping in each other's arms, he'd suddenly crush me tight. Still sleeping, he'd bite my flesh – there'd be bruises, sometimes blood –

It was Emily who told me – I never knew until then – that his mother was mad, perhaps his father as well. "And your brother?" I'd whisper, "was your brother mad too?"

"I don't know," she'd say. "Sometimes I'm not even sure about myself."

It's getting cold. I get up from the table to turn on the electric fire, then make another cup of coffee. Smoke another cigarette. The rain has stopped, but it's still grey, it's given a metal tinge to everything I can see out of the window: a dog nosing about papers in the gutter, empty cars, windows still curtained shut, a tree that's thrived somehow on the pollution. The music on the radio is annoying me. It sounds tinny and empty. Emily likes it though.

I have dreams, Martin had said, "Something terrible is going to happen. Strange angels come and sit by my bedside. Leaves are bursting brown and withered out of buds –"

I didn't believe him, of course. I should have him seen by a doctor: maybe it would have rescued him from the factory, at least. I countered this with fears of my own, that they would take him away, that in the future I'd only see him in those wards where the mad fall deeper into unreality by the proximity of each other's delusions. At the worst times, he began to accuse me of tampering with his food.

Perhaps, I told myself, he's only eccentric. What's eccentric? It's a madness that only afflicts the rich. Not eccentric then. With him curled up in bed beside me, asleep, I'd whisper, "I'm sorry," without knowing what I was sorry for. He seemed so frail and alone. It was the three a.m. terrors, the time of day when the world seems most grim.

Sanity came with the daylight, for me at least. For him too, but the uncertainties had accumulated during the day, and by the time we got home they'd spill out, abundant, growing and feeding on the day's events.

He – we- began to drink heavily towards bedtime. It was an easy anaesthetic. He'd talk to me then, and tell me stories, parts of his life I'd never known before. How they'd grown up. The strangeness of those early years, in which everything was odd, but his were odder still. Growing up, in that strange claustrophobic house they'd inherited. No wonder he turned out the way he did.

There are children playing now, in the streets. It's still chilly and wet, but at that age you're impervious to the weather. They throw stones at a barking dog, and one hits it on the muzzle so that it streaks away. Across the road a man pokes his head out of a window and shouts something I can't hear. The children scatter. Somewhere else, far off, a car alarm signals the moment.

I light another cigarette. Emily says, "You smoke too much," and I nod, agreeing, inhaling, opening the window a crack to let the fug out. The man calls again, but the children are gone. The rains grows heavier – it's drumming –

He had joked, "I think I'm allergic to the wet," and I had laughed but it was true. Last summer, when the rains swept in heavily and clouds tumbled, colliding, he cried, "I'm in pain," clutching his side, nearly doubled over. It was where the scar was. "It's the meal we had. Someone's put something in it." That familiar paranoia.

"Don't be silly," I said. "who would want to hurt you?" It was a different sort of poison that'd made him that way, the poison of the past, it made him delirious. Lightning blue and flickering to accompany his nonsense talk. I put him to bed and he twisted beneath the covers, a slow motion movement, his mouth opening and closing like a stranded fish. Who knows what he intended saying. His breath sounded like the last of the air squeezed out of a balloon. A definite fever, from the way he shivered. The sheets were stuck by sweat to his skin – the rain brought strange humours –

Bathing his face to lower his temperature. Outside, dark, no noise. I stayed awake to attend to him, the wettened towel on his forehead heating so quickly. I turned on a radio for company, its low murmur, but all the stations merged into one, a single voice. It was the voice of madness – speaking in tongues –

Lavender in next door's window box carrying in a cloying scent of nostalgia. Petrol spilled rainbow on the streets. Insomniacs identifiable by lighted window panes. I remained awake all night, beside his bed, renewing the cooling towels, the fever seeping though. Flecks of spittle dried around his mouth, his breath seemed ready to ignite. Two in the morning then four, six easing in. The worst of the storm past, and seeing the room through heavy-lidded eyes, I was drifting off to sleep, but then Martin was awake and he was calling my name over and over, sitting up in bed and twisting, the bedsheets rumpled, and I was holding his body hot against my own, the sweat, his breath, the fire, his body collapsed and firm both, hair wet, tears on cheeks, me pushing down saying stupid, reassuring words, "It's all right, it's all right, it'll be better soon," not believing any of it, too scared even to leave him and phone for the doctor.

But then he calmed down and slept until noon. I remained by his bed, hunched, shocked, not daring to move.

Three weeks of illness until the rains ceased. Thunderstorms flourished in the damp and clammy air. Black clouds merged into one. Flashes and balls of lightning flared better than fireworks. All the time by Martin's bedside, tending the fever. Lifting and guiding his body when he staggered, delirious, to the toilet. Cleaning up the thin, soupy vomit he emitted, the room filled with the dry, sour odour of sickness. His body trembling in spasms. Wondering, not always consciously, if he was going to die.

The doctor coming and going, checking on his progress. Sometimes hospital was mentioned, but I wouldn't let him, for Martin's sake, not mine – the madness would show up so black against that white –

In his fever he spoke strange languages, whole sentences. I had never heard them before. His eyes rolled so far back in his head, only the white showed – hands clenching and unclenching the bedsheets – the movement of the clock slow and endless – their sighing and ticking seeming to fill the whole room. I longed to escape the responsibility, staring out of the window into the grey, endless wash of rain –

Even after the fever had lifted I had to accompany him everywhere – he was so weak –

When he was well enough to speak, he told me about the body. It seemed important somehow for him to recount it. Lying there in bed, whispering through cracked lips – "And even then I could see that he looked like me," his belief in finding the body real enough, and although I wondered if this was only delirium, the story was probably true in essence. The war's touch was everywhere back then. Then as now. It haunted me too. It wouldn't take much – a fever say, or time's erosion - to graft the face of the body he found onto his own, to allow it take on his own features, more pertinent now he had felt death drifting by close enough to feel its touch –

Emily would know – trade her secret for mine – I look at her asleep and wonder what she would say, my sleepy blue-eyed girl looking so vulnerable – tongue protruding nipped between her teeth. My mouth remained closed –

It was the usual pattern. After the rains came a drought. The sky was unable to hold any more. Cloud was replaced by a white, burning sun. Martin would open the window and hold out his hands as though catching its rays. We went for walks and he tottered like an old woman. When he was strong enough he went out on his own, long, solitary walks, returning home hours later. The sudden, irrational outbursts were gone, and I persuaded myself that the fever had burnt them away.

We were happiest then. There had been lust before, a strangled love, and a simmering distrust, but then it all combined in an emotion that was entirely unfamiliar, and it was like an ache when he was gone, even for a few hours. In our spare time we'd explore side streets of the city we hadn't been in before, finding charity shops that sold clothes for almost-nothing – which was all we could afford in any case – laughing at their window displays that invariably held sun-faded board games and hideous pottery dishes. Martin bought a long tweed coat that reached down to his toes, and a thick black scarf that wrapped around and obscured part of his face. He left the shop wearing these in the sweltering heat and we giggled at the reactions of passers-by. It was rebellion that we were regaining, after so long, after the factory had worn it out of us.

Once he took me to a church. "You're not getting religion, are you?" I asked, thinking about his father. "No," he said, "but I wanted to see it –"

The interior was dimly-lit and smelled of damp and old wood, and in that it was the same as any church I have been to. It held three columns of pews, and unremarkable stained-glass windows. There were a few people in there already.

"Why are we here?" I asked. Martin indicated one of the pews. "This," he said, "is where Katherine seduced me." I started laughing at the absurdity of the idea, but an old woman in the pew in front of us turned and glared, and I dropped my voice to a whisper. "Martin, you didn't. Not in here. Not with her." He nodded, grinning. "I swear. Right in that pew. She arranged to meet me here and practically raped me on the spot." We were unable to suppress our laughter then. "Oh, you didn't. How blasphemous!"

He had told me about Katherine before, but when he had said they had lived together I had thought it was – well, not what it evidently had been. I was unable to stop giggling, like a schoolchild, and even when the footsteps approached I was unable to stop. "Ssh," said Martin, "that's probably the curate."

It was, and he threw us out.

On the way home, I kept on asking Martin the same question. "You're not making it up? Really? And he'd shake his head, and giggle again. "That first time I only did it because she owned the room I was living in. I thought I might get a reduction on the rent –"

I wasn't jealous. I swear I wasn't. It was the absurdity of the situation that struck me, because he'd told me before, how aloof and proper she was, and even then I couldn't understand what had brought them together. I should have known though, because people are always more complex than you imagine. Of course, she was very beautiful, in a repressed schoolmistress sort of way. Her revenge, for example – that certainly didn't fit into his description of her –

"- hands on head. Don't move –"

The heat wave continued, temperatures seeming to rise daily. It was so hot the ground cracked. Thin, jagged fissures released dead soil smells. Plants withered to brown crisps. Work in the factory became unbearable. Shifting about anonymous components for unnamed weapons. The air a sweating steel stench. Around the factory, a bleached and dusty landscape. A desert scene.

I first saw Emily then. She was stretched out on a slab of concrete like a pallid lizard, near to the factory. The air was blazing, warped and disfigured in the way it is when there's great heat. I was outside, near the perimeter fence, when I saw her. I thought, *There's been deaths from the heat already*, but it didn't occur to me to ask why she was there, why she chose this oddest of places to lie almost-naked in the mid-day sun, so close to a compound that was at best toxic, and at worst dangerous. Maybe she thought she was invisible. Or maybe the security guards just chose to alleviate their boredom by looking at her. It maybe wasn't so unusual: so many of the city's vagrants haunted the dereliction of its outskirts, first and second-generation victims of war. Old age came quickly to them, and sanity cracked early. They formed an elite corps of the destitute, and they numbered in their thousands. Looking at them, you knew we were turning into a new third world.

That evening, I mentioned it to Martin. He hadn't seen her, because now he only worked part-time at the factory. It was the one good thing to come out of his illness, I suppose. "Maybe she's looking as well," he said. "maybe she's looking for the body too."

That was the first intimation I had that he was not as well as he seemed. I hadn't made the connection before, not really, between the ruins and the place where he had found the body, but once it had been said it became obvious. And what did it mean, "Maybe she's looking for the body too?" I began to wonder what he did all day, when I was at work. Now I suspected. I thought: if he could hide his paranoia from others before, couldn't he hide it from me too? Had he simply become more adept in his deception?

A few days after that, I swapped shifts and came home early. When I arrived he was gone. He could, of course, be out on a stroll in the park. Maybe he was seeing friends (I knew he had friends, though I never met them). So many maybes, and all of them improbable. Still, I knew where he had gone.

I returned the way I had come, back to the factory with its high wire fences, its guards and patrolling dogs. This was my point of departure. From here the ruins stood on either side, remnants of buildings that stood in vast miles of berubbled landscape. Untouched since the early days of the war, it had taken on its own character. Now it was like a desert scene, with its own fauna and vegetation. Strange wiry grasses grew between the fallen timbers and lizards baked on the stones with an enviable placidity. It was not a safe place. Packs of feral dogs had colonised it, and there were rumours too of other, more exotic creatures that had escaped from zoos: pumas and lynx among other, less believable, inhabitants.

I walked, directionless. There were no clues as to where he might have gone, although I was sure he was out there somewhere. All the buildings seemed identical, hollow and crumbling. Listening for sounds, but there was nothing unfamiliar. No footfalls lightly falling. No noises from the factory in the distance, its constant beat. I chose perilous routes leading through canopies of rotting wood bent under the weight of fallen concrete and iron. A memory of habitation. Inside, charred remnants of furniture, electrical goods blackened and warped. Evidence of animal or human occupancy in the shit dried out on the rubble. Flies buzzing furiously. Several times I found I had walked full circle, and then I would stop, regain my bearings and begin again. I longed for something to drink.

Eventually I came upon him, as I turned a corner behind a block of houses. He was a short way ahead of me, digging in the debris. He lifted objects that had lain undisturbed from the time they had fallen: a rusted bedstead, a fridge without a door, a mound of papers bound together and reduced now to a black sludge. I hid behind a partially-demolished wall, observing. The items he found seemed to be of no interest to him, but yet he was evidently hunting for something. Hunting for what? Not dreams of buried treasure. It's only now I think I know. The stink of his sweat was ripe in the air. His face and hands were grey with dust. Once he stopped, cursing, shouting words I was unable to catch. He gestured angrily at something or someone I couldn't see. It was frightening to see him this way. I didn't know what to do. I watched. Eventually he left, in the direction in which I had come, and I waited until he was far ahead before following. He was heading home. Once out of the ruins, I caught a bus back, tired and sunburnt and the sweat drying on me in a distinctly unpleasant fashion. Other passengers looked at me with an undisguised contempt. On the street some old codger came up to me to beg money and I told him to fuck off. I was exhausted and close to tears. He spat a yellow-green gobbet at me by way of reprisal. I thought I would never reach home.

We slept apart that night. I didn't say anything, but he must have known. What could I say? I saw you, digging in the rubble? For God's sake, what were you looking for? I think you need help. I'm afraid you don't really love me. I think you're afraid, too and you don't even know what you're afraid of. All of those things. But I said none of them.

Eventually I fell asleep. When I woke it was a clammy, overcast day. I lay on the bed, still tired and sore from the journey the day before. The heat was humid and intense, the way it becomes when it signals the arrival of a storm. When I opened the curtains, the sky was clustered with black and curdled cloud. The radio buzzed with static.

Martin had already left by the time I rose. Maybe he had gone to work early to avoid my questions. He must have known they were coming. Breakfast was a bitter cup of coffee with soured milk. Pouring it, I found my hand jittered so much it sent water spilling over the tabletop. On the radio, too-happy music and worried commentators. I turned it off. It was nothing new. I wondered how it had all managed to so quickly unravel in this way, and could find too many answers but no solutions. I poured another cup of coffee, trying to put off going to work for as long as possible.

Leaving the house, I found a letter slipped through the letter box. It was a pink and perfumed envelope, addressed to Martin in minute writing. But nobody ever wrote to Martin. I opened it. Inside was a letter from Katherine – blue pen, neat uniform characters – written in Mills and Boon language, and it begged him to return. It was full of recriminations and apologies, *and I never meant to do any of those things to you, it was so spiteful. You must understand though, how jealous I was.* I read it twice and then set in on fire with my lighter, watching as the paper blackened and flaked, before washing the ashes down the sink with a swirl of water. There was such a strong smell of burning, and it's hard now not to see it as a premonition. I felt better though, once I had done it.

On the way to work, I imagined what I would say to Martin when we arrived home that night. It was unavoidable now: he would have to see a doctor. Or not let's mince words, he would have to see a psychotherapist. I'd have to keep him away from the ruins, make sure he took whatever medication they prescribed for him. I wouldn't let them take him away though, never that. I'd look after him. These were good images, they suggested a future that, although difficult, was achievable. They battled against what I had seen yesterday, Martin bent amongst the ruins, lifting the dross of past lives, the rubble, sweating in the sunlight. I felt almost optimistic.

The storm clouds grew. It became airless and oppressive. Thunder clattered away in the distance. I hurried, afraid I would get caught out in the inevitable rain. The city itself seemed to melt in the heat.

At work, Martin pretended normality, just as I did. I was impatient for the day to pass, even though it had hardly begun. I wanted to bring everything to its conclusion, the point where we could stop everything that had gone before, and then carry on. How naive that was. How stupid to think there'd be a happy ending.

At mid-day, the alarm sounded, driving us from the building with its insistence. My first reaction was to think, *They're bombing us again!* but that had stopped nearly a decade before. It was the fire alarm. Not just a practice either. There was real panic in the guard's voices, and the smell of burning was strong and acrid.

The air filled with smoke, making it difficult to see. We were all pushing out through the fire doors, a glut of pressing bodies trying not to give in entirely to fear. I looked, but could not see Martin, and turned to enter the building again, before someone grabbed my arm.

"Don't be stupid. You can't go back in there, love. This way."

I shouted, "Martin?" then "Martin!" but my voice couldn't even be heard above the noise.

"Don't worry. He'll be all right."

When we got outside, it was raining. It was a torrential rain that bounced off stone and tarmacadam. A joke: "That'll put the fire out if nothing else will." There was nervous laughter that I joined in with, despite myself. Someone asked, "What started it?" To which the answer came, "It was the lightning. I was there when it happened. It hit the roof and just exploded. Just like you see in a film, it was." In confirmation, the lightning flashed again, and the sky broke open with thunder. Smoke seeped through the factory doorways, through which people continued to emerge. And then no more. We stood and watched the factory burn. Flames orange and flaring.

"Shouldn't we be getting away from here? What if it blows?"

I looked around about for Martin. Everyone seemed to be there, apart from him. Who was taking the roll call? Nobody, it seemed.

"It's more the toxins we should be worried about. You breathe in that stuff and you're done for."

I began to feel myself shake, and couldn't stop. It was shock, not that far from hysteria. He'd be trapped in there, near the vats, breathing in the smoke –

Cold and shivering, I searched for faces I recognised in that sea of unfamiliarity, asked, "Isn't anyone coming to put it out?" Flames red and surging.

"Oh, let it burn." Laughter. "Nobody's left in there, I hope. Does anyone know?"

"Wouldn't be alive by now, anyway."

It was hard to see through the rain, and the smoke. I doubled over coughing, and when I looked up again, a retreat was in progress.

There was a sulphurous smell and a man beside me was vomiting – it was the fumes.

A tug at my shirt. "Are you looking for Martin? He's over there." I turned my head and saw momentarily his face slipped into the crowd. The tumble of emotions – relief, anger, terror, pity, love – sent me running in his direction. I called out his name, but in the crush and noise he must not have heard. So many people. Was that his hand, his hair, his face? The crowd seemed deliberate in its obstructions. The smoke had risen to mix with the low cloud, and faces were lit with fire and lightning.

At last I saw him again. He was breaking free from the others, head bent, ploughing through the steel rain. His natural instinct: away from the others, away from the factory, towards the ruins. I should have guessed.

My own feet clattering over the stones. Scudding through mud. The stalks of withered plants sharp against my legs, the rain in my eyes. My breath raw from running. I would catch him, I would!

(but when I got there, all I found was Emily, who ran, and a body -)

For a while there the sun tried hard to shine but it's given way to rain again. Emily's gone back to sleep on the couch. Her hands are folded beneath her head for a pillow. Her hair's all in a tangle. She breathes through her mouth and her breath makes a whistling noise, it goes *eee eee*. Yesterday's paper is crushed beneath her legs. When I prise it away, the ink comes off on my fingers. It's so overcast, the day seems old already, but it's only now the others will be arriving for work. Cars in a mad rush on the road, headlights showing. People queuing for a bus. When I sit down alongside her, Emily stirs and murmurs, drawing her legs up towards her body. The rain lashes so hard it sounds like hail. Gutters are full and overflowing. Litter floats on the brown water. Martin's still on my mind. I can see his face and he's crying. I would hold him through the night. His features are in Emily's, you can pick them out. A hint in the nose, the shape of the jaw, the texture of the hair. I'm smoking a cigarette and feeling lonely. The room's cluttered with furniture but still it seems bare. If I could be bothered I'd get up, turn on the light. Maybe the day would be worse with the sun. The gloom in the corners holds pockets of memory. Martin laughing, Martin frightened, at home or working. I lie down beside Emily, slipping my body behind hers. The smell of her skin and morning coffee. The rain breaking hard over the roof, an ominous, comforting rumble. Emily moans. And then the tears do come, creeping down her closed eyelids and sliding down her plain face, leaving a gleaming path. In my arms I hold her fast, I rock a little. I wipe the tears from her cheeks, I sing a lullaby in a soft voice. It goes: "Rock-a-bye baby on the tree top. When the wind blows –"

And that's how the two of us remain, waiting for the day to pass.

About this revised edition

It's an odd experience, revisiting work that is now nearly quarter of a century old, and not always a pleasurable one.

The short stories that make up *Approaching Our Destination* needed minor alterations – glaring errors here and there, and minor editing – but essentially they remain unchanged.

It was a more difficult decision to include *Blowing Hot and Cold* in this edition. The earliest work included here, it's flaws are very evident.

For that reason, it has been more heavily revised and reformatted, though I have resisted the temptation to restructure it completely.

Other people, whose judgement I respect, think highly of it, and it is in deference to their opinion that it is included here: my own inclination would have been to leave it out altogether.

Also By Peter Campbell

This Time We Go Down to the Green Together

A woman is dying. A reclusive actress finds herself at the centre of a mystery. A hand is severed. A dead goldfish talks. Birds fall from the sky. A girl drowns. It's the end of the world, perhaps. The end of someone's world, certainly.

Moreover, what WILL we do with the drunken sailor?

Singular, bewildering and downright perverse, This Time We Go Down To the Green Together resembles a Scottish Last Year at Marienbad. Except it's stranger, dirtier, and contains more swearing.

A novel in twenty three apparently unrelated parts.

ISBN: 978-0-9930314-0-3

Front cover photograph: Jake Hills
Image licence: Unsplash.

Back cover photograph: 'Une Maison' - Nicolas Vigier
Image licence: public domain dedication